"*Cats of ThunderClan!*" *Bramblestar called from* the Highledge. "Alderpaw has had a vision—and this vision is to set him off on an important quest. The medicine cats' prophecy told us that unless we embrace what we find in the shadows, the sky will never clear. Alderpaw's vision gives us hope that the cats of ThunderClan can find what lies in the shadows, and if so, then our Clan will prosper."

The whole of ThunderClan erupted into enthusiastic yowling. "Alderpaw! Alderpaw!"

Alderpaw froze, almost wishing that a big owl would swoop down and carry him off. Then Sparkpaw gave him a nudge. "Come on, slow mole!" she meowed, giving him an affectionate glance. "It's time to go."

WARRIORS

THE PROPHECIES BEGIN

Book One: Into the Wild

Book Two: Fire and Ice

Book Three: Forest of Secrets

Book Four: Rising Storm

Book Five: A Dangerous Path

Book Six: The Darkest Hour

THE NEW PROPHECY

Book One: Midnight

Book Two: Moonrise

Book Three: Dawn

Book Four: Starlight

Book Five: Twilight

Book Six: Sunset

POWER OF THREE

Book One: The Sight

Book Two: Dark River

Book Three: Outcast

Book Four: Eclipse

Book Five: Long Shadows

Book Six: Sunrise

OMEN OF THE STARS

Book One: The Fourth Apprentice

Book Two: Fading Echoes

Book Three: Night Whispers

Book Four: Sign of the Moon

Book Five: The Forgotten Warrior

Book Six: The Last Hope

Also by Erin Hunter

SEEKERS

RETURN TO THE WILD

MANGA

SURVIVORS

THE GATHERING DARKNESS

NOVELLAS

A VISION OF SHADOWS

WARRIORS

THE
APPRENTICE'S
QUEST

ERIN
HUNTER

HARPER
An Imprint of HarperCollinsPublishers

Special thanks to Cherith Baldry

The Apprentice's Quest
Copyright © 2016 by Working Partners Limited
Series created by Working Partners Limited
All rights reserved. Printed in the United States of America. No part of
this book may be used or reproduced in any manner whatsoever without
written permission except in the case of brief quotations embodied in
critical articles and reviews. For information address HarperCollins
Children's Books, a division of HarperCollins Publishers, 195 Broadway,
New York, NY 10007.
www.harpercollinschildrens.com

ISBN 978-0-06-238639-7

Typography by Ellice M. Lee
19   20   CG/BRR   10   9
❖
First paperback edition, 2017

THUNDERCLAN

LEADER   **BRAMBLESTAR**—dark brown tabby tom with amber eyes

DEPUTY   **SQUIRRELFLIGHT**—dark ginger she-cat with green eyes and one white paw

MEDIGINE GATS   **LEAFPOOL**—light brown tabby she-cat with amber eyes and white paws and chest

    JAYFEATHER—gray tabby tom with blind blue eyes

WARRIORS   (toms and she-cats without kits)

    BRACKENFUR—golden-brown tabby tom

    CLOUDTAIL—long-haired white tom with blue eyes

    BRIGHTHEART—white she-cat with ginger patches

    THORNCLAW—golden-brown tabby tom

    WHITEWING—white she-cat with green eyes

    BIRCHFALL—light brown tabby tom

    BERRYNOSE—cream-colored tom with a stump for a tail

    MOUSEWHISKER—gray-and-white tom

    POPPYFROST—tortoiseshell she-cat

    CINDERHEART—gray tabby she-cat

    LIONBLAZE—golden tabby tom with amber eyes

    ROSEPETAL—dark cream she-cat

BRIARLIGHT—dark brown she-cat, paralyzed in her hindquarters

BLOSSOMFALL—tortoiseshell-and-white she-cat with petal-shaped white patches

BUMBLESTRIPE—very pale gray tom with black stripes

IVYPOOL—silver-and-white tabby she-cat with dark blue eyes

DOVEWING—pale gray she-cat with green eyes

CHERRYFALL—ginger she-cat
APPRENTICE, SPARKPAW (orange tabby she-cat)

MOLEWHISKER—brown-and-cream tom
APPRENTICE, ALDERPAW (dark ginger tom with amber eyes)

SNOWBUSH—white, fluffy tom

AMBERMOON—pale ginger she-cat

DEWNOSE—gray-and-white tom

STORMCLOUD—(formerly Frankie); gray tabby tom

HOLLYTUFT—black she-cat

FERNSONG—yellow tabby tom

SORRELSTRIPE—dark brown she-cat

QUEENS   (she-cats expecting or nursing kits)

DAISY—cream, long-furred cat from the horseplace

LILYHEART—tortoiseshell-and-white she-cat (mother to Leafkit, a tortoiseshell she-kit, Larkkit, a black tom-kit, and Honeykit, a white she-kit with yellow splotches)

ELDERS (former warriors and queens, now retired)

PURDY—plump tabby, former loner with a gray muzzle

GRAYSTRIPE—long-haired gray tom

SANDSTORM—pale ginger she-cat with green eyes

MILLIE—striped gray tabby she-cat with blue eyes

SHADOWCLAN

LEADER **ROWANSTAR**—ginger tom

DEPUTY **CROWFROST**—black-and-white tom

MEDICINE CAT **LITTLECLOUD**—very small tabby tom

WARRIORS **TAWNYPELT**—tortoiseshell she-cat with green eyes
APPRENTICE, NEEDLEPAW

TIGERHEART—dark brown tabby tom
APPRENTICE, SLEEKPAW

STONEWING—white tom
APPRENTICE, JUNIPERPAW

SPIKEFUR—dark brown tom with tufty fur on his head
APPRENTICE, YARROWPAW

WASPTAIL—yellow tabby she-cat with green eyes
APPRENTICE, STRIKEPAW

DAWNPELT—cream-furred she-cat
APPRENTICE, BEEPAW

SNOWBIRD—sleek, lithe, well-muscled, pure white she-cat with green eyes

SCORCHFUR—dark gray tom with slashed ears, one of which is torn

BERRYHEART—black and white she-cat

CLOVERFOOT—gray tabby she-cat

RIPPLETAIL—white tom

SPARROWTAIL—large tabby tom

MISTCLOUD—spiky-furred, pale gray she-cat

QUEENS   **GRASSHEART**—pale brown tabby she-cat

PINENOSE—black she-cat (mother to Birchkit, a beige tom-kit, Lionkit, a yellow she-kit with amber eyes, Puddlekit, a brown tom-kit with white splotches, and Slatekit, a sleek, gray tom-kit)

ELDERS   **OAKFUR**—small brown tom

KINKFUR—tabby she-cat, with long fur that sticks out at all angles

RATSCAR—brown tom with long scar across his back

WINDCLAN

LEADER   **ONESTAR**—brown tabby tom

DEPUTY   **HARESPRING**—brown-and-white tom

MEDICINE CAT   **KESTRELFLIGHT**—mottled gray tom with white splotches like kestrel feathers

WARRIORS   **NIGHTCLOUD**—black she-cat

GORSETAIL—very pale gray-and-white she-cat with blue eyes

CROWFEATHER—dark gray tom

APPRENTICE, FERNPAW (dark brown she-cat)

LEAFTAIL—dark tabby tom, amber eyes

EMBERFOOT—gray tom with two dark paws

BREEZEPELT—black tom with amber eyes

FURZEPELT—gray-and-white she-cat

LARKWING—pale brown tabby she-cat

SEDGEWHISKER—light brown tabby she-cat

SLIGHTFOOT—black tom with white flash on his chest

OATCLAW—pale brown tabby tom

FEATHERPELT—gray tabby she-cat

HOOTWHISKER—dark gray tom

QUEENS   **HEATHERTAIL**—light brown tabby she-cat with blue eyes (mother to Smokekit, a gray she-kit, and Brindlekit, a mottled brown she-kit)

ELDERS   **WHITETAIL**—small white she-cat

RIVERCLAN

LEADER   **MISTYSTAR**—gray she-cat with blue eyes

DEPUTY   **REEDWHISKER**—black tom

MEDICINE CATS   **MOTHWING**—dappled golden she-cat

       WILLOWSHINE—gray tabby she-cat

WARRIORS   **MINTFUR**—light gray tabby tom

       DUSKFUR—brown tabby she-cat
       APPRENTICE, SHADEPAW (dark brown she-cat)

MINNOWTAIL—dark gray she-cat

MALLOWNOSE—light brown tabby tom

PETALFUR—gray-and-white she-cat

BEETLEWHISKER—brown-and-white tabby tom

CURLFEATHER—pale brown she-cat

PODLIGHT—gray-and-white tom

HERONWING—dark gray-and-black tom

SHIMMERPELT—silver she-cat

LIZARDTAIL—light brown tom
APPRENTICE, FOXPAW (russet tabby tom)

HAVENPELT—black-and-white she-cat

PERCHWING—gray-and-white she-cat

SNEEZECLOUD—gray-and-white tom

BRACKENPELT—tortoiseshell she-cat

JAYCLAW—gray tom

OWLNOSE—brown tabby tom

QUEENS

LAKEHEART—gray tabby she-cat

ICEWING—white she-cat with blue eyes (mother to Nightkit and Breezekit)

ELDERS

MOSSPELT—tortoiseshell-and-white she-cat

A VISION OF SHADOWS

WARRIORS

THE
APPRENTICE'S
QUEST

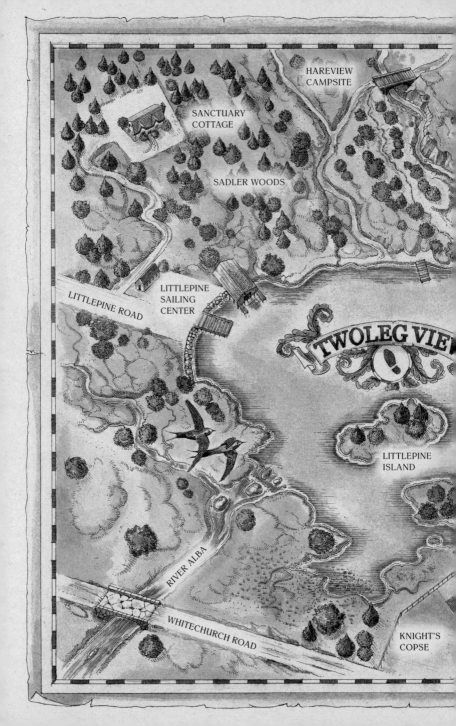

PROLOGUE

❧

Jayfeather scrambled up the slope that led to the Moonpool, his paws skidding on the damp stones. A chill breeze ruffled his fur, and he shivered as his mother, Leafpool, hauled herself up the rocks to stand at his side.

"Greenleaf is almost over," she said. "We'll need to stock up on herbs while we still can. Catmint, especially."

"Catmint!" Jayfeather's tail-tip twitched impatiently. "You're always meowing on about catmint. If you had your way, we'd fill our den with it and not leave room for anything else."

Leafpool gave him a friendly shove. "We could do worse. You know how quickly whitecough can turn to greencough if it's not treated properly. The elders—"

"Sandstorm, Graystripe, Millie, and Purdy are perfectly healthy," Jayfeather interrupted. "Honestly, Leafpool, you coddle them too much. Besides, we have plenty of catmint growing by the old Twoleg nest. Enough even for you! So don't expect me to go out gathering more."

As he finished speaking, he heard the scuffling of paws farther down the slope. The powerful watery scent of RiverClan swept over him as Mothwing and Willowshine, the River-Clan medicine cats, climbed up to join them.

"We have plenty of catmint," Mothwing announced mildly. "Just let us know if ThunderClan runs into problems."

"Thanks, Mothwing," Leafpool meowed, while Jayfeather bit back a sharp retort.

Like ThunderClan needs to rely on RiverClan for herbs!

"Let's get moving," he urged the other medicine cats. "Littlecloud and Kestrelflight are ahead of us. I can scent their trail."

Taking the lead, Jayfeather bounded up the rest of the slope, sure-pawed in spite of his blindness, and pushed his way through the thick bushes that surrounded the hollow of the Moonpool. As he emerged, shaking his pelt, he could hear the splashing of the stream as it poured down the rocks, and he imagined the glitter of starshine on the surface of the water.

"Welcome!" Littlecloud, the ShadowClan medicine cat, called out from the water's edge below. "Kestrelflight and I thought you were never coming."

"Well, we're here now," Jayfeather responded.

He began to descend the spiral path that led to the pool, his paws slipping easily into the prints left by the cats who used to live by the lake countless seasons before.

"So long ago . . . ," he whispered to himself, struggling with bittersweet memories of the time he had walked the same path with those ancient cats. The time he had set their paws on the journey that led them to the mountains. *The time I shared tongues with Half Moon . . .*

Forcing himself back to the present, he joined Littlecloud and Kestrelflight beside the pool and waited for Leafpool, Mothwing, and Willowshine to pad down the path in turn. Then he settled himself at the water's edge. He could hear the other medicine cats doing the same, spaced out along the bank.

Even Mothwing, he thought, wondering once again how she could be a medicine cat when she didn't believe in StarClan. *All she's going to get out of this is a nice, peaceful nap!*

Gradually the sound of cats shifting around faded, leaving only the endless cascade of falling water. Beneath the torrent Jayfeather's acute hearing picked up the sound of Littlecloud's breathing. There was a faint rasp in it, and now and then a hitch that reminded Jayfeather uncomfortably of how old the ShadowClan medicine cat was getting.

He hasn't taken an apprentice since Flametail's death, Jayfeather reminded himself with a frown. *ShadowClan is crawling with young cats. Surely one of them must be suitable?*

Determinedly Jayfeather banished his worries. Whatever might happen in the future, life was good in the Clans now. There had been plenty of prey throughout greenleaf, and every cat was healthy. Contentment crept over him like the taste of succulent prey as he closed his eyes, stretched out his neck, and touched his nose to the water of the Moonpool.

Jayfeather became aware of sunlight beating down on his fur. His nose twitched at the scent of green, growing things, carried to him on a warm breeze. Stretching luxuriously, he opened his eyes.

What in the name of StarClan . . . ?

Springing to his paws, Jayfeather stared around him. He was standing in the middle of a stretch of lush grass, bordered by leaf-laden trees. Somewhere in the distance he could hear the gentle bubbling of a stream. And all around him, blinking at one another in confusion, were his fellow medicine cats.

This can't be right, Jayfeather told himself, every hair on his pelt rising in apprehension. Once he had been able to walk in the dreams of other cats, but he had lost that power after the battle against the cats of the Dark Forest, almost eighteen moons ago. *And now we're walking in one another's dreams.* The medicine cats of all four Clans stood together on the sunny grass of StarClan's hunting grounds. *Does that mean StarClan has an important message for* all *of us?*

"What's happening?" Kestrelflight asked, his eyes wide and scared.

Littlecloud shook his head in bewilderment. "It's very odd . . . ," he mewed.

Leafpool and Willowshine had their heads together and were talking in quick, anxious murmurs. Jayfeather padded toward them, only to halt as he spotted a group of cats approaching from beyond the trees. They moved in a haze of starshine, with a frosty glitter at their paws and around their ears. A noble tom with a flame-colored pelt paced in the lead. A shiver ran through Jayfeather's pelt as he recognized the former ThunderClan leader.

Leafpool let out a cry of joy. "Firestar!"

A wave of affection flooded over Jayfeather as he watched

her race across the grass to touch noses with her father.

Kestrelflight bounded after her to meet Barkface, who had been his mentor in WindClan; the two medicine cats immediately fell into deep conversation. Willowshine padded up to Leopardstar and dipped her head respectfully as she greeted the previous RiverClan leader. Littlecloud and Flametail settled down together on the grass, sharing tongues and purring with delight, while ShadowClan's former leader Blackstar looked on approvingly.

Jayfeather set off more slowly to greet the StarClan cats. Though he was pleased to see them, his paws still prickled with uneasiness. *I want to know what all this is about.*

He noticed more cats standing in the shade of the trees, barely visible except as glimmers of starlight. Scanning them closely, Jayfeather realized that he didn't recognize any of them. Parting his jaws, he inhaled deeply to draw their scent into his mouth, and he tasted something he had never encountered before.

Narrowing his eyes, Jayfeather strode up to Firestar. "What's going on?" he demanded. "Who are those strange cats?"

"Greetings to you too, Jayfeather," Firestar responded.

Jayfeather's tail-tip twitched impatiently. "Well?"

Firestar cleared his throat and glanced at the other StarClan cats, who broke off their conversations to cluster around him.

"I suppose you can go ahead and speak for us all this time," Leopardstar remarked drily to the flame-colored tom. "You're obviously planning to anyway."

The other medicine cats had drawn closer to Jayfeather, who saw Kestrelflight shifting his paws uneasily, as if he wanted to speak but was uncomfortable with this shared vision.

Jayfeather gave him a prod. "Spit it out," he growled.

"Maybe each of us medicine cats should speak privately with our own Clanmates," Kestrelflight suggested diffidently. "There might be things to discuss that are private to our Clans."

"No," Barkface meowed gently, touching his nose to Kestrelflight's shoulder. "We have a prophecy for all of you—one that concerns all the Clans."

Jayfeather felt his heart start to beat faster. *Not another prophecy!* he groaned inwardly. *Does this mean our seasons of peace are coming to an end?*

"A prophecy, and a promise too," Firestar meowed. He was staring directly into Jayfeather's eyes, as if he knew the words Jayfeather hadn't spoken aloud. "A time of great change is coming for all the Clans. *Embrace what you find in the shadows, for only they can clear the sky.*"

He stopped speaking, while the StarClan ancestors gazed impressively at the medicine cats.

When the silence had stretched out for several heartbeats, Jayfeather lashed his tail in frustration. "What does *that* mean?" he demanded, glaring at Firestar. Sarcasm filled his voice like a scratching claw as he added, "If you try really hard, do you think you could be a bit more obscure?"

Firestar gazed at Jayfeather with a mixture of affection and irritation. But the vision was already beginning to fade. The shapes of the StarClan cats shone out in a blaze of starlight, dazzling Jayfeather and the other medicine cats. The sky darkened as if clouds were racing to cover the sun.

But before his vision left him, Jayfeather spotted from the corner of his eye another cat he did not immediately recognize: a very young tom standing a pace or two back from the circle of medicine cats. As Jayfeather turned to face him, he bounded away, so that all Jayfeather saw clearly was the flick of a white-tipped tail.

Jayfeather took a breath to catch his scent. *That's a living cat!* he realized. *And he smells strongly of ThunderClan.*

CHAPTER 1

♣

Alderkit stood in front of the nursery, nervously shifting his weight. He unsheathed his claws, digging them into the beaten earth of the stone hollow, then sheathed them again and shook dust from his paws.

Now what happens? he asked himself, his belly churning as he thought about his apprentice ceremony, which was only moments away. *What if there's some sort of assessment before I can be an apprentice?*

Alderkit thought he had heard something about an assessment once. Perhaps it had been a few moons ago when Hollytuft, Fernsong, and Sorrelstripe had been made warriors. *But I can't really remember. . . . I was so little then.*

His heart started to pound faster and faster. He tried to convince himself that some cat would have told him if he was supposed to prove that he was ready. *Because I'm not sure that I am ready to become an apprentice. Not sure at all. What if I can't do it?*

Deep in his own thoughts, Alderkit jumped in surprise as a cat nudged him hard from behind. Spinning around, he saw his sister Sparkkit, her orange tabby fur bushing out in all directions.

"Aren't you excited?" she asked with an enthusiastic bounce. "Don't you want to know who your mentor will be? I hope I get someone *fun*! Not a bossy cat like Berrynose, or one like Whitewing. She sticks so close to the rules I think she must recite the warrior code in her sleep!"

"That's enough." The kits' mother, Squirrelflight, emerged from the nursery in time to hear Sparkkit's last words. "You're not supposed to *have fun* with your mentors," she added, licking one paw and smoothing it over Sparkkit's pelt. "You're supposed to *learn* from them. Berrynose and Whitewing are both fine warriors. You'd be very lucky to have either of them as your mentor."

Though Squirrelflight's voice was sharp, her green gaze shone with love for her kits. Alderkit knew how much his mother adored him and his sister. He was only a kit, but he understood that Squirrelflight was old to have her first litter, and he remembered their shared grief for his lost littermates: Juniperkit, who had barely taken a breath before he died, and Dandelionkit, who had never been strong, and who had slowly weakened until she also died two moons later.

Sparkkit and I have to be the best cats we can be for Squirrelflight and Bramblestar.

Sparkkit, meanwhile, wasn't at all cowed by her mother's scolding. She twitched her tail and cheerfully shook her pelt until her fur fluffed up again.

Alderkit wished he had her confidence. He hadn't wondered until now who his mentor would be, and he gazed around the clearing at the other cats with new and curious eyes. *Ivypool would be an okay mentor,* he thought, spotting the silver-and-white tabby she-cat returning from a hunting patrol with Lionblaze and Blossomfall. *She's friendly and a good hunter. Lionblaze is a bit scary, though.* Alderkit suppressed a shiver at the sight of the muscles rippling beneath the golden warrior's pelt. *And it won't be Blossomfall, because she was just mentor for Hollytuft. Or Brackenfur or Rosepetal, because they mentored Sorrelstripe and Fernsong.*

Lost in thought, Alderkit watched Thornclaw, who had paused in the middle of the clearing to give himself a good scratch behind one ear. *He'd probably be okay, though he's sort of short-tempered . . .*

"Hey, wake up!" Sparkkit trod down hard on Alderkit's paw. "It's starting!"

Alderkit realized that Bramblestar had appeared on the Highledge outside his den, way above their heads on the wall of the stone hollow.

"Let all cats old enough to catch their own prey join here beneath the Highledge for a Clan meeting!" Bramblestar yowled.

As the cats in the clearing turned their attention to Bramblestar and began to gather together, Alderpaw thought that his father seemed to stand taller and stronger than all of them—even brave warriors like Lionblaze and Dovewing.

He's so confident and strong. I'm lucky to be his son.

Bramblestar ran lightly down the tumbled rocks and took his place in the center of the ragged circle of cats that was forming at the foot of the rock wall. Graystripe, the Clan's previous deputy, purred as the kits passed him, and Sorrelstripe, one of the youngest warriors, held her head high, as if proud to have finished her own apprenticeship. Squirrelflight gently nudged her two kits forward until they too stood in the circle.

Alderkit's belly began to churn even harder, and he tightened all his muscles to stop himself from trembling. *I can't do this!* he thought, struggling not to panic.

Then he caught sight of his father's gaze on him: such a warm, proud look that Alderkit instantly felt comforted. He took a few deep breaths, forcing himself to relax.

"Cats of ThunderClan," Bramblestar began, "this is a good day for us, because it's time to make two new apprentices. Sparkkit, come here, please."

Instantly Sparkkit bounced into the center of the circle, her tail standing straight up and her fur bristling with excitement. She gazed confidently at her leader.

"From this day forward," Bramblestar meowed, touching Sparkkit on her shoulder with his tail-tip, "this apprentice will be known as Sparkpaw. Cherryfall, you will be her mentor. I trust that you will share with her your dedication to your Clan, your quick mind, and your excellent hunting skills."

Sparkpaw dashed across the circle to Cherryfall, bouncing with happiness, and the ginger she-cat bent her head to touch noses with her.

"Sparkpaw! Sparkpaw!" the Clan began to yowl.

Sparkpaw gave a pleased little hop as her Clanmates chanted her new name, her eyes shining as she stood beside her mentor.

Alderkit joined in the acclamation, pleased to see how

happy his sister looked. *Thank StarClan! There wasn't any kind of test to prove that she was ready.*

As the yowling died away, Bramblestar beckoned to Alderkit with his tail. "Your turn," he meowed, his gaze encouraging Alderkit on.

Alderkit's legs were suddenly wobbly as he staggered into the center of the circle. His chest felt tight, as if he couldn't breathe properly. But as he halted in front of Bramblestar, his father gave him a slight nod to steady him, and he stood with his head raised as Bramblestar rested the tip of his tail on his shoulder.

"From this day forward, this apprentice will be known as Alderpaw," Bramblestar announced. "Molewhisker, you will be his mentor. You are loyal, determined, and brave, and I know that you will do your best to pass on these qualities to your apprentice."

As he padded across the clearing to join his mentor, Alderpaw wasn't sure how he felt. He knew that Molewhisker was Cherryfall's littermate, but the big cream-and-brown tom was much quieter than his sister, and had never shown much interest in the kits. His gaze was solemn as he bent to touch noses with Alderpaw.

I hope I can make you proud of me, Alderpaw thought. *I'm going to try my hardest!*

"Alderpaw! Alderpaw!"

Alderpaw ducked his head and gave his chest fur a few embarrassed licks as he heard his Clan caterwauling his name. At the same time, he thought he would burst with happiness.

At last the chanting died away and the crowd of cats began to disperse, heading toward their dens or the fresh-kill pile. Squirrelflight and Bramblestar padded over to join their kits.

"Well done," Bramblestar meowed. "It wasn't so scary, was it?"

"It was great!" Sparkpaw responded, her tail waving in the air. "I can't wait to go hunting!"

"We're so proud of both of you," Squirrelflight purred, giving Sparkpaw and then Alderpaw a lick around the ears. "I'm sure you'll be wonderful warriors one day."

Bramblestar dipped his head in agreement. "I know you both have so much to give your Clan." He stepped back as he finished speaking, and waved his tail to draw Molewhisker and Cherryfall closer. "Listen to your mentors," he told the two new apprentices. "I'm looking forward to hearing good things about your progress."

With an affectionate nuzzle he turned away and headed toward his den. Squirrelflight too gave her kits a quick cuddle, and then she followed him. Alderpaw and Sparkpaw were left alone with Molewhisker and Cherryfall.

Molewhisker faced Alderpaw, blinking solemnly. "It's a big responsibility, being an apprentice," he meowed. "You must pay close attention to everything you're taught, because one day your Clan may depend on your fighting or hunting skills."

Alderpaw nodded solemnly.

"You'll have to work hard to prove you have what it takes to be a warrior," Molewhisker went on.

His head held high, Alderpaw tried to look worthy, but was

afraid he wasn't doing a very good job of it. Hearing Cherryfall talking to Sparkpaw just behind him didn't help at all.

". . . and we'll have such fun exploring the territory!" the ginger she-cat mewed enthusiastically. "And now you'll get to go to Gatherings."

Alderpaw couldn't help wishing that his own mentor were a little more enthusiastic, like his littermate's.

"Can we start learning to hunt now?" Sparkpaw asked eagerly.

It was Molewhisker who replied. "Not right now. In addition to learning how to be warriors, apprentices have special duties for the well-being of the whole Clan."

"What do we have to do?" Alderpaw asked, hoping to impress on his mentor that he was ready for anything.

There was a guilty look on Cherryfall's face as she meowed, "Today you're going to make the elders more comfortable by getting rid of their ticks."

Molewhisker waved his tail in the direction of the medicine cats' den. "Go and ask Leafpool or Jayfeather for some mouse bile. They'll tell you how to use it."

"Mouse bile!" Sparkpaw wrinkled her nose in disgust. "Yuck!"

Alderpaw's heart sank further. *If this is being an apprentice, I'm not sure I'm going to like it.*

Sunlight shone into the den beneath the hazel bushes where the elders lived. Alderpaw wished that he could curl up in the warmth and take a nap. Instead he combed his claws painstakingly through Graystripe's long pelt, searching for ticks. Sparkpaw was doing the same for Purdy, while Sandstorm and Millie looked on, patiently waiting their turn.

"Wow, there's a massive tick here!" Sparkpaw exclaimed. "Hold still, Purdy, and I'll get it off."

With clenched teeth she picked up the twig Jayfeather had given her, which had a ball of moss soaked in mouse bile stuck on one end, and awkwardly maneuvered it until she could dab the moss onto Purdy's tick.

The old tabby shook his pelt and sighed with relief as the tick fell off. "That's much better, young 'un," he purred.

"But this stuff smells *horrible*!" Sparkpaw mumbled around the twig. "I don't know how you elders can stand it." Suppressing a sigh, she began parting Purdy's clumped, untidy fur in search of more ticks.

"Now you listen to me, youngster," Purdy meowed. "There's not a cat in ThunderClan who wasn't an apprentice once, takin' off ticks, just like you."

"Even Bramblestar?" Alderpaw asked, pausing with one paw sunk deep in Graystripe's pelt.

"Even *Firestar*," Graystripe responded. "He and I were apprentices together, and I've lost count of the number of ticks we pulled. Hey!" he added, giving Alderpaw a prod. "Watch what you're doing. Your claws are digging in my shoulder!"

"Sorry!" Alderpaw replied.

In spite of being scolded, he felt quite content. Cleaning off ticks was a messy job, but there were worse things than sitting in a shaft of sunlight and listening to the elders. He looked up briefly to see Sandstorm's green gaze resting lovingly on him and his sister as she settled herself more comfortably in the bracken of her nest.

"I remember when your mother was first made an apprentice," she mewed. "Dustpelt was her mentor. You never knew him—he died in the Great Storm—but he was one of our best warriors, and he didn't put up with any nonsense. Even so, Squirrelflight was a match for him!"

"What did she do?" Alderpaw asked, intrigued to think of his serious, businesslike mother as a difficult young apprentice. "Go on, tell us!"

Sandstorm sighed. "What *didn't* she do? Slipping out of camp to hunt on her own . . . getting stuck in bushes, falling into streams . . . I remember Dustpelt saying to me once, 'If that kit of yours doesn't shape up, I'm going to claw her pelt off and hang it on a bush to frighten the foxes!'"

Sparkpaw stared at Sandstorm with her mouth gaping. "He wouldn't have!"

"No, of course not," Sandstorm responded, her green eyes alight with amusement, "but Dustpelt had to be tough with her. He saw how much she had to offer her Clan, but he knew she wouldn't live up to her potential unless she learned discipline."

"She sure did that," Alderpaw meowed.

"Hey!" Graystripe gave Alderpaw another prod. "What about my ticks, huh?"

"And ours," Millie put in, with a glance at Sandstorm. "We've been waiting *moons*!"

"Sorry . . ."

Alderpaw began rapidly searching through Graystripe's pelt, and almost at once he came across a huge swollen tick. *That must be making Graystripe really uncomfortable.*

Picking up his stick with the bile-soaked moss, he dabbed at the tick. At the same moment, he happened to glance up, and spotted Leafpool and Jayfeather talking intently to each other just outside the medicine cats' den.

As Alderpaw wondered vaguely what was so important, both medicine cats turned toward him. Suddenly he felt trapped by Jayfeather's blind gaze and Leafpool's searching one.

A worm of uneasiness began to gnaw at Alderpaw's belly. *Great StarClan! Are they talking about* me*? Have I messed something up already?*

CHAPTER 2

Alderpaw scarcely slept at all on his first night in the apprentices'
den. He missed the warm scents of the nursery and the familiar shapes of his mother and Daisy sleeping beside him. The
hollow beneath the ferns seemed empty with only him and his
sister occupying it.

Sparkpaw had curled up at once with her tail wrapped over
her nose, but Alderpaw dozed uneasily, caught between excitement and apprehension at what the new day would bring. He
was fully awake again by the time the first pale light of dawn
began to filter through the ferns.

He sprang up as the arching fronds parted and a head
appeared, but relaxed when he recognized Cherryfall.

"Hi!" the ginger she-cat meowed. "Give Sparkpaw a prod.
It's time for our tour of the territory!"

"Me too?" Alderpaw asked.

"Yes, of course. Molewhisker is here waiting. Hurry!"

Alderpaw poked one paw into his sister's side, and her
soft, rhythmic snoring broke off with a squeak of alarm. "Is
it foxes?" she asked, sitting up and shaking scraps of moss off
her pelt. "Badgers?"

"No, it's our mentors," Alderpaw told her. "They're going to show us the territory."

"Great!" Sparkpaw shot upward, scrabbling hard with her hind paws as she pushed her way out through the ferns. "Let's go!"

Alderpaw followed more slowly, shivering in the chilly air of dawn. Outside the den Molewhisker and Cherryfall stood waiting side by side. Beyond them he spotted Bumblestripe, Rosepetal, and Cloudtail emerging from the warriors' den. After a quick grooming they set off, with Cloudtail in the lead, and vanished through the thorn tunnel.

"There goes the dawn patrol," Molewhisker meowed. "We'll wait a few moments to let them get on their way. If you want, you can take something from the fresh-kill pile."

Alderpaw suddenly realized how hungry he was. With Sparkpaw at his side, he raced across the camp.

"There's not much here," Sparkpaw complained, prodding with one paw at a scrawny mouse.

"The hunting patrols haven't gone out yet," Alderpaw pointed out. He took a blackbird from the scanty prey that remained and began gulping it down.

"Wait till *we're* hunters!" Sparkpaw mumbled around a mouthful of mouse. "Then the fresh-kill pile will *always* be full."

Alderpaw hoped that she was right.

Molewhisker waved his tail from the opposite side of the camp. Swallowing the last of their prey, the two apprentices bounded back to join him and Cherryfall, who took the lead as they pushed their way through the tunnel in the barrier of thorns that blocked the entrance to the camp.

Alderpaw's pads tingled with anticipation as he slid through the narrow space and set his paws in the forest for the first time.

By now the dawn light had strengthened, and a reddish glow through the trees showed where the sun would rise. Ragged scraps of mist still floated among the undergrowth, and the grass was heavy with dew.

Sparkpaw's eyes stretched wide as she gazed around her. "It's so big!" she squealed.

Alderpaw was silent, unable to find words for what he could see. Except for the thorn barrier behind him, and the walls of the stone hollow beyond, trees stretched away in every direction, until they faded into a shadowy distance. Their trunks rose many fox-lengths above his head, their branches intertwining. The air was full of tantalizing prey-scents, and he could hear the scuffling of small creatures in the thick undergrowth among the trees.

"Can we hunt?" Sparkpaw asked eagerly.

"Maybe later," Cherryfall told her. "To begin with, we're going to tour the territory. By the time you're made warriors, you'll need to know every paw step of it."

Molewhisker nodded seriously. "Every tree, every rock, every stream . . ."

Alderpaw blinked. *All of it? Surely no cat could ever know all of it?*

"This way," Cherryfall meowed briskly. "We'll start by heading for the ShadowClan border."

"Will we meet ShadowClan cats?" Sparkpaw asked. "What happens if we do?"

"Nothing happens," Molewhisker replied sternly. "They stay on their side; we stay on ours."

Cherryfall set out at a good pace, with Sparkpaw bouncing along beside her. Alderpaw followed, and Molewhisker brought up the rear.

Before they had taken many paw steps, they came to a spot where a wide path led away into the forest, covered only with short grass and small creeping plants. Longer grass and ferns bordered it on either side.

"Where does that go?" Alderpaw asked, angling his ears toward the path. "And why doesn't anything much grow there?"

"Good question," Molewhisker responded. Alderpaw was pleased at his mentor's approving tone. "That path was made by Twolegs many, many seasons ago. The same Twolegs who cut out the stone to make the hollow where we camp. It leads to the old Twoleg den, where Leafpool and Jayfeather grow their herbs."

"But we aren't going that way today," Cherryfall added.

Heading farther away from the camp, Alderpaw noticed that the trees ahead seemed to be thinning out. A bright, silvery light was shining through them.

"What's that?" Sparkpaw asked.

Neither of their mentors replied; they just kept walking until they reached the edge of the trees. Then they pushed through a thick barrier of holly bushes. Alderpaw emerged onto a stretch of short, soft grass. Beyond it was a strip of pebbles and sandy soil, and beyond that . . .

"Wow!" Sparkpaw gasped. "Is that the lake?"

Alderpaw blinked at the shining expanse of water that lay in front of him. He had heard his Clanmates back in the camp talking about the lake, and he had imagined something a bit bigger than the puddles that formed on the floor of the hollow when it rained. He would never have believed that there was this much water in the whole world.

"There's no end to it!" he exclaimed.

"Oh, yes, there is," Molewhisker assured him. "Some cats have traveled all the way around it. Look over there," he continued, pointing with his tail. "Can you see those trees and bushes? That's RiverClan territory."

Alderpaw narrowed his eyes and could just make out the trees his mentor was talking about, hazy with the distance.

"RiverClan cats love the lake," Cherryfall mewed. "They swim in it and catch fish."

"Weird!" Sparkpaw responded. Giving a little bounce, she added, "Can I catch a fish?" Without waiting for her mentor to reply, she dashed across the pebbles and skidded to a halt with her forepaws splashing at the edge of the water. "Cold!" she yowled, leaping backward with her neck fur bristling. Then she let out a little huff of laughter and bounced to the edge again, her tail waving excitedly. "I can't see any fish," she meowed.

Molewhisker heaved a sigh. "You won't, if you go on like that. Or anything else, for that matter. Yowling and prancing around like that, you'll scare away all the prey in the forest."

Sparkpaw backed away from the water again and joined her Clanmates beside the bushes, her tail drooping. "Sorry," she muttered.

"That's okay." Cherryfall rested her tail briefly on her apprentice's shoulders. "We're not hunting right now. And I know how exciting it is to see the lake for the first time."

Molewhisker flicked his ears. "Let's move on."

He took the lead as the cats padded along the lakeshore. Soon they came to a stream, which emerged from the forest and flowed into the lake.

"This is the ShadowClan border," Cherryfall announced.

Alderpaw wrinkled his nose at a strong, unfamiliar reek that came from the opposite side of the stream.

"Yuck! What's that?" Sparkpaw asked, taking a pace back and passing her tongue over her jaws as if she could taste something nasty.

"That's the scent of ShadowClan," Molewhisker answered.

"That's *cat* scent?" Sparkpaw sounded outraged. "I thought only foxes stank like that."

"It only smells bad because we're not used to it," Molewhisker pointed out, beginning to lead the way upstream, back into the shelter of the trees. "We probably smell just as bad to them."

"No way!" Sparkpaw muttered under her breath.

"You know that all the Clans scent-mark their boundaries," Cherryfall explained as they continued to follow the stream. "Of course, we all know where the borders are, but marking them reminds every cat that they aren't supposed to enter another Clan's territory without permission."

"You should be able to pick up the ThunderClan scent markers, too," Molewhisker mewed. "We'll show you how to set them. Before long, you'll be doing it as part of a border patrol."

"Cool!" Alderpaw exclaimed. For the first time he imagined himself as a warrior, maybe even leading a patrol, setting scent markers to protect his Clan's territory. *I'm learning so much today! I feel like I'm becoming a real part of my Clan.*

After they had traveled some distance into the forest, the stream veered sharply away, but the line of ShadowClan and ThunderClan scent markers continued in the same direction across the ground. On the ShadowClan side the leafy trees and thick undergrowth soon gave way to dark pines, the ground covered by a thick layer of needles.

"Now we'll show you something really different," Cherryfall promised. She beckoned the two apprentices into a hazel thicket, signaling with her tail for them to keep quiet. "What do you think of that?"

Alderpaw gazed out into a clearing dotted with weird structures: they looked like little dens made of strange green pelts. Tasting the air, he realized they were right on the border between the two Clans. As well as the scent markings, he managed to pick up another scent he had never encountered before.

"Is this some sort of Twoleg stuff?" he asked. "I've never

seen a Twoleg, but Squirrelflight says they come into the forest sometimes."

"Exactly right," Molewhisker purred, giving Alderpaw a light flick over his ear with his tail. Alderpaw felt his chest swell with pride. "In greenleaf, Twolegs come and live here in these little dens."

"Why do they do that?" Sparkpaw asked, sounding as if she didn't believe him.

Molewhisker shrugged. "StarClan knows."

"Are they here now?" Alderpaw asked.

"They're probably still asleep in there," Cherryfall mewed. "Lazy lot. Anyway, this clearing is in ShadowClan territory, so they're ShadowClan's problem. Let's be on our way."

Alderpaw's legs were beginning to get tired as the mentors turned away from the border and plunged into deeper woodland. They seemed to walk for seasons, crossing leafy glades, skirting bramble thickets, and leaping across small streams. His belly started to feel hollow. It had been a long time since he had eaten the blackbird back in the camp.

Eventually he began to hear the sound of flowing water up ahead, as if they were coming to a wider stream. Before it came into sight, Cherryfall signaled for them to halt. "What can you smell?" she asked.

Alderpaw and Sparkpaw stood side by side, their jaws wide as they drew in air over their scent glands. Alderpaw concentrated hard, trying to separate all the different scents that seemed to be attacking him.

"Mouse!" Sparkpaw exclaimed as he was still trying to focus. "*Please* can we hunt now? I'm starving!"

"Yes, mouse," Cherryfall mewed, ignoring her apprentice's pleading. "What else?"

Alderpaw forced his hunger down, focusing all his attention on what he could smell. "There are two scents close together," he began hesitantly, afraid that he was going to get it wrong. "And they're really strong. ThunderClan and . . ." The other scent was vaguely unpleasant, and he remembered what they had learned at the ShadowClan border. "Is it the scent of another Clan?"

Molewhisker and Cherryfall exchanged a glance. "That's right," Molewhisker meowed. "Do you know which Clan?"

How am I supposed to know? Alderpaw asked himself. *I've never smelled it before!* Then he remembered something else.

"You told us RiverClan is way over on the other side of the lake. So this one must be WindClan."

"Excellent!" Cherryfall purred. "Let's go and see the border."

She led the way to the bank of another stream, this time running at the bottom of a deep cleft covered in lush vegetation. "Over there is WindClan territory," she mewed with a wave of her tail.

Beyond the stream the trees quickly gave way to a steep hill covered in short, tough grass, the slope rearing up like the arched back of a cat.

"WindClan cats live *there*?" Sparkpaw asked.

Molewhisker nodded. "Yes, on the moor."

"It looks bleak," Alderpaw murmured with a shiver. "They must have their camp somewhere in these woods, right?"

"Wrong," his mentor responded. "They camp in a hollow on the moor, surrounded by gorse bushes. It wouldn't do for ThunderClan, but they seem to like it."

"I'd hate to be out there without any trees," Sparkpaw mewed. "I think—"

She broke off as a rabbit appeared, dashing over the brow of the hill. A moment later a thin, leggy tabby crested the rise, racing along in pursuit, her belly fur brushing the moorland grass and her tail streaming out behind her. Both creatures disappeared into a hollow, but a thin shriek, abruptly cut off, told the ThunderClan cats that the tabby had caught her prey.

"They're pretty fast," Molewhisker commented.

"I could just eat a rabbit," Sparkpaw sighed, licking her lips as if a piece of succulent prey were lying in front of her.

"Then we'll get back to camp," Cherryfall meowed. "It's not far from here."

"But I thought we were going to practice hunting!" Sparkpaw protested.

Alderpaw twitched his tail, hoping the mentors would say no. He felt nervous enough about remembering all the new things they'd learned without adding a hunting lesson to the mix. But Cherryfall and Molewhisker glanced at each other. "Okay," Molewhisker agreed after a moment. "But even if you catch something, you can't eat it. Everything goes back to the fresh-kill pile. The Clan must be fed first."

Alderpaw's heart sank. His belly was already rumbling.

But he tried to hide his disappointment.

Sparkpaw shrugged. "Fine. But we can still try, right?"

Heading away from the stream, the cats reached the edge of a clearing where a huge oak tree stood, its roots writhing up above the surface of the ground. Thick clumps of fern grew around it.

"This is a good place for prey," Molewhisker mewed, halting. "See what you can pick up."

Alderpaw closed his eyes, feeling a little overwhelmed by all the different scents flooding over him, and the different sounds he could hear in the undergrowth and the branches above his head. *This is a lot harder than picking out the WindClan scent. That was so strong it was hard to miss.*

Finally Alderpaw managed to home in on a scent he recognized: a shrew. He could hear a tiny scratching noise in the undergrowth, coming from the right direction. Opening his eyes, he spotted movement in the grass stems.

But am I sure . . . ? he asked himself, hesitating to point it out.

Before he decided whether to speak, Sparkpaw pointed with her tail. "There's a shrew over there."

"I can scent it too," Alderpaw agreed, hoping his mentor would believe he had spotted it for himself.

"Okay, you can try catching it," Cherryfall meowed, her gaze flicking from Alderpaw to Sparkpaw. "You've seen the hunter's crouch, haven't you—like this?" She demonstrated, pressing herself close to the ground with her muscles bunched, ready to move forward.

Alderpaw and Sparkpaw did their best to copy her.

"Good," Cherryfall went on. "Now, remember to keep low, and set your paws down really lightly. Careful you don't tread on a twig."

"And watch your tail," Molewhisker added. "If you let it wave around, your prey will know where you are."

"Sparkpaw, you try first," Cherryfall mewed.

Barely hesitating, Sparkpaw began to creep forward, her eyes gleaming with excitement. She kept her paws tucked in close to her body and her tail wrapped along her side. Suddenly she leaped forward, disappearing into the thickest part of the undergrowth.

A heartbeat later Sparkpaw reappeared, the limp body of a shrew dangling from her jaws. She paced back toward the others, her head raised proudly and her tail straight up in the air.

"Wow!" Cherryfall exclaimed as Sparkpaw dropped the shrew at her paws. "I've never heard of an apprentice catching something on her very first try."

"Neither have I," Molewhisker agreed. "Good job, Sparkpaw."

"Great catch," Alderpaw meowed.

"Oh, it was easy," Sparkpaw boasted. "I just did what you told me."

Molewhisker turned to his apprentice. "Let's see if Alderpaw can do as well."

Alderpaw felt himself stiffen with anxiety. *I sort of wish she'd missed that catch. Then I wouldn't have to worry about missing mine.* But he forced himself to push the envious thoughts aside.

"We'll move on," Cherryfall decided. "We've probably

scared all the prey away around here."

Alderpaw felt his paws growing heavier with every paw step as he followed the mentors. *I just know I'm going to mess up.* His belly was churning by the time they halted beside a small pool, with bushes and long grass growing around its edge.

"We should find something here," Molewhisker meowed. "Okay, both of you, show me the hunter's crouch."

Alderpaw squatted beside his sister, his pelt prickling with anxiety as both mentors padded around them, observing them closely.

"Good, Sparkpaw," Cherryfall mewed. "But keep your tail a bit closer."

"And Alderpaw, tuck your paws in a bit more," Molewhisker added.

"Yes, you can't have your hindpaws sticking out if you want a good pounce," Sparkpaw put in.

I know that, Alderpaw thought, giving her a glare.

"And you have to be really, really quick," Sparkpaw went on. "Your prey won't wait around for you. And your claws—"

"Sparkpaw, knock it off." Molewhisker's tone was irritable. "You're not the mentor here. You're a brand-new apprentice, just like Alderpaw."

Sparkpaw flattened her ears, then nodded reluctantly, while Alderpaw gave his mentor a grateful look. Molewhisker responded by brushing his tail over Alderpaw's shoulders.

"Remember what we told you about keeping low," Cherryfall continued. "And watch where you're putting your paws.

The snap of a twig, the wave of a fern frond, and your prey's gone."

Alderpaw nodded, trying to take in all the information. Then the moment he had dreaded finally arrived.

"Now, Alderpaw," Molewhisker meowed. "See if you can find some prey."

Alderpaw narrowed his eyes and concentrated, tasting the air. The scents here weren't quite so complicated, and he soon pinpointed a vole underneath a bush close to the water.

"There's a vole under there," he murmured to Molewhisker, angling his ears toward the bush.

Molewhisker gave him an approving nod. "Good. Go after it, then."

Alderpaw adjusted his crouch and began to creep forward, then hesitated. *Is the vole really under that bush, or in the clump of long grass just beside it? Should I go straight for it, or loop around the grass so it can't see me coming?*

"What's the matter?" Molewhisker hissed impatiently. "Go!"

Alderpaw was frozen with indecision. *I have to get this right, but I don't know how!*

While he was still hesitating, unable to move, the vole suddenly scampered out of the depths of the bush, plopped into the water, and vanished.

"Mouse-brain!" Sparkpaw exclaimed.

I probably deserve that, Alderpaw admitted to himself. He hung his head in shame as Molewhisker padded up to him. "A good hunter doesn't hesitate," his mentor meowed. "You need to trust your instincts." Then he relaxed a little and touched Alderpaw on the shoulder with his tail. "Never mind. There'll be other prey."

His mentor's kindness only made Alderpaw feel more ashamed. *I've let Molewhisker down.*

Sparkpaw suddenly darted off into the bushes, and Alderpaw looked up, startled. She emerged a moment later, swinging the body of a plump mouse by its tail.

"Sparkpaw, that's amazing!" Cherryfall's eyes were sparkling with delight. "You're going to be a great hunter."

"Yeah, good catch," Molewhisker muttered, his tail-tip twitching in annoyance.

I've let him down again, Alderpaw thought wretchedly. *I wanted so much to make him proud of me!*

Cherryfall picked up Sparkpaw's shrew and led the way as the cats headed back toward camp. Alderpaw trudged along with his head down, feeling more miserable and disgraced with every paw step. *I can't believe this is happening!*

"Don't worry," Molewhisker meowed briskly, padding along beside him. "You'll learn. You just have to go for it, not hesitate like you did back there."

"I know," Alderpaw murmured. *But that's easy enough to say.*

He didn't want to look at Cherryfall and Sparkpaw bouncing along ahead of them, carrying Sparkpaw's prey. And just when he thought he couldn't possibly feel more depressed, Ivypool, Birchfall, and Sorrelstripe emerged from the undergrowth. They were also heading for the camp, and also carrying prey.

"You've had good hunting," Cherryfall remarked, nodding toward the couple of squirrels and the rabbit the patrol were carrying.

"So have you, by the look of it," Ivypool responded.

"Oh, these are Sparkpaw's," Cherryfall meowed. "And it's her first day out of camp. Not bad, huh?"

"Wow, that's amazing!" Sorrelstripe exclaimed. "Good job, Sparkpaw."

"You've got a good apprentice there," Birchfall added.

"It's because Cherryfall is such a good mentor," Sparkpaw mewed.

No cat took any notice of Alderpaw, which suited him just fine. His tail drooped lower and lower with disappointment in himself, and he wished he could sink into the forest floor and disappear.

As they entered the camp, Alderpaw spotted Bramble-star standing on the Highledge outside his den, talking to Graystripe. As soon as he saw the returning cats, he broke off his conversation, ran lightly down the tumbled rocks and bounded across the clearing to meet them.

"How did your first day out of camp go?" he asked.

Cherryfall and Molewhisker exchanged a glance; Alder-paw could see they were amused by Bramblestar's eagerness to find out how his kits had done.

"I caught a shrew *and* a mouse!" Sparkpaw announced, puffing out her chest with pride.

"Excellent!" Bramblestar exclaimed, giving his daughter a lick around her ears. "And how about you, Alderpaw?"

Alderpaw was silent, looking down at his paws.

The awkward silence stretched out for a few heartbeats. It was Sparkpaw who spoke first. "Oh, he really listened to his mentor, and he learned all about ThunderClan's territory."

But there's nothing special about that, Alderpaw thought miserably.

"I'm sure Alderpaw will get the hang of hunting," Molewhisker meowed. "He's trying hard."

Alderpaw felt even worse to think that was the best his littermate and his mentor could find to say about him. *I just want Bramblestar to be proud of me!* With a desperate struggle he managed to raise his head and look at his father, bracing himself to meet disappointment in his gaze.

But Bramblestar's eyes revealed nothing. He hesitated for a moment, then gave a little nod. "Cherryfall and Molewhisker, you and Sparkpaw take the prey to the fresh-kill pile," he directed. "I'm sure you're hungry. Alderpaw, I want a word with you alone."

Sparkpaw shot Alderpaw a sympathetic glance as she and the other cats left. Alderpaw stood once more with his head lowered. "Are you angry with me?" he asked Bramblestar in a low voice. "I tried. I really did." He kept his gaze fixed on the ground; he couldn't bring himself to look up at his father again.

Bramblestar bent and touched Alderpaw's head gently with his nose. "I'm sure you tried hard," he told Alderpaw. "This is only the first day you've been out of camp. And I'm proud to hear that you're paying attention to your mentor and doing your best to learn."

Alderpaw still couldn't manage to meet his father's gaze. *He's just being nice. And I don't want to look up and see pity in his eyes.*

Bramblestar was silent for a few heartbeats. "Did I ever tell you much about my own apprentice days?" he meowed at last.

"I know Firestar was your mentor," Alderpaw mumbled, still looking down at his paws. "He must have thought you were pretty great, to mentor you when he was Clan leader."

Bramblestar sighed. "I think Firestar just wanted to keep a close eye on me. It took him a long time to trust me, because Tigerstar was my father." His voice had grown tight, as if he didn't want to think about the evil cat who had fathered him, the cat who had tried to murder his own Clan leader and make himself ruler of the whole forest. "Anyway," he went on after a moment, sounding more relaxed, "the first time I went hunting with Firestar, I really wanted to impress him. I ran so hard after a squirrel that I slipped on some wet leaves, went nose over paws, and crashed into a tree. Great StarClan, it hurt! And what hurt even more was that I was pretty sure Firestar had to stop himself from laughing."

"Really?" At last Alderpaw was able to look up without feeling ashamed or embarrassed. "Did that really happen?"

"It really did," Bramblestar confirmed. "It was an awful first try at hunting, but I soon got much better, and I'm sure you will too."

Gazing up into his father's gentle eyes, Alderpaw felt as

though a heavy weight were lifting off his back, and he began to look forward to going out with his mentor again. *I will get better,* he promised himself. *And one day I will be a warrior and make my Clan proud of me!*

CHAPTER 3

❧

The sun had gone down, and the outlines of the forest trees above the stone hollow had begun to fade into the twilight. Alderpaw sat outside the apprentices' den, giving himself a thorough grooming.

This is a special night. I have to look my best.

He and Sparkpaw had been apprentices for almost a half-moon. Looking back, Alderpaw felt that he hadn't done too badly. Molewhisker had praised him for being responsible about helping the elders and doing his share of the chores, like collecting moss to make every cat's nest comfortable, along with all the other tasks apprentices had to do. He had gone out on a border patrol, paid attention to the leader, and done everything he was supposed to.

Even though I haven't caught any prey yet, I almost caught a bird yesterday, and Molewhisker told me birds are especially hard to catch.

But Alderpaw had to admit that even though he was doing well, Sparkpaw was doing better. She never came back from hunting empty-pawed, and she seemed to find it so easy to learn battle moves.

But just because she's brilliant at everything doesn't mean that I'm awful,

Alderpaw told himself, trying hard to believe it. *I wonder what it would be like if I weren't an apprentice at the same time as Sparkpaw. Then I wouldn't have to compare myself with her all the time.* But the thought felt disloyal to his littermate, and he thrust it away, his pelt hot with guilt. *She's my sister! Of course I want to be with her!*

At that moment Sparkpaw appeared out of the gloom. "Are you ready?" she asked, bouncing on her paws with excitement. "Bramblestar is gathering the Clan by the thorn tunnel."

Alderpaw sprang up, pushing away his worries. Anticipation tingled through him from ears to tail-tip. "This is going to be so great!" he meowed. "Our first full-moon Gathering!"

"And we get to be introduced to the other Clans," Sparkpaw added as she and her brother scampered across the clearing side by side. "I can't wait!"

Joining the crowd of cats who clustered around the tunnel entrance, Alderpaw wondered what the other Clans would be like. Apart from glimpses across the border when he was on patrol, he'd only seen cats from another Clan once, when he was still a kit and two medicine cats from RiverClan had come to talk to Jayfeather and Leafpool. They had looked just like normal cats, except that their pelts were especially thick and sleek, and they had left a funny, fishy smell behind them. And while they were in the camp, all the ThunderClan cats had been tense, casting sidelong glances at them, with their neck fur bristling.

Anyway, medicine cats are different from real warriors, Alderpaw told himself. It was hard for him to imagine whole other Clans full of cats.

At last Bramblestar raised his tail to lead the cats who had been chosen to go to the Gathering. As Alderpaw padded through the tunnel near the back of the group, his excitement began to ebb. *I hope I don't do something stupid in front of all those strange cats.*

By now Alderpaw was becoming used to the forest in daylight, but he realized when he slid out through the thorn tunnel that it looked quite different in twilight. The trees seemed thicker and more mysterious; the air was cooler and carried different scents. The darkness was full of new sounds, and it was hard to work out where they were coming from.

By the time he and his Clanmates emerged onto the lake-shore, Alderpaw's heart was pounding. He had barely left the shelter of the trees when he heard a hooting sound above his head. Flinching, he whipped around to stare up into the darkness. A pale wing swept across his vision, and then the owl was gone.

Suppressing a shiver, Alderpaw turned to Squirrelflight, who was padding along beside him. "I've heard stories about huge owls," he began nervously, "big enough to snatch up a cat. Is it true?"

Squirrelflight's green eyes glinted in the dusk with a mixture of kindness and amusement. "The owls in these woods aren't big enough to attack a cat," she replied.

Alderpaw mulled over her answer. He was only partly comforted: Did his mother mean that somewhere else there *were* owls big enough to take cats as their prey? And if there were, couldn't they come to the forest one day?

Molewhisker, who was walking on Alderpaw's other side, flicked his apprentice's ear with his tail. "Someday Cherry-fall and I will take you and Sparkpaw hunting at night," he meowed. "There's a lot of prey that's out of its nest at night instead of during the day."

"That's . . . er . . . great," Alderpaw responded weakly.

Just then he heard a shocked, excited sound from Spark-paw, who was just behind him along with Cherryfall. Glancing back, Alderpaw spotted little lights flickering on and off in the darkness, as if little scraps of sunlight were dancing in the air.

"What are those?" Sparkpaw asked, staring at the lights as if she couldn't believe what she was seeing.

"They're called fireflies," Cherryfall explained. "Insects that light up just like the stars. Isn't that cool?"

"It's fantastic!" Alderpaw mewed.

Sparkpaw shot off toward the lights, and Alderpaw hesitated less than a moment before he followed her. Excitement filled him as he leaped up, batting at the fireflies with his paws as if he could catch the little sparks of sunlight. Beside him his sister was leaping up too, twisting in the air, but the tiny glints of light were always just out of reach.

"Sparkpaw! Alderpaw!" Squirrelflight's stern voice rang out after a few heartbeats. "Come back here right now."

Alderpaw and Sparkpaw dropped to their paws and pad-ded back to the group of cats, panting and disheveled.

"What do you think you're doing?" Squirrelflight asked as they rejoined her. "When you're on your way to a full-moon

Gathering, you're representing ThunderClan, and when you meet the other Clans you had better behave *perfectly*."

Alderpaw dipped his head. "We will. I'm sorry."

"Sorry," Sparkpaw echoed.

"I should think so!" Squirrelflight stalked on ahead.

The two apprentices followed, but as soon as Squirrelflight was out of earshot, Sparkpaw leaned closer to Alderpaw. "Wasn't that *amazing*?" she whispered. "We never saw stuff like that when we were stuck in camp all the time!"

The ThunderClan cats skirted the lake, keeping close to the edge as they passed through WindClan territory. On the way, they watched the moon emerge from behind thick clouds, shedding a cold silver light over the surface of the water.

"Good," Molewhisker meowed. "If StarClan is angry, they cover the moon. This means the Gathering can go ahead."

At the far side of WindClan territory, Alderpaw spotted a cluster of Twoleg dens in the frosty moonlight. "That must be the horseplace," he murmured to Sparkpaw. "Remember Daisy telling us about it in the nursery?"

Sparkpaw paused a moment, scanning the ground beyond the Twoleg fence. "I can't see any horses," she mewed, sounding disappointed. "Maybe they go into their dens when—"

She broke off as Squirrelflight gave her a prod. "Keep moving. We're almost there."

Alderpaw's excitement mounted as they crossed a stretch of marshy ground and the tree-bridge leading to the Gathering island came into view. Another group of cats was milling around the shore near the end of the fallen tree.

"That's WindClan," Cherryfall told the two apprentices. "Take a good sniff so you can learn their scent."

Alderpaw had encountered the WindClan scent on their border with ThunderClan, but it was much stronger here: a scent that suggested cool air and tough, scraggly plants. There was a hint of rabbit, too, he decided. The WindClan cats looked fairly ordinary, though they were thinner than most of his Clanmates, with long legs and wiry, muscular bodies.

Bramblestar paced forward through the crowd of cats and dipped his head politely to a brown tabby tom whose graying muzzle told of his age.

"Greetings, Onestar," Bramblestar meowed. "How's the prey running in WindClan?"

"Well enough, I suppose," the WindClan leader replied gruffly. "I hope your warriors kept close to the lake when you passed through our territory."

"Of course." Bramblestar's tone was calm. "ThunderClan would never dream of trespassing."

Onestar's only response was a grunt.

Bramblestar signaled to his cats to stay back while the WindClan cats crossed the tree-bridge to the island. Alderpaw's paws prickled with nervousness as he watched them balancing along the trunk and leaping to the ground at the far end.

I wonder if any cat has ever fallen into the lake, he thought. *That would be so embarrassing!*

As Bramblestar began to lead the ThunderClan cats across, Alderpaw kept his head high. When it came to Sparkpaw's turn she raced across and hurled herself onto the shore of the island with a yowl of triumph.

Cherryfall, who was next, rolled her eyes. "I'll have to say something to her about taking risks," she muttered.

Alderpaw clambered onto the tree trunk and was relieved to find that it was much wider and steadier than he expected. He didn't like the sight of the dark water just below him, or the sucking sound it made as it lapped against the tree, but he kept his gaze fixed on the island ahead of him and was massively relieved when he reached the tree roots. He jumped down beside Sparkpaw, who had waited for him.

"Come on, slow mole!" she urged him. "We're missing all the fun!"

Alderpaw saw that the ThunderClan warriors were pushing their way through a thick line of bushes at the top of a slope that led up from the beach. With Sparkpaw beside him, he raced up the slope and thrust himself into the bushes after his Clanmates. As the thorns raked through his pelt he reflected that he hadn't needed to spend so much time grooming himself.

On the other side of the bushes Alderpaw found himself at the edge of a wide circle of grass. A huge, gnarled oak tree stood in the center, its roots as thick as a cat's body. All around it cats were milling around; some were talking together in clusters, while others found comfortable spots and settled down facing the oak tree. Their mingled scents caught Alderpaw in the throat so that he almost choked.

"It looks like all the other Clans are already here," Sparkpaw murmured into his ear. "I've never seen so many cats!"

Alderpaw nodded in agreement. He was especially astonished to see a crowd of young cats—*probably apprentices like us,* he thought—yowling and tussling together in the shelter of the bushes. *I thought you were supposed to behave perfectly at a Gathering,* he thought, remembering what Squirrelflight had told him. *But maybe other Clans have different rules.*

"Well, what do you think?" Molewhisker asked; he had padded up unnoticed while Alderpaw was staring at the rowdy young cats.

"It's amazing!" Alderpaw breathed out.

"It sure is," Cherryfall agreed, emerging from the bushes and giving her pelt a shake. "Especially your first time."

"Look," Molewhisker meowed, pointing with his tail. "That's Rowanstar, the ShadowClan leader, climbing into the Great Oak."

Alderpaw blinked as he looked up at the powerful ginger tom who settled himself in the fork between two branches and gazed around commandingly. *He looks like a cat I wouldn't want to cross.*

"You've already seen Onestar, there on the branch just above Rowanstar," Molewhisker went on, indicating the brown tabby tom. "And here comes Mistystar, the RiverClan leader."

Alderpaw saw a gray-blue she-cat leap gracefully into the tree; several leaves fluttered down as she found a spot on a lower branch. He noticed that Bramblestar too was heading for the tree, and felt a thrill of pride to see his father ready to take his place with the other leaders. *He's so important!*

"The deputies sit on the roots," Cherryfall told the apprentices. "The brown-and-white tom is WindClan's deputy, Harespring, and the black tom next to him is Reedwhisker from RiverClan. The cat just joining them is Crowfrost from ShadowClan."

"And I'd better get my tail over there, too," Squirrelflight meowed as she padded past. Pausing briefly, she added to the apprentices, "This is your chance to get to know cats in other Clans. Go and introduce yourselves."

Alderpaw saw that the older ThunderClan cats were mixing with the other Clans already, settling down with their friends and eagerly exchanging gossip. Squirrelflight joined the other deputies, while Bramblestar swarmed up the tree and sat on a branch near Mistystar.

Alderpaw looked around nervously, not knowing which of this milling crowd of cats he dared approach. *I'd rather just stick with Sparkpaw,* he told himself.

"I'll introduce you to a few cats, if you like," Cherryfall offered.

Alderpaw was about to accept gratefully when Sparkpaw's ears twitched. "We don't need help, thanks," she mewed. "We'll manage just fine on our own."

"Okay." Cherryfall dipped her head. "See you later." She padded off and plopped herself down beside a rangy tabby she-cat who looked as if she belonged to WindClan.

Alderpaw turned to glare at his littermate. "Why did you say that?" he demanded. "I'd much rather be introduced by

Cherryfall than walk up to a strange cat and have to introduce myself."

Sparkpaw returned his glare. "I'm not going to hide behind an older cat like I'm some kind of *kit*," she hissed. "What would the cats from the other Clans think of me then?"

"Fine," Alderpaw retorted. "But who are we going to talk to?"

Sparkpaw let her head and tail droop a little, as if she was only just now thinking that through. Then she raised her chin high again and looked around.

Almost at once Alderpaw spotted another cat gesturing to them with her tail. She seemed to be an apprentice by her size, a sleek silver-gray she-cat with white chest fur. Her bold green eyes sparkled as she called out, "Hey! Over here!"

Relieved that another cat had made the first move, Alderpaw trotted over with Sparkpaw by his side. He picked up the weird reek that was familiar from the ShadowClan border, but was too polite to wrinkle his nose.

"I'm Needlepaw," the silver she-cat announced. "This is Sleekpaw, and that's Beepaw."

The two apprentices she was with nodded in greeting. Sleekpaw was a yellow she-cat, and Beepaw a plump white she-cat with black ears.

"Hi," Beepaw meowed, shifting to make room for the two ThunderClan apprentices under the bush where they were crouching. "We're from ShadowClan."

"Is this your first Gathering?" Needlepaw asked. "It's my second—I've been an apprentice for three moons."

"Yes, it's our first," Alderpaw responded. "I'm Alderpaw, and this is Sparkpaw."

"We're from ThunderClan," Sparkpaw added.

"Are you really?" Needlepaw's brilliant green eyes widened. "Does that mean you want to boss all the other cats in the forest around?"

"No, it does *not*!" Sparkpaw exclaimed with a lash of her tail, while Alderpaw's neck fur bristled. "What are you even talking about?" Sparkpaw went on. "Why would you insult us like that?"

"All right, keep your fur on," Needlepaw meowed, with an amused glance at her Clanmates. "I was only teasing. All the Clans have reputations with the others. ThunderClan cats are bossy, WindClan cats get scared and run away, and RiverClan cats are too fat and lazy to hunt properly."

Alderpaw narrowly stopped himself from gaping, exchanging a scandalized glance with Sparkpaw. *Who does she think she is, talking about other Clans like that?*

"Well, *I* think it's stupid," Sleekpaw added, licking one paw and drawing it over her ear. "What Clan you're in doesn't decide what you're like. It's just where you're born. Some of the cats in ShadowClan are every bit as bossy as Thunder-Clan cats."

Sparkpaw's ears pricked forward in shock at Sleekpaw's idea, though Alderpaw had the feeling that she might be right.

Before Sparkpaw could argue, a cat's voice rang out across the clearing. "Cats of all Clans!" It was Rowanstar, standing tall and proud on his branch. "Welcome to the Gathering.

Mistystar, would you like to speak first?"

The gray-blue she-cat dipped her head as she rose to her paws. "RiverClan is doing well," she began. "The lake is full of fish . . ."

"RiverClan cats eat fish!" exclaimed Beepaw. "Can you imagine? No wonder they're so smelly."

Alderpaw glanced around to see if any ShadowClan warriors would correct Beepaw's behavior, but there were none within earshot. He hoped furiously that Mistystar hadn't heard the comment, but if she had, she ignored it.

"A new litter of four kits has been born to Lakeheart," she announced, then dipped her head again to Rowanstar before resuming her seat.

"Onestar?" Rowanstar gestured to the WindClan leader.

"Hunting has been good on the moor," Onestar announced.

"I bet *he* hasn't done much hunting," Needlepaw muttered. "Creaky old mange-pelt!"

"Yeah, my mentor said he couldn't catch a blind hedgehog, never mind a rabbit," Sleekpaw responded.

They're talking about a Clan leader! Alderpaw couldn't help but be amused, and he heard a suppressed snort of laughter from Sparkpaw. But he was shocked by their comments, and even more shocked that ShadowClan warriors would talk like that in front of apprentices.

"Some rogues passed through the edges of our territory," Onestar continued. "Crowfeather led a patrol to keep an eye on them, and the rogues left without making any trouble. They'll be a long way away by now."

"I'd have clawed their ears off if they'd come to Shad-owClan," Beepaw murmured, sliding out her claws. "That'd teach them not to trespass on our territory."

"WindClan has always been weak," Needlepaw added. "That's what I heard Tawnypelt telling Crowfrost, anyway."

Sleekpaw bent forward to mutter something into Needlepaw's ear, but Alderpaw stopped listening, as Bramblestar had just risen to make his report.

"The prey is running well in ThunderClan," the tabby tom meowed. "And two new apprentices, Alderpaw and Sparkpaw, have begun training with their mentors, Molewhisker and Cherryfall."

Alderpaw was aware of every cat turning to look at him and his littermate. Some of them yowled out their names. "Alderpaw! Sparkpaw!" Utterly embarrassed, he lowered his head to lick his chest fur. *It was bad enough being the center of attention when it was just my own Clan!*

Sparkpaw, however, was preening, thoroughly enjoying the welcoming yowls of the other cats.

Bramblestar had taken his seat on the branch again, and Rowanstar stepped forward.

"Prey is plentiful in ShadowClan," he reported.

"Honestly!" Needlepaw whispered. "Does any cat expect him to say anything else? If we were all starving, he'd say just the same. He must think we're all mouse-brained."

Alderpaw was shocked all over again at the disrespectful way Needlepaw spoke. *Don't these cats even respect their own leader? I would never talk about Bramblestar like that!* He was sure that

Rowanstar wasn't lying. These sleek she-cats obviously had all the prey they could eat.

"Twolegs are still using the greenleaf Twolegplace on our territory," Rowanstar went on. "But they haven't caused much trouble, and as the weather gets colder over the next couple of moons, we don't expect to see much of them."

"And it can't be soon enough for me," Needlepaw muttered.

"Two of our apprentices have been made warriors." Rowanstar glanced down proudly, sweeping his tail around to indicate a white tom and a yellow she-cat, who stood close together near the Great Oak. "Stonewing and Wasptail."

The two new warriors stood up straighter, their eyes gleaming, as their Clanmates yowled their names enthusiastically. Most of the other cats joined in.

"Also," Rowanstar continued when the clamor had died down, "four kits have been made apprentices. Beepaw is apprenticed to Dawnpelt, Sleekpaw to Tigerheart, Juniperpaw to Stonewing, and Strikepaw to Wasptail."

Instead of yowling to acclaim the new apprentices, a murmur of surprise arose from all the cats. Onestar looked sharply at the ginger tom. "Is ShadowClan really giving apprentices to brand-new warriors now?" he asked disapprovingly.

"By the time ShadowClan cats are warriors," Rowanstar retorted, the faintest suggestion of a growl in his voice, "they're ready for anything. Other Clans need to stay out of ShadowClan business."

Alderpaw noticed that the ShadowClan apprentices sitting beside him were looking a bit smug.

"ShadowClan has *lots* of apprentices," Needlepaw informed him loftily. "Rowanstar doesn't know what to do with us all."

"That's nice for you," Sparkpaw mewed pertly.

Alderpaw felt even more strongly that it was weird, both the way the ShadowClan apprentices talked about their leader and the fact that an apprentice would be so casual about sharing her Clan's weaknesses with others.

He was distracted from his thoughts when he noticed that the four Clan leaders had drawn closer together in the branches of the oak tree and were speaking to one another in low tones.

A moment later Rowanstar stepped forward again. "The medicine cats have something to say to all the Clans," he announced. "Something important that they have only discussed with their leaders so far."

A tense silence fell among the Clans as the medicine cats gathered together in front of the Great Oak. As well as Leafpool and Jayfeather, Alderpaw recognized Mothwing and her apprentice, Willowshine, from when they had visited the ThunderClan camp.

"That old tom must be Littlecloud from ShadowClan," he murmured to Sparkpaw.

"So the cat with the splotchy gray fur is Kestrelflight from WindClan," Sparkpaw responded.

The medicine cats conferred together rapidly before Kestrelflight leaped up onto one of the oak roots beside the deputies.

"All of us have shared a vision," he began. "We received a

prophecy that is vital to all our Clans."

Meows of shock and confusion rose from the cats around him as he finished speaking.

"Why would StarClan give you a *shared* vision?" some cat called out.

"Which cat spoke to you all?"

"It's been *seasons* since we had a prophecy!"

The clamor grew louder and louder until Jayfeather stood up, lashing his tail. "For StarClan's sake, shut up and listen!" he snapped.

Gradually the noise died down, until Kestrelflight could make himself heard again. "Firestar spoke to us first," he reported.

"Oh, yeah, it *would* be Firestar!" Needlepaw muttered. "He has his tail in every cat's business, even now he's dead."

"He said, 'Embrace what you find in the shadows, for only they can clear the sky.'"

"And what did he mean by that?" Harespring, the Wind-Clan deputy, asked.

"We don't know," Kestrelflight replied.

Harespring sniffed. "Well, great."

As he listened to Kestrelflight, Alderpaw couldn't shake off the feeling that all this was somehow familiar. He could almost picture a large cat with a flame-colored pelt—a cat he had never seen—speaking the words. *Could that have been Firestar?* But everything was vague, like a half-remembered dream; he tried to push the shadowy memory away and focus on what was being said.

When Kestrelflight fell silent, agitated voices rose all around him.

"What does it mean?"

"What would we find 'in the shadows'?"

"And how are we supposed to find it if we don't know what it is?"

"Maybe it's ShadowClan?"

"If you ask me," a scarred ShadowClan elder hissed, "what should be *embraced* is a bit more respect for senior warriors."

Beepaw and Needlepaw shared a quiet purr of laughter. "Ratscar's always saying that!" Beepaw murmured.

A pretty RiverClan apprentice raised her tail. "I found some really beautiful blue feathers that I decorated my nest with in a shady glen," she meowed. "Do you think they could be important?"

An older RiverClan tabby—her mentor, Alderpaw guessed—gave her a sharp cuff over the ear. "Stupid furball!"

"Our old territory, back in the forest, was filled with shadows," Onestar murmured. He looked old and frail, his eyes full of memories. "So much was lost to us when we left."

"But how could we possibly find our old territory?" Mistystar asked. Her voice was warm and sympathetic, and she stretched out her tail to draw the tip down the WindClan leader's flank. "It's gone."

"I've got a question." Cloudtail rose from where he was sitting beside Brightheart and Whitewing and faced the medicine cats. "Do we think this prophecy applies to all the Clans? Or was it meant for Jayfeather specifically?"

"Good question," Littlecloud responded.

"Firestar prefaced it with 'a time of great change is coming for all the Clans,'" Jayfeather replied. "Which would seem to mean, yes, this is meant for all of us."

A new swell of voices, confused and angry, rose from all four Clans.

"Is StarClan saying that we *all* must embrace what we find in the shadows—whatever that is?" Crowfrost demanded.

Alderpaw could feel the tension in the clearing, as if a covering of cold, dark fog had suddenly descended. Cats were sharing uneasy glances and muttering to one another in low voices.

"This is so exciting!" Sparkpaw whispered. "Maybe *we'll* find the shadowy thing and save ThunderClan."

"I doubt it," Alderpaw responded. *I don't feel ready to be heroic.*

"What?" Needlepaw had obviously overheard. "*No* ThunderClan cat is better at finding things than *any* ShadowClan cat!"

"You *would* say that!" Sparkpaw flashed back at her. "Just you wait and see!"

"I think the whole idea is silly," Sleekpaw mewed disdainfully, though Alderpaw noticed that she kept her voice low while she said it. "Prophecies and StarClan and all that stuff are just ridiculous!"

Alderpaw and Sparkpaw exchanged a shocked glance. *Does Sleekpaw not believe in StarClan?* Alderpaw wondered. *That's terrible!* He thought that Needlepaw and Beepaw were shocked too, silent for a few heartbeats, even though they finally forced out short purrs of laughter.

A sudden prickling sensation at the back of his neck made Alderpaw feel that some cat was looking at him. He glanced over his shoulder toward the Great Oak, and his pelt began to prickle with alarm. Seated at the foot of the tree with the other medicine cats, Leafpool was staring directly at him.

Why?

CHAPTER 4

"Alderpaw, will you concentrate!" Molewhisker gave an irritable lash of his tail. "Any kit could learn this move."

The two apprentices were battle training with their mentors in a clearing near the camp. Molewhisker was teaching them to rear up on their hind paws so they could attack their opponent from above. Sparkpaw had gotten the idea right away, and Alderpaw's ears were smarting from the blows she had landed on him. But somehow every time he tried it, he would overbalance, or Sparkpaw would slip aside before his blows could connect.

Alderpaw knew exactly why he couldn't give all his attention to training. He couldn't shake the uneasy feeling Leafpool's gaze had given him at the Gathering the night before. Why was she always *staring* at him? Until recently, neither of the medicine cats had paid any attention to him, apart from the time he had gotten a thorn in his paw when he was a kit. Now he felt as if they were aware of him all the time. *I don't like it,* he told himself.

"That's enough battle training for today," Molewhisker meowed with a sigh. "Cherryfall, why don't you and Sparkpaw collect your prey from earlier? Alderpaw, you and I will try hunting in another part of the forest."

"Okay," Cherryfall agreed. "We might see what else we can catch on the way back. Good luck, Alderpaw."

She and Sparkpaw headed back toward the camp. Sparkpaw had a bounce in her step; in the earlier hunting session she had caught a fat thrush and a squirrel, and Cherryfall couldn't praise her highly enough.

"Come on, Alderpaw." Molewhisker turned to pad deeper into the forest. "Maybe you'll hunt better without your littermate close by."

Fat chance, Alderpaw thought gloomily as he followed his mentor. *I haven't caught anything yet. Not just today, but ever. Sparkpaw catches stuff all the time.*

Once again his thoughts drifted back to Leafpool's steady gaze on him. *Medicine cats know things,* he reflected. *Maybe she knows that there's something wrong with me, and I'll never be a good warrior.*

He was worrying so much that he didn't realize Molewhisker had halted and was speaking to him. All he heard was the final words: ". . . try doing it that way."

"Sorry," he mewed. "Would you mind saying that again?"

Molewhisker flexed his claws, and his voice was sharp as he replied. "Alderpaw, you need to pay attention. A cat who can't hunt is no good to his Clan."

Alderpaw flinched at the harsh tone. Molewhisker gazed at him and sighed, shaking his head slightly. He was obviously making a massive effort to regain his patience.

"I want you to focus very intensely on one small area at a time while you're looking for prey," he meowed. "Don't open your ears and nose to all the territory around you."

"Okay, I'll try," Alderpaw responded.

After glancing around, he picked out the undergrowth at the foot of an oak tree and concentrated all his senses on it. Eventually he heard something scratching among the tree roots; tasting the air, he recognized the scent of mouse.

Alderpaw dropped into the hunter's crouch and crept forward. He remembered everything Molewhisker had taught him: to keep low, his belly fur brushing the ground, and to keep his tail curled against his side.

He set down his paws as lightly as he could, and as he drew closer to the tree, his whole pelt tingled with the thought of victory. *This time I'm going to do it. . . . I'm sure of it!*

Now he could see the small, gray body of the mouse crouched behind a tuft of long grass. His jaws were already watering at the anticipated taste of prey. But just as he was readying himself to pounce, a twig cracked underneath his forepaw. With a flicker, the mouse was gone.

Alderpaw halted, letting out a growl of frustration. He didn't dare look at Molewhisker until his mentor stood right over him.

Molewhisker's tail-tip was twitching in agitation. "Maybe that's enough for today," he meowed, his voice tightly controlled.

He was silent as he led the way back to camp, and Alderpaw followed in a fog of despair. *It's all going wrong! Whoever heard of a warrior who can't fight and can't hunt?*

As soon as they emerged from the thorn tunnel into the camp, Bramblestar bounded over to them. "Molewhisker, I need a word with you," he meowed. "Come up to my den."

"Okay, Bramblestar." Molewhisker glanced back as he followed his leader toward the tumbled rocks. "Alderpaw, you can get something to eat."

Alderpaw trudged over to the fresh-kill pile. Sparkpaw was already there, tucking into the thrush she had caught. "How did it go?" she asked.

"Awful," Alderpaw replied. "I missed *another* really easy catch."

"Oh, mouse dung!" Sparkpaw's gaze was sympathetic, and she pressed her muzzle briefly into Alderpaw's shoulder. "Never mind. You can share this thrush. There's plenty."

"Thanks," Alderpaw mewed miserably. *Am I always going to depend on other cats for food?*

As he took his first bite, Sparkpaw glanced curiously up at Bramblestar's den on the Highledge. "Are you in trouble?" she asked. "Is that why Bramblestar is talking to Molewhisker?"

Alderpaw's belly lurched. *I never thought of that. I was just so relieved to have the training over.* "Of course not," he responded, gazing nervously up at the Highledge. But he couldn't keep a quaver out of his voice, and he knew Sparkpaw realized he didn't believe what he was saying.

As he watched, Bramblestar and Molewhisker emerged from the den, Jayfeather and Leafpool walking in their wake. All four cats climbed down the tumbled rocks to the ground.

Bramblestar waved his tail to beckon Alderpaw. *Oh, StarClan! It is about me,* Alderpaw thought. Exchanging a glance with his sister, he swallowed and headed toward his Clan leader.

"I know you've been working hard as an apprentice," Bramblestar began as Alderpaw joined him. His voice and his eyes were kind. "I'm really proud of all you've learned. But sometimes a cat can find himself halfway down the wrong path."

Alderpaw blinked at his father. "I don't understand."

Bramblestar's eyes softened. "It appears that you now have a new destiny: you're going to be a medicine-cat apprentice."

Alderpaw gaped. "What?" He had expected to be punished for his failure, but never that he would be taken away from Molewhisker altogether. "I'm not going to be a warrior anymore?"

Bramblestar nodded to the two medicine cats. "Leafpool and Jayfeather saw your new destiny in a vision."

"But I *can't!*" Alderpaw had never in his wildest imaginings thought of being a medicine cat. *I'd be even more useless at that!*

Besides, he couldn't really believe in this vision. Surely it was just an excuse so that Bramblestar could protect his feelings. *Leafpool and Jayfeather don't need another medicine cat,* he thought. He was so horrified and humiliated that he wanted to flee from the camp and run and run until he was far away from any cat who knew about his failure.

"*Please,*" he begged. "I promise I'll do better. I'll listen to Molewhisker and try really hard!"

"I know you've already been trying hard," Molewhisker told him sympathetically. "I'm not angry with you."

Leafpool took a step forward. "This isn't a punishment," she explained. "Jayfeather and I asked Bramblestar for this."

"They said they believe you'll be able to talk with StarClan," Bramblestar put in.

Alderpaw began to realize that his Clan leader, his *father*, wouldn't lie to him. But he was still doubtful. *I can't think what's given Leafpool and Jayfeather the idea that I can speak to StarClan.* "Isn't there anything I can do to make you change your mind?" he asked desperately.

Bramblestar shook his head. "It has nothing to do with *me*," he replied. "It is the will of StarClan. This is what you are meant to do."

Realizing it would do no good to keep on arguing, Alderpaw took a deep breath. "Okay," he sighed. When Bramblestar dismissed him with a nod, he staggered back to where Sparkpaw was still eating, and stared blankly at the remains of the thrush. *I'm not hungry anymore.*

"What did Bramblestar and Molewhisker want to tell you?" Sparkpaw asked curiously.

"They said . . ." Alderpaw's voice was trembling; he took a breath and started again. "They said I have to be a medicine-cat apprentice."

Sparkpaw's eyes stretched wide with amazement. "That's great!" she exclaimed. "Medicine cats are really important." Then she seemed to realize how unhappy Alderpaw was feeling and added more sympathetically, "But it doesn't seem like it's as much *fun* to be a medicine cat as it is to be a regular warrior. All those icky herbs!" She blinked thoughtfully for a moment. "Maybe that's why you're so bad at hunting—you're meant to be a medicine cat."

Alderpaw felt as if he wanted to retch up every piece of prey he had ever eaten. *I'm sure that's why they want me to be a medicine cat: not because I'm special and important, but because I'm no good as a warrior apprentice.*

He swallowed hard, feeling as if there were a tight knot in his chest. *Well, I'll just show them! I'm going to be the best medicine-cat apprentice I can be,* he resolved. *I'll try really hard, and make Bramblestar and Squirrelflight proud.*

But deep down inside, Alderpaw wasn't sure he could do it. *I'm not really a medicine cat. I'm not . . . special enough.*

A chilly dawn mist filled the stone hollow as Alderpaw tumbled out of his den. Sparkpaw was still snoring peacefully in her mossy nest. He arched his back in a good long stretch, then headed out into the camp.

Most of his Clanmates were still asleep, though Squirrelflight was standing outside the warriors' den, organizing the dawn patrol with Brackenfur, Berrynose, and Brightheart.

"You're up early," she remarked to Alderpaw as he padded past.

"Jayfeather wants me in the medicine cats' den," Alderpaw responded.

"Best not be late, then," his mother mewed, giving him a swift lick around the ears. "But get yourself some fresh-kill first. You can't learn on an empty belly."

"Thanks!" Alderpaw darted to the fresh-kill pile, grabbed a shrew, and gulped it down.

This was Alderpaw's second day as a medicine-cat apprentice. The day before, he had sat in a corner of the den, watching and trying to keep out of the way. But Leafpool had said that today he would start helping.

Part of him was looking forward to that, but Alderpaw was sure that Jayfeather, who was always so snappy and short-tempered, didn't really want him there. *Leafpool is much kinder,* he thought with a sigh, *but I wish she would stop giving me funny looks.*

Both medicine cats slept in the den, along with Briarlight, whose hind legs didn't work, and any other sick cats who needed constant attention. It was so crowded that Jayfeather and Leafpool had decided that for the time being Alderpaw should still sleep in the apprentices' den with Sparkpaw. Alderpaw was glad to be with his littermate, but it made him feel even more that he wasn't a real medicine cat. His pelt felt hot with jealousy all over again when he remembered the previous night: Sparkpaw had told him all about going on a border patrol with Cherryfall and the other cats. *Why can't I just be normal and a good warrior apprentice like Sparkpaw?* he thought with a sigh. Then he braced himself. *I won't think like that anymore. I'm going to do the best I can. I'm not going to fail at this too.*

As soon as Alderpaw pushed his way past the bramble screen in front of the medicine cats' den, Jayfeather turned from where he was rooting among the herbs in the cleft at the back. "You're late," he snapped.

"Oh, come on, Jayfeather," Leafpool meowed, looking up from massaging Briarlight's hindquarters. "The sun isn't up yet."

Jayfeather bared his teeth in the beginning of a snarl. "I'll say what I like," he retorted. "I'm not your apprentice now. Did you sleep well?" he asked Alderpaw.

"Yes, thanks," Alderpaw responded, taken aback by the sudden change in Jayfeather's tone from irritable to intense.

Jayfeather turned to face him. "Do you have strange dreams sometimes?"

Alderpaw felt awkward under Jayfeather's blind gaze. It seemed almost rude to stare at him when he knew Jayfeather couldn't see. He glanced aside, only to meet Leafpool's gaze, also fixed intently on him.

Alderpaw's skin crawled as if a whole nest of ants was living in his fur. "I—I guess I do, sometimes," he stammered. "Doesn't every cat?"

"I do!" Briarlight interrupted, hauling herself up onto her forepaws. "I dreamed just the other night that I remembered I could fly, and I went soaring off over Clan territory. It was great!"

Alderpaw was thoroughly relieved to have the attention taken away from him.

Jayfeather and Leafpool exchanged a glance; then Jayfeather shrugged and turned back to the stored herbs. "Come over here," he meowed to Alderpaw. "It's time you started to learn about herbs."

Alderpaw joined him and peered at the herbs piled up in

little heaps. They looked like so many dead leaves to him, but he had the good sense not to say so.

"This is goldenrod," Jayfeather began, sniffing at a plant with bright yellow flowers. "We use it for cleaning wounds. And this is tansy, which is good for coughs—not as good as catmint, which is this plant here."

"But useful all the same," Leafpool put in. She had finished giving Briarlight her massage and was helping her exercise by tossing a ball of moss for Briarlight to catch. "And it helps with back pain, too."

"This is watermint," Jayfeather went on, angling his ears toward a plant with hairy stems and spikes of purple flowers. "We give that for bellyache."

"Let him have a sniff," Leafpool suggested. "So much of what we do depends on scent," she added to Alderpaw.

Jayfeather edged backward so that Alderpaw could reach the cleft and sniff at the various herbs. *They all smell alike to me,* Alderpaw thought. *Sort of . . . herby.*

"And this one is yarrow," Jayfeather continued. "It makes a cat vomit if they've swallowed poison, and we also make an ointment of it to heal cracked pads. Got that?" he asked, turning swiftly back to Alderpaw.

"Uh . . . I think so," Alderpaw mewed. In fact his brain was whirling, and he thought he would never manage to remember all the different herbs and their uses. *And this is only a small part of them!*

Jayfeather continued to point out different herbs and let Alderpaw sniff them, until Alderpaw felt he had been concentrating for moons. His shoulders ached and his eyes stung in the scent-laden air.

The sun was well up when the bramble screen was pushed aside again and Sparkpaw padded into the den.

"What do you want?" Jayfeather asked. "We're busy here, so it had better be good."

"Cherryfall sent me," Sparkpaw replied, sounding not at all bothered by Jayfeather's unfriendly tone. "Purdy has a belly-ache, and I've come to get herbs for it."

"Oh, poor Purdy!" Leafpool exclaimed. "I'll come to the elders' den and check on him."

Jayfeather swung around on Alderpaw. "Well? What herb should Leafpool take with her? What's good for bellyache?"

"Uh . . . that would be . . ." Alderpaw knew that Jayfeather had told him. But his head was stuffed with quickly recited herb names, and he couldn't pull out the one he wanted. Panicking, he glanced wildly around and spotted Briarlight mouthing *watermint* at him.

"Watermint," Alderpaw meowed, with a grateful look at Briarlight.

He felt warmed to notice that Sparkpaw looked impressed. *It's nice to show her what I can do, for a change.*

"Okay," Jayfeather mewed briskly. "Now find it in the stores."

Alderpaw stared at the piles of herbs. He had no idea which one was watermint. Aware of Jayfeather twitching impatiently beside him, he pulled out a stem with bright yellow flowers.

Jayfeather sighed. "No, that's goldenrod. Purdy had better

not eat that; we put it on wounds. This is watermint."

He snagged the purple-flowered plant in his claws and gave it to Leafpool, who headed out of the den with Sparkpaw following.

"You need to pay close attention," Jayfeather told Alderpaw sharply. "Cats' lives depend on us getting things right."

"I know . . . ," Alderpaw sighed.

How will I ever learn all this?

CHAPTER 5

Alderpaw paused in front of the herb store for a moment, then confidently drew out a few leaves of tansy. "Here you are, Dovewing," he mewed. "These should help your sore throat."

The pale gray she-cat dipped her head. "Thanks, Alderpaw." She licked up the leaves and began chewing them as she left. "It feels better already," she mumbled around the mouthful.

"Good job," Jayfeather mewed briskly to Alderpaw.

Alderpaw felt a small burst of warmth in his chest. *That's the first time Jayfeather has sounded approving!* He had been a medicine-cat apprentice for several sunrises now, and his new life didn't feel quite as impossible as it had in the beginning. Even so, he still found it hard to think of himself ever becoming a full medicine cat.

As he began to tidy up the remaining tansy leaves, Squirrelflight pushed past the bramble screen and entered the den. "Is Leafpool back yet?" she asked Jayfeather.

"No, she isn't," Jayfeather grumbled. "And why she has to trek across to ShadowClan because Littlecloud isn't feeling well, I do not know."

"She only wants to help him," Squirrelflight meowed.

Jayfeather snorted. "Now *there's* a cat who could use an apprentice. ShadowClan is overflowing with them; you would think they could find one for Littlecloud. But no, they have to borrow a ThunderClan medicine cat."

"You know as well as I do," Squirrelflight responded mildly, "that a medicine-cat apprentice has to be just the right cat."

She shot an affectionate glance at Alderpaw, who warmed at her words.

"Bramblestar and I want to talk to you in his den," Squirrelflight told Jayfeather. "Are you busy right now?"

"Nothing that won't wait," Jayfeather replied. "Alderpaw, you can help Briarlight with her exercises. I'll be back soon."

When he was gone, Alderpaw rolled up a ball of moss and began tossing it to Briarlight to help her stretch her forelegs and chest. He was amazed by how agile she was, catching the ball when he was sure he had thrown it out of her reach.

"You're *good* at this!" he exclaimed.

"I've had a lot of practice," Briarlight mewed. "It really helps with my breathing. How's your training going?" she asked after a moment.

Alderpaw shook his head. "I feel like I'm doing a little bit better now, but I'm not sure I can ever be a full medicine cat."

"You'll be fine," Briarlight reassured him. "Think how much you've learned, and you've been apprenticed for less than a half-moon."

Alderpaw hoped that she was right. He felt guilty about being anxious, when Briarlight had so many obstacles and was often in pain. *She never gives up, and she hardly ever seems to feel sorry for herself.*

"Jayfeather! Jayfeather!"

Alderpaw stiffened as he heard his sister's frantic yowling in the camp outside. A heartbeat later she came tearing into the den, wild-eyed and panting. "Where's Jayfeather?" she demanded. "I was out in the woods with Cherryfall and Sorrelstripe, and Cherryfall is hurt—she cut her leg. She needs help right away!"

Alderpaw froze for a moment, on the edge of panic. *This is the first time I've had an emergency, and I'm here on my own! What do I do?*

"Jayfeather is in Bramblestar's den," Briarlight meowed steadily. "Sparkpaw, go and get him."

Sparkpaw dashed out immediately. While he waited, Alderpaw wondered what he should do. *Should I get some herbs out of the stores? What's the right herb for a cut leg?*

He was relieved a few moments later when he heard Sparkpaw calling to him from outside. He slid out of the den to find her waiting there with Jayfeather.

"Come on!" Jayfeather ordered. "Sparkpaw, show us where you left Cherryfall."

Sparkpaw led the way out of the camp and headed toward the ShadowClan border. Alderpaw followed with Jayfeather, guiding the blind medicine cat around tree stumps and bramble thickets. Even though he was worried about Cherryfall, he was relieved to be out in the forest again instead of being cooped up all day in the medicine cats' den.

"Can't you get a move on?" Jayfeather asked him irritably. "Cherryfall could be bleeding to death!"

"I'm doing the best I can," Alderpaw responded. He felt a spurt of annoyance, because he could have gone a lot faster if he hadn't been guiding a blind cat. But he knew that Jayfeather was only bad-tempered because he hated needing help, so Alderpaw kept calm and looked ahead to work out the easiest route.

"How did Cherryfall hurt herself?" Jayfeather asked as they emerged onto the lakeshore where the going was easier.

"Well, we were talking about the prophecy," Sparkpaw began, "and Cherryfall wondered if 'what you find in the shadows' could mean the kittypets who stayed with Thunder-Clan during the Great Storm. We were going to go try and find the ones who left after, and see if they wanted to come back."

Alderpaw wasn't surprised. Since the Gathering he had been too busy to think much about the prophecy, but the rest of his Clanmates seemed to talk of nothing else.

Jayfeather let out a snort. "That was a mouse-brained idea! Kittypets have nothing to do with StarClan. They are no use to Clan cats."

"Cherryfall thought it was worth a try," Sparkpaw mewed defensively.

"Besides, you would have to cross ShadowClan to get to the Twolegplace," Jayfeather growled, letting out a hiss of annoyance as he stumbled over a fallen branch. "You should have asked permission before just wandering out of ThunderClan territory. Stupid furballs!"

"It was only an idea." Sparkpaw's neck fur bristled at Jayfeather's dismissive tone. "Anyway, we didn't get near ShadowClan territory. Cherryfall slipped and cut herself on some Twoleg rubbish before we came in sight of the border."

Jayfeather made no response, though he still looked angry.

"We just thought if we made it to the Twolegplace, maybe we'd find some kittypets who knew the cats we wanted to talk to," Sparkpaw added.

Jayfeather rolled his eyes. "StarClan help us! Mouse-brains!"

Sparkpaw clamped her jaws together as if she was biting back a furious retort. Alderpaw felt sorry for her, though he couldn't help thinking that Jayfeather was right. *Surely kittypets couldn't be part of a prophecy from StarClan.*

"It's this way," Sparkpaw meowed after a moment. She veered away from the shore, through a stand of hazel saplings, and into a grassy hollow shaded by a spreading beech tree. Cherryfall was lying at the foot of the tree with one leg stretched out, while Sorrelstripe paced up and down anxiously beside her.

"Thank StarClan you're here!" Sorrelstripe exclaimed as Sparkpaw led the way down into the hollow.

Alderpaw followed and stood beside Jayfeather as the medicine cat examined Cherryfall's paw. There was a deep cut across her pads, and blood was oozing out of it. Clots of blood had soaked the grass beside her, and Alderpaw spotted some scraps of hard, clear Twoleg stuff close beside her. He dabbed at it experimentally and felt the sharp edge.

"Careful!" Sorrelstripe warned him. "That's what hurt Cherryfall."

"Why can't the Twolegs take their stuff back to their own dens instead of leaving it here to injure cats?" Sparkpaw asked angrily.

"Alderpaw!" Jayfeather beckoned with his tail. "We need some cobweb to stop the bleeding. Go and find some."

Alderpaw froze, glancing around wildly. *Cobweb? Where?* The sight and reek of the blood, and Cherryfall's face screwed up with pain, worried him so much that his paws felt stuck to the ground.

"Over there!" Sparkpaw pointed to an oak tree at the far side of the hollow. "There's a cleft in that tree—there should be cobwebs inside it."

Before Alderpaw could move, his littermate darted off, closely followed by Sorrelstripe. *Now Sparkpaw is better than me at being a medicine cat!* Alderpaw thought, furious with himself. He was even angrier when she turned out to be right, and she and Sorrelstripe returned across the hollow with pawfuls of cobweb.

"Oh, for StarClan's sake, Alderpaw!" Jayfeather hissed in exasperation. "Come here. Put your paw there." He pointed with his tail to a spot on Cherryfall's leg. "Press down hard— no, harder than that. Don't worry about hurting her. We've got to stop this bleeding."

"It's okay, Alderpaw," Cherryfall gasped.

Alderpaw put all his strength into pressing down where

Jayfeather had shown him, and to his relief the flow of blood from Cherryfall's paw slowed and then dwindled away completely.

"Good," Jayfeather grunted. "Now the cobweb."

Alderpaw couldn't believe how deft Jayfeather's paws were in wrapping Cherryfall's wound, especially considering he was blind.

"Now release the pressure," Jayfeather instructed Alderpaw when all the cobweb was wound around the injured paw. "And—please, StarClan—let's hope the bleeding doesn't start again."

Alderpaw lifted his paw and stared at the cobweb covering, afraid that he would see a red blotch spreading on the gray webs. "There's no more blood," he mewed after a few heartbeats.

"Right." Jayfeather sounded satisfied. "Cherryfall, let's get you back to camp. And don't even think about putting that paw to the ground. Sparkpaw and Sorrelstripe, support her."

Back in the camp, Jayfeather had the other cats take Cherryfall to the medicine cats' den. Alderpaw arranged a nest for her beside Briarlight, and she sank into it with a sigh of relief.

"Thanks, Jayfeather," she mewed. "And you, Alderpaw. I'm sorry to be such a nuisance."

"Just remember that the next time you want to do something mouse-brained," Jayfeather muttered. "Now, Alderpaw, unwrap the cobwebs. I want to get a better idea of the wound."

"What if the bleeding starts again?" Alderpaw asked nervously.

"Then we put more cobweb on, bee-brain!"

As carefully as he could, snagging his claws delicately into the cobweb wrapping, Alderpaw laid the wound bare. He hardly dared to breathe as he tore away the last of the cobwebs, but to his relief there was no more bleeding.

Meanwhile Jayfeather had gone to the herb store, and he came back carrying a piece of comfrey root. "We'll put a poultice of this on the wound," he meowed, dropping it at Alderpaw's paws. "You can chew it up, and Cherryfall, give that wound a good lick."

Alderpaw began chewing the root, blinking at its tangy taste. When he thought it was fine enough, he spat it out again. Jayfeather bent his head to sniff at it.

"It'll do," he commented. "Now spread it on Cherryfall's paw."

Alderpaw noticed how Cherryfall began to relax as he patted the poultice into place and the comfrey juices sank into her wound. "That feels so good . . . ," she murmured.

"You should get some sleep," Jayfeather told her when the poultice was in place. Turning to Alderpaw, he added, "And you're done for the day. Go and get something to eat."

"Thanks, Jayfeather."

Alderpaw slipped out of the den, his legs shaky with exhaustion. Spotting his sister over by the fresh-kill pile, he padded across to join her.

"Come and share this vole," Sparkpaw invited him as he drew near. "I caught it when I went hunting with Cherryfall earlier today. Doesn't it look good?"

Alderpaw felt his jaws watering as he looked at the plump piece of prey, and he realized that his belly was bawling with hunger. At the same time a hot wave of embarrassment flooded through his pelt.

"I really freaked out when I saw Cherryfall's wound," he confessed. "I couldn't do a simple thing like finding cobwebs." He let out a long sigh. "How am I going to be a good medicine cat if I freeze up at the sight of blood?"

"Oh, mouse dung!" Sparkpaw mewed cheerfully. "I don't know why any cat would *want* to be a medicine cat, but I was really impressed with the way you stopped Cherryfall's wound bleeding. You just need to trust yourself," she went on, brushing her tail against Alderpaw's side. "The way I do when I'm hunting. It's when you stop to worry that you miss your prey, and it was the same thing with the cobweb. But then you did the right thing. So I think in the end you'll be a pretty good medicine cat."

"Do you really believe that?" Alderpaw asked.

Sparkpaw gave him a nudge. "Of course I do, you daft furball!"

Taking a bite of the succulent vole, Alderpaw realized that he was beginning to feel better.

CHAPTER 6

When Alderpaw arrived at the medicine cats' den the following morning, he saw that Leafpool had returned and was giving Cherryfall's wound a good sniff. "That looks fine," she told the ginger she-cat. "But you can tell Squirrelflight you're off warrior duties for today. Go to your den and rest."

Cherryfall dipped her head in thanks and brushed past Alderpaw on her way out of the den.

"Hi, Leafpool," Alderpaw meowed. "How is Littlecloud?"

Leafpool straightened up. "Better," she replied. "He just had a touch of whitecough. I'm still worried about him, though. He's getting older, and there's no cat in ShadowClan to help him."

"Surely StarClan must have sent a sign to *some* cat," Alderpaw murmured.

"Huh!" Jayfeather turned from where he was sorting herbs at the back of the den. "ShadowClan cats are all so keen to be warriors that they might not pay any attention to signs."

I know how they feel, Alderpaw told himself, even though he was becoming more comfortable in his new life.

"Anyway," Leafpool mewed, "you'll meet Littlecloud and

the other medicine cats tonight. It's time for the half-moon meeting at the Moonpool."

Alderpaw stiffened. The medicine cats had all seemed so important when he had seen them at the Gathering, giving the prophecy to the Clans. *What will I say to them? I don't feel like I really belong with them.*

At the same time, a tingle of excitement ran through his pelt. *No cat besides the medicine cats knows what happens at their meetings.* "What will we do there?" he asked.

"You'll find out," Jayfeather told him. "Now, what about doing some work? We're almost out of catmint, since you took some over to ShadowClan," he added, narrowing his eyes at Leafpool.

"Do you want me to collect some from the old Twoleg nest?" Alderpaw offered.

"No," Jayfeather growled with a lash of his tail. "Moles have been digging through our herb patch. I bet they've made a real mess of it. *Moles!*" he spat, digging his claws into the ground. "I'd strip the pelt off every last one of them."

"Don't get so worked up." Leafpool brushed her tail along Jayfeather's side. "We can replant the herbs."

Jayfeather gave an ill-tempered grunt. "And meanwhile we're short of catmint just when leaf-fall is coming and we're likely to get more greencough. We'll have to cross Shadow-Clan territory to get catmint from that Twoleg garden beside RiverClan."

Alderpaw was surprised and a little disconcerted. "But you scolded Sparkpaw because she and Cherryfall and Sorrelstripe were going to those Twoleg nests," he reminded Jayfeather.

It was Leafpool who replied. "Rules are different for medicine cats. Besides, any cat can cross territory if they stay within three fox-lengths of the lake."

So Jayfeather just likes to be cranky, Alderpaw thought. *I guess I knew that already.*

"Anyway," Leafpool went on briskly, "I've just spent time with ShadowClan, helping Littlecloud. They're not going to bother me, are they? Alderpaw, you and I will go together."

When Leafpool and Alderpaw crossed the stream at the ShadowClan border, there was a strong, fresh scent of ShadowClan cats. Before they had taken many paw steps along the lakeshore, a ShadowClan patrol emerged from the bushes above the beach.

"Tigerheart," Leafpool mewed politely, dipping her head to the dark tabby tom who was in the lead. "How's the prey running in ShadowClan?"

"Why do you want to know?" the tabby warrior challenged her. "You're not hoping to steal some of it, are you?"

Alderpaw felt his neck fur bristling at the hostile tone, but Leafpool was unmoved. "You know better than that, Tigerheart," she responded.

Tigerheart's tail-tip twitched to and fro. "I know you're always meddling in ShadowClan business," he meowed. "Just like a ThunderClan cat."

"Yeah, especially one related to Firestar," one of the other ShadowClan cats put in: a hefty brown tom with a tuft of fur on the top of his head.

"Spikefur, I'm proud that Firestar was my father." Leaf-pool's tone was still calm.

Alderpaw was so riveted by this exchange, wondering if it was going to end in a fight, that he hadn't paid much attention to the rest of the ShadowClan patrol. He jumped, startled, as one of them came up and nudged him. Turning, he recognized Needlepaw.

"Oh, it's you," he mewed, not sure if he was pleased to see her.

"Hi, Alderpaw." Needlepaw gave him a friendly nod. "I thought I might be seeing you again soon. You've met Sleek-paw, and this other furball is Yarrowpaw."

"Furball yourself!" the third apprentice growled.

"Okay, Leafpool." Tigerheart took a pace back. Alder-paw had missed the next part of the conversation, but he was relieved that the ShadowClan tom sounded less hostile. "You can pass," he went on. "But we'll escort you to the edge of our territory."

Leafpool dipped her head in acknowledgment. "Thank you."

The whole patrol set off along the edge of the lake, with Leafpool and Tigerheart in the lead. The apprentices brought up the rear; Needlepaw padded along beside Alderpaw.

"Toms!" she muttered. "Always making trouble. Spikefur's a real pain in the tail." She hopped along on three paws while she used the fourth to ruffle up the fur on her head, and spoke in Spikefur's lower tone. "'Go and fetch me more moss, lowly apprentice! And catch me a blackbird while you're at it.'"

Alderpaw stifled a snort of laughter. "You shouldn't talk like that about your mentor."

"He's not my mentor, thank StarClan!" Needlepaw meowed. "I'm Tawnypelt's apprentice, but she's helping reinforce the camp walls today, so I get to go out with Spikefur." She rolled her eyes. "I'm so *lucky*! Anyway," she went on, "what are you doing here with Leafpool?"

"She's my mentor now," Alderpaw replied. "We're going to—"

"You're a *medicine*-cat apprentice?" Needlepaw's eyes stretched wide with amazement. "You didn't say that when we met before."

"I wasn't, then," Alderpaw explained.

"Wow, that's really cool!" Needlepaw sounded impressed. "You must get to learn lots of stuff."

"Oh, yes, lots. Different kinds of herbs and what they're used for, and how to stop wounds from bleeding . . ." For the first time Alderpaw found himself boasting, proud of his position as a medicine-cat apprentice. "Tonight Leafpool is taking me to the Moonpool to meet with StarClan," he finished.

"That's *awesome*," Needlepaw breathed out. "Do you have visions? Do you know anything special about the prophecy?"

Alderpaw shook his head. "I did have a sort of weird dream . . . ," he began.

"Alderpaw!" Leafpool glanced back, and gestured with her tail for Alderpaw to come and walk beside her.

Embarrassed, Alderpaw realized he had almost gotten

carried away and told Needlepaw stuff he wasn't supposed to mention. For the rest of their journey across ShadowClan territory, he padded in silence beside his mentor.

At the far border, Tigerheart waved his tail toward Leafpool and Alderpaw. "You have permission to cross back to your own Clan," he mewed loftily. "But don't take too long about it."

Like we'd want to hang around in your *territory,* Alderpaw thought.

"Good-bye, Alderpaw." Needlepaw gave him a friendly swipe around the ear with her tail. "I'll be seeing you."

Alderpaw wasn't sure if he was looking forward to that or not.

The half-moon shed a bright light over the forest as Jayfeather, Leafpool, and Alderpaw trekked alongside the stream that separated ThunderClan from WindClan. Alderpaw felt every hair in his pelt rise as they crossed a set of ThunderClan scent markers, and he realized that they were leaving behind not just their own territory, but the territories of all the Clans, and setting off into the unexplored hills.

"Is it much farther?" he panted.

"Oh, yes, we've a long way to go yet," Jayfeather told him.

Alderpaw sighed, half excited and half afraid. They had left the sheltering trees behind, and now rolling moorland stretched away in all directions, bare except for clumps of gorse, or reeds growing around a pool.

"How did the medicine cats know to come up here to the Moonpool?" Alderpaw asked.

"Actually, I was the cat who found it." Leafpool sounded slightly embarrassed. "Spottedleaf—she was a ThunderClan medicine cat many seasons ago, when Firestar first came to the forest—came from StarClan to show me the way."

"Wow, that means you're really special!" Alderpaw mewed admiringly.

Leafpool ducked her head. "Not at all. Just the right cat in the right place. Besides, lots of cats gathered at the Moonpool before the Clans ever came to the lake."

"Will we meet them?" Alderpaw blinked nervously.

"You may meet them in StarClan," Leafpool replied. "But they left this place many, many seasons ago."

Alderpaw shivered. "That's weird."

The journey to the Moonpool seemed to take forever. Then, scrambling up a steep slope, Alderpaw began to realize that he could hear the sound of falling water from somewhere up ahead.

"We're almost there," Leafpool told him.

Leafpool kept climbing upward, and Alderpaw padded after her. Jayfeather brought up the rear; glancing back to make sure he was okay, Alderpaw was impressed to notice how he set down his paws instinctively in the right places. It was as though he knew this path so well that he didn't need to see it.

Before they reached the top of the slope, Alderpaw heard a yowling cry coming from some way behind them. He paused and looked back to see all the other medicine cats, tiny in the distance, making their way along the path.

"We'll wait for them," Leafpool mewed, standing at Alder-paw's shoulder.

As the other cats drew closer, Alderpaw could pick out each one and recognize them. Kestrelflight, the mottled gray tom from WindClan, was in the lead. Mothwing followed him, with her apprentice, Willowshine, beside her. Last of all came Littlecloud; the old tom was obviously finding the climb strenuous, and he stood panting when he reached the place where Alderpaw and the others were waiting.

"Greetings," Mothwing meowed, dipping her head politely, then giving Alderpaw a curious glance. "Who is this, Leaf-pool?"

"This is Alderpaw," Leafpool replied. "He's our new apprentice."

A murmur of surprise came from the other medicine cats. "Really?" Kestrelflight responded. "I should have thought the *last* thing ThunderClan needed was another medicine cat!"

"We don't question the will of StarClan," Leafpool replied levelly, while Jayfeather flicked his whiskers irritably.

Alderpaw tried not to feel intimidated. It helped when Willowshine gave him a kind look and mewed, "I'm sure there can never be too many cats taking care of their Clan."

Littlecloud said nothing, though Alderpaw thought he was looking slightly envious. *I hope StarClan sends him an apprentice soon.*

"Are we doing this, or are we just going to stand here all night?" Jayfeather asked testily. He moved into the lead, springing confidently up the last part of the slope.

At the top a thick line of bushes barred their path. Jay-feather and Leafpool pushed their way through without hesitating. Alderpaw paused for a moment, then struggled through the stiff branches, pausing to shake his pelt when he emerged on the other side. Then he looked up, and he drew in his breath in a soundless gasp of astonishment.

In front of the line of bushes the ground dropped away into a deep hollow. A spring of water gushed from the rocks oppo-site, plunging down through moss and fern into a pool. The surface of the water glittered with the broken reflections of moon and stars. Alderpaw thought he had never seen any-thing so beautiful.

"It's amazing, isn't it?" Willowshine murmured, emerging from the bushes at his side. "I'll never forget the first time I saw it. And it still takes my breath away."

Leafpool and Jayfeather had already begun to pad down the spiraling path that led to the pool. Alderpaw followed them, awestruck as his paws slid into the impressions made by those ancient cats so long ago. His pelt tingled. The ancient cats, who had left . . . *many, many seasons ago* . . .

The other medicine cats followed him down the path and gathered at the edge of the pool. Leafpool beckoned Alder-paw to come and stand beside her. "Alderpaw," she meowed, "is it your wish to share the deepest knowledge of StarClan as a ThunderClan medicine cat?"

This is it, Alderpaw thought. "It is," he replied, his voice sounding as if a claw were scratching his throat.

Leafpool gazed up at the stars, her amber eyes glowing like

small fires in the night. "Warriors of StarClan," she began, "I present to you this apprentice. He has chosen the path of a medicine cat. Grant him your wisdom and insight so that he may understand your ways and heal his Clan in accordance with your will."

Alderpaw stood there blinking, aware that something tremendous was happening. He almost thought he could see the assembly of starry warriors, seated around him on the slopes of the hollow. Then Leafpool touched his shoulder with her tail.

"Crouch down beside the water, lap a few drops, and then touch the surface with your nose," she instructed.

As Alderpaw obeyed, he could see the other medicine cats around the Moonpool, their noses lowering to the water. It felt icy cold when he lapped it, and when he touched his nose to it, he thought that an icicle was stabbing him to the heart. Biting back a yowl, he closed his eyes and waited.

Alderpaw wasn't aware of the passing of time, but he found himself walking alongside a shallow, sparkling stream with no clear idea of how he had gotten there. Lush vegetation grew on the banks, and the air was full of rich scents. Alderpaw wondered if he should be afraid, but he felt too peaceful, and he wandered on, enjoying the warmth of the sun on his pelt.

After a little while, he saw that a large tom with a flame-colored pelt was walking along beside him. "Greetings," the tom said. "I'm so happy to finally meet one of Squirrelflight's kits."

Alderpaw's belly lurched as he realized that this must be

Firestar, his mother's famous father, who died in the Great Battle before he and his sister were born. Alderpaw would have expected to be overcome with shyness in the presence of such an awesome cat, but instead he felt at ease with him right away. There was something about Firestar that seemed oddly familiar.

Is this the same cat that I had that weird dream about?

"Come," Firestar meowed, leading Alderpaw farther along the stream until they reached a place where the water spread out into a pool. Firestar motioned to Alderpaw to stand right on the edge. "Look into the water," he instructed.

At first all Alderpaw could see was the pebbly bottom of the pool, and a few tiny fish darting here and there. Then the water and the pebbles seem to dissolve, and he found himself staring down into a deep gorge, with a river edged by bare, sandy rocks. Cats were moving here and there among the rocks, gathering into a ragged circle with one cat in the middle.

It's like I'm a bird, looking down on it all.

As if the bird were swooping lower, Alderpaw found himself suddenly much closer, so that he could see the individual cats more clearly. The cat in the center of the circle was a mottled brown-and-cream she-cat with a noble air, and she beckoned with her tail to some cat at the edge of the circle.

Two cats moved forward: a powerful ginger tom and a smaller black-and-white she-cat. The brown-and-cream she-cat and the ginger tom spoke to each other. Alderpaw felt frustrated; although he could see, he couldn't hear what the cats were saying.

Then the ginger tom stepped back. The older she-cat spoke to the younger one, and the younger one replied. Alderpaw suddenly realized what he was seeing.

"It's a warrior ceremony!"

Firestar touched his shoulder lightly with his tail. "Watch."

The Clan leader—for Alderpaw knew that was who the older she-cat must be—rested her muzzle on the new warrior's head, and the new warrior gave her leader's shoulder a respectful lick.

The cats who were gathered around erupted into joyful yowls, pressing around the new warrior and brushing her pelt with their tails and muzzles. The young she-cat looked overwhelmed but very happy.

As the ceremony broke up, Alderpaw noticed a small silver tabby she-cat pad up to the Clan leader and exchange a few words with her. Then the silver tabby looked up, and Alderpaw caught a flash of green eyes before the vision faded and all he could see was the bottom of the pool again.

It's almost like she could see me!

Trembling, Alderpaw backed away from the edge of the pool. "Firestar, who are they?" he asked urgently. "They look like Clan cats—they were holding a warrior ceremony, just like Clan cats—but they're not from any of the Clans around the lake. Where are they? Are they cats from the past, or the future? What are you trying to tell me?"

Firestar dipped his head toward Alderpaw, his green eyes filled with meaning, but he did not reply to any of his questions. If he was trying to tell Alderpaw something without words, Alderpaw couldn't understand what it was.

A moment later, a white mist drifted around him, blotting out the pool and the flame-colored figure of Firestar. Alderpaw found himself back beside the Moonpool, with the other medicine cats beginning to wake all around him.

Happiness thrilled through Alderpaw, warming him from ears to tail-tip. *I've had a vision! That proves I* am *meant to be a medicine cat.* He opened his jaws to tell the other cats about it, but before he spoke, doubts crowded in on him. *I don't know if it was a real vision. It could have been just a weird dream, like the one I had before.*

His doubts increased when none of the other cats said anything about what they had seen. *I'll keep my dream to myself for now,* he decided. *At least until I'm sure what it was.*

CHAPTER 7

✿

Alderpaw was alone in the medicine-cat den, except for Briarlight, who was curled up in her nest, asleep.

"She had such a restless, painful night," Leafpool had told him when he arrived in the den to start work. "Try not to wake her."

Jayfeather had straightened up from where he was bent over Briarlight, listening to her breathing. "I think she'll be okay now. We're going into the forest to collect herbs," he added to Alderpaw. "You can stay here and organize the store. Throw out anything that looks too withered to be useful."

Now that the two medicine cats had gone, Alderpaw was left to get on with the boring job. But for once he didn't mind. It gave him a chance to think over his dream at the Moonpool the night before.

I'm sure it was just a dream, he assured himself. *It's not even worth telling Jayfeather and Leafpool about. They'd think I was crazy!*

Instead Alderpaw had decided to make himself useful. In the last few days, he felt he was actually starting to get the hang of being a medicine cat.

Maybe I'll be a good medicine cat after all, he told himself. *Or at least I'll be good enough.*

Absorbed in separating the catmint from the tansy, and in picking out the wrinkled juniper berries that had lost their healing juices, Alderpaw was startled to hear the paw steps of another cat approaching the den. He turned to see Cherryfall brush back the bramble screen and limp inside.

"Hi," he mewed, pointing with his tail at Briarlight and signaling to Cherryfall to keep quiet. He was glad to see her, though he didn't like the pained expression on her face. "Is anything the matter?"

"It's my paw," Cherryfall replied, holding it up. "It hasn't healed yet, and it's still painful. Could you take a look at it?"

"Sure," Alderpaw responded. "But it's early days for it to heal."

With a sigh of relief Cherryfall lay on her side in a nest of moss and fern and stretched out her injured paw. Alderpaw examined it, giving it a good sniff and noting that the wound was clean and hadn't started bleeding again. He was especially careful to look for the signs of infection that Jayfeather had told him about.

It's not red, and it's not hot to the touch.

"It's not infected," he told Cherryfall. "It's just a deep cut and it's taking time to heal." He hesitated, then added, "That's normal."

"I'm glad it's not serious," Cherryfall meowed, "but is there anything you can give me to help the pain? It isn't terrible, but it's distracting me, and I want to get back to warrior duties."

Alderpaw padded back to the store and began to look through the herbs, touching each one and trying to remember what they were for. There were a lot of different kinds, but he knew what he wanted to find. He was sure that comfrey root was what Cherryfall needed. He remembered chewing up the root for a poultice when they first brought Cherryfall back to camp, and Jayfeather had told him that comfrey root helped soothe the pain of a wound.

Soon he spotted the pile of black roots and bit off a piece, remembering the tangy taste from last time as he chewed it into a poultice. When it was mashed up fine, he spat it out and spread it onto Cherryfall's wound.

Cherryfall's pained expression faded and a look of relief spread over her face. Alderpaw watched her carefully, thinking how important it was for a medicine cat to be aware of how other cats were feeling.

"I think it's already starting to work," Cherryfall mewed after a moment. "Thanks, Alderpaw. I'm so glad to be rid of the pain."

"It's nothing," Alderpaw mumbled, embarrassed.

Cherryfall got up, keeping her injured paw off the ground, and touched her nose to Alderpaw's ear. "I'm so pleased you've found your place as a medicine cat," she told him. "Jayfeather and Leafpool will be very proud of you."

Alderpaw watched Cherryfall as she left the den, feeling his pelt tingle with pride at her words. *I've treated my first injury all on my own!*

Voices sounded from outside the den, and Alderpaw realized that Jayfeather had returned. He couldn't hear what he and Cherryfall were saying, but he could guess.

Cherryfall must be telling Jayfeather what a great job I'm doing!

But when Jayfeather entered the den with a bundle of yarrow in his jaws, his neck fur was bristling and his tail-tip was twitching to and fro. "Is it true what Cherryfall just told me?" he demanded, dropping the herbs. "Did you give out a remedy without asking?"

Alderpaw felt his heart plummeting and his whole pelt burning with shame as he realized he had managed to do the wrong thing again. "Well . . . y-yes," he stammered. "But Cherryfall said her wound hurt, and I remembered you said a poultice of comfrey root would help. I chewed it up really well, just like you taught me." When Jayfeather made no comment, he added more desperately, "I wouldn't have given her anything if I wasn't very, *very* sure I knew what it would do. But I was certain that's what comfrey root is *for*. And it helped! She felt much better!"

Jayfeather let out a long growl deep in his throat. "Yes, it will help with the pain. But sometimes pain is a warning sign, telling a cat that something is wrong. What if Cherryfall had an infection and you dulled the pain? Then her infection would have gotten worse, without any cat knowing. Infections can be very dangerous."

"But . . . but . . ." Alderpaw tried to protest, but he felt so guilty it was hard to get the words out. "I *checked* for infection, and Cherryfall showed no signs of it."

I was only trying to help, he thought. *I didn't realize I could have made things worse.*

"I'm so sorry," he mewed miserably. "I never should have done it. I won't ever do it again!"

Jayfeather relaxed slightly, angling his ears toward the sleeping Briarlight, and Alderpaw realized that his voice had risen on the last few words.

"You were right," Jayfeather conceded. "I checked Cherryfall myself, and she didn't have an infection. But sometimes the signs can be hard to spot, especially if a medicine cat is still learning . . . which you will be for quite some time. Until you've had more training, you should stick to doing only whatever Leafpool and I tell you."

Alderpaw bowed his head. "Okay, Jayfeather."

"So for now," Jayfeather went on more briskly, "you can get some mouse bile and go do the elders' ticks."

Alderpaw stifled a sigh. "Yes, Jayfeather."

When Alderpaw reached the elders' den under the hazel bushes, carrying a twig with a ball of bile-soaked moss dangling from the tip, only Sandstorm was there.

"Hi," she meowed, a friendly look in her green eyes. "I'm glad to see you. Graystripe and Millie have gone for a walk, and Purdy is sunning himself somewhere. I've got a huge tick on my shoulder, just where I can't get at it."

Alderpaw parted Sandstorm's fur to find the tick, then

dabbed mouse bile on it. This time he couldn't suppress a sigh, to think that he was back on tick duty just as if he had never become a medicine-cat apprentice.

Sandstorm wriggled her shoulders gratefully as the tick fell off. "That's much better, Alderpaw. But there's something wrong, isn't there? Would it help to tell me about it?"

Alderpaw shook his head, embarrassed that he hadn't hidden his feelings.

Sandstorm brushed her tail along his side. "There's no shame in being sad sometimes," she mewed. "No reason not to show it. And besides," she added with a faint *mrrow* of amusement, "you're not very good at hiding it!"

Her joke made Alderpaw feel a little better. He kept searching her fur for more ticks as Sandstorm went on talking to him in a gentle voice.

"You're my kin, and you should feel comfortable telling me things. Maybe I can help. And as the others aren't here just now, it can stay just between us."

Alderpaw relaxed. He dabbed mouse bile on the tick he had just found, then set the twig down. "I gave Cherryfall a poultice of comfrey root when Leafpool and Jayfeather were out," he confessed. "Jayfeather was furious."

"Wow!" Sandstorm exclaimed. "What a dreadful thing to do! Bramblestar will certainly throw you out of the Clan."

For one horrible moment Alderpaw thought she meant it. Then he realized that she was joking.

"You shouldn't feel bad," the old she-cat went on more

seriously. "You were trying to do your best, and you deserve praise for that. Now you'll know better for next time. Being an apprentice is all about learning and growing, and aren't you lucky to have the opportunity? And to have Leafpool and Jayfeather, such wise cats, to guide you?"

"I . . . I don't want to disappoint them," Alderpaw stammered.

"Did Jayfeather seem upset?" Sandstorm asked him. "I don't mean cranky—Jayfeather is always cranky—but *upset*?"

Alderpaw thought about that for a moment. "No," he meowed at last. "He didn't."

"Because he just wants you to learn," the ginger she-cat went on. "And you're doing that. You shouldn't expect to understand everything right away. You're thoughtful and cautious, and that will serve you well as a medicine cat."

She really knows me well! Alderpaw thought, beginning to feel a bit better. *It's so good to have older, wiser cats to give me advice.*

"Is anything else bothering you?" Sandstorm asked after a moment.

Alderpaw's mind flashed back to the strange vision at the Moonpool. *I'm almost sure it was just a dream . . . but what if it was more?*

Sandstorm's guidance had inspired him, and the encouraging look in her eyes made him want to confide in her. "Something happened last night at the Moonpool," he began, and went on to tell her about his meeting with Firestar and how he had watched the unfamiliar Clan in the water of the pool.

"It was so strange . . . ," he told Sandstorm. "These other cats seem to live in a rocky gorge with a river running through it. And it looked like their leader was making a new warrior."

Sandstorm narrowed her eyes, her green gaze suddenly intense. "Describe these cats to me," she meowed. "Tell me as much as you can remember."

"Well," Alderpaw began. "The cat I thought was the leader was a cream-and-pale brown tabby she-cat with amber eyes. And there was a big powerful ginger tom, and a small silver-gray tabby she-cat with dark gray paws and deep green eyes." He shivered. "She looked up at me; it was like she knew I was there."

Sandstorm jumped to her paws, her pelt bristling with excitement. "I know those cats! They sound like Leafstar and her deputy, Sharpclaw—and the small silver tabby is Echosong, their medicine cat."

"That's really weird," Alderpaw murmured. "Why would I dream about real cats I've never met—never even heard of?"

Sandstorm's green eyes glowed. "That wasn't a dream . . . *it was a vision.*"

"Really?" Alderpaw began to share the older cat's excitement. "So who are the cats that I saw?"

"They are from another Clan, SkyClan," Sandstorm replied. "And they may need our help."

Alderpaw gaped at her. There was another Clan he'd never heard of? He had to believe Sandstorm, because he knew how wise she was. And he was excited to have had a vision, like a real medicine cat. But at the same time he felt that the vision was wasted on him. "Why me?" he blurted out.

"Why not?" Sandstorm's voice was calm. "If you weren't supposed to have the vision, you wouldn't have had it. StarClan chose you, and you must honor their choice. And that means you must tell Leafpool and Jayfeather."

Alderpaw's belly lurched with nervousness. He shrank from the idea of telling his mentors. *Jayfeather already thinks I'm doing stuff I'm not ready for. . . . What will he think when I tell him about my vision? Won't he think this is more of the same?*

"Jayfeather will claw my ears off," he muttered.

"Nonsense!" Sandstorm mewed briskly. "Alderpaw, you need to stop getting your tail in a twist and go tell the others."

Alderpaw's paw steps dragged as he headed across the stone hollow to the medicine cats' den. By the time he reached it, Leafpool had returned and was bending over the sleeping Briarlight.

"I . . . uh . . . I need to talk to you about something important," he began.

Jayfeather twitched his whiskers. "What now?"

Leafpool flicked his ear with her tail. "Of course you can talk to us, Alderpaw, but let's go outside. Briarlight just woke up and ate something, but she's sleeping again now, and I don't want her disturbed."

"Make it quick," Jayfeather meowed.

Outside the den, Alderpaw spoke in a low voice as he told his mentors about his vision at the Moonpool. "Sandstorm said she recognized those cats," he finished.

To his amazement, Leafpool was gazing at him with glowing amber eyes, while Jayfeather clawed at the ground in his excitement. *They're* both *really pleased,* Alderpaw thought, *not just Leafpool.*

"Do you think this might be my first vision?" he asked.

"No," Jayfeather responded, "this wasn't your *first* vision. Remember when the medicine cats were given the prophecy from StarClan? Didn't I see you there?"

Alderpaw gazed at him in wonder. Maybe he really *had* seen Firestar before! "That was a *vision?*"

Jayfeather rolled his eyes. "StarClan give me strength!"

"Yes, it was a vision," Leafpool replied. "And that's why it was clear to us that you should become a medicine-cat apprentice. Alderpaw, StarClan obviously has big plans for you!"

Alderpaw found that hard to take in. He felt so excited that he was tingling from nose to tail-tip, and his claws flexed in and out. *I wasn't chosen to be a medicine cat just because I was a terrible hunter—I was chosen because I have these special powers!*

"We'll have to go and discuss this with Bramblestar," Leafpool announced.

"Good," Alderpaw meowed, turning toward his leader's den. *I can't wait to hear what Bramblestar thinks about this!*

Leafpool shook her head, while Jayfeather raised a paw to halt Alderpaw. "No, we're going alone," he rasped. "You may have had the vision, but you're too inexperienced to discuss what it means. We'll tell you what happens."

Alderpaw's sensation of being special faded. "Oh," he

muttered, feeling young and silly again. He stayed outside the den, watching Leafpool and Jayfeather as they headed toward the tumbled rocks that led up to the Highledge.

I guess whatever my vision was trying to tell me, the older cats will take care of it.

CHAPTER 8

Left alone in the den, Alderpaw went back to the tasks of sorting dried herbs and putting away the fresh ones Leafpool and Jayfeather had brought back. Once his excitement had died down, he felt as if his pelt didn't quite fit him anymore. He wasn't sure that he wanted to be a cat who had important visions, and he wished he knew how Bramblestar would react to what Alderpaw's mentors were telling him.

He had almost finished the task when he heard limping paw steps approaching the den. *Oh no—that must be Cherryfall!*

Alderpaw had no idea what he would say to her. He didn't know whether to apologize about treating her without asking advice, or to ask how she was doing, or just ignore the whole thing.

But when Cherryfall poked her head around the bramble screen, he had no chance to say anything. "Alderpaw!" she blurted out. "You have to come quickly—Sparkpaw's hurt!"

Terror tore through Alderpaw like a massive claw. Remembering what had happened when he treated Cherryfall, he wondered whether he should get the other medicine cats.

No—it's my sister! I have to help her now!

"Show me where," he mewed to Cherryfall.

Racing out of the den, he followed the ginger she-cat toward the ShadowClan border. They pelted through the forest, dodging around bramble thickets and leaping over fallen branches. As they drew closer, Alderpaw could hear his sister's agonized yowling. The sound grew louder as they barreled through a clump of ferns and emerged near the greenleaf Twolegplace.

Sparkpaw was lying in a heap at the foot of a tree. Hollytuft was crouched beside her, gently stroking her shoulder, while Ivypool was encouraging her to lap from a bunch of soaked moss. Both warriors stood up and took a pace back as Alderpaw bounded up to his littermate.

"What happened?" he panted.

"She was climbing on a thin branch, trying to catch a bird," Cherryfall explained. "She fell right out of the tree, and now her foreleg . . ." She winced, her voice dying away.

"Oowwww!" Sparkpaw mewled; her whole body was twisted with agony.

Alderpaw started to shake at the sight of his sister—bright, capable Sparkpaw—in such pain and distress. *I've never seen her like this! She's always so confident and in control.* Now that he was close enough, he could see her foreleg was pointing at an awkward angle, not natural at all.

His heart pounded as he remembered Purdy telling him a story about Cinderheart: how she had fallen from a tree and broken her leg, and how she had had to spend moons in the medicine cats' den before she could use it again.

Please, StarClan, don't let that happen to Sparkpaw.

Steadying himself, Alderpaw crouched down beside his sister. "I have to examine your leg," he meowed. "It might hurt."

Sparkpaw nodded. "Just do it," she mewed through clenched teeth.

Alderpaw ran his paws over Sparkpaw's leg and shoulder. At once relief washed over him like a warm tide. *It's not broken—only dislocated. And I know how to fix that!*

Leafpool had taught him what to do, telling him of when the same thing had happened to Berrynose when he was out hunting and had fallen over the edge of a rocky bank. Suddenly Alderpaw felt much more confident.

"Don't worry," he reassured Sparkpaw. He tried to sound sure of himself, even though his paws were shaking. "You're going to feel much better very quickly."

As he spoke, he saw Ivypool lean closer to Hollytuft, and heard her whispering, "Does he *really* know what he's doing?"

Hollytuft just shook her head uncertainly.

Alderpaw hesitated for a moment. *Do I know?*

Then Sparkpaw let out another yowl of pain, and he gave himself a mental shake. "Cherryfall," he directed, "put your paw on her other shoulder, just there. Ivypool and Hollytuft, keep her hind legs still. Don't worry, Sparkpaw," he added. "It'll all be over in the time it takes you to catch a mouse."

Bending over Sparkpaw, Alderpaw took hold of her injured leg with one paw and her shoulder with the other. *You can't overthink it,* he remembered Leafpool saying. *Just do it quickly, with a forceful push.*

Just as his mentor had told him, Alderpaw forced his sister's leg back into its socket with a quick, sure motion. Sparkpaw convulsed under his paws and let out a shriek. But beneath her cry, Alderpaw heard the *pop* as her leg slipped back into position.

Did that do the trick? he wondered. He had heard gasps of horror from Ivypool and Hollytuft, as if they thought he had made things worse.

"You can let her go now," he told the warriors. "Sparkpaw, try standing up."

Sparkpaw blinked at him, then slowly staggered to her paws and began to pad back and forth. Alderpaw watched her, hardly daring to breathe. She still looked shaky, and she was limping a little, but she could put weight on the leg.

"That's amazing!" Sparkpaw exclaimed, turning toward her brother. "It feels *so* much better. Thanks so much, Alderpaw. You're turning out to be a great medicine cat."

"You sure are," Cherryfall agreed.

Hollytuft and Ivypool were looking impressed, too. Alderpaw licked his chest fur in embarrassment as they congratulated him, though he reveled in their looks of approval.

"I'd better get back to my herbs," he mewed shyly. "Sparkpaw, you need to have Leafpool or Jayfeather check you out when you get back to camp."

Alderpaw felt like his paws were hardly touching the

ground as he padded back through the forest. *I treated Spark-paw's injury! And she's okay!*

Then, as he passed the old Twoleg path, he realized with a start that he had left without permission. His pelt prickled with anxiety, though as he drew close to the camp, he tried to throw off his worries.

Maybe I can sneak back in without any cat noticing.

But as he rounded an old tree stump and came within sight of the thorn barrier, he spotted Bramblestar waiting for him beside the entrance to the tunnel.

Oh, no! Alderpaw thought. *Am I in trouble again? I shouldn't have left camp . . . and didn't Jayfeather just tell me that I shouldn't be doing anything without asking him or Leafpool?*

"I'm sorry! I'm really sorry!" he burst out as he bounded up to Bramblestar. "I won't—"

"I don't know what you're apologizing for," Bramblestar interrupted with a confused look. "I'm not here because you're in trouble. I need to talk to you because Jayfeather and Leafpool have told me about your vision."

Startled, Alderpaw stretched his eyes wide. In all the stress of helping Sparkpaw, he had forgotten that his mentors were discussing that with Bramblestar.

"Let's sit over here." Bramblestar pointed with his tail at a shady spot underneath an arching clump of ferns. When both cats were comfortably settled, he went on, "We think the vision means that you've been chosen for a very special quest."

Alderpaw felt warm all over at the look of pride in his father's eyes, so that at first he didn't really take in what he was saying.

"So you must leave ThunderClan and go on this quest," Bramblestar added.

Wait . . . a quest?

Every hair on Alderpaw's pelt rose in shock at what his Clan leader was telling him. "But . . . but I can't!" he gasped.

Bramblestar curled his tail around to rest it on Alderpaw's shoulder. "StarClan wouldn't have sent you the vision if you weren't ready," he meowed. "We believe the vision you had was about the prophecy. As Sandstorm told you, the cats you saw are from another Clan, called SkyClan. Since the prophecy mentioned the sky clearing, we think they may be in trouble. Jayfeather, Leafpool, and I agree that you must go on a quest to find them."

Alderpaw realized that he was gaping like a blackbird chick waiting for food. He tried hard to speak calmly, and to ask sensible questions that would help him understand.

"Sandstorm told me that the cats I saw belong to SkyClan," he began. "But I don't see why they should need *my* help. And how am I ever going to find them?"

"It's a long story." Bramblestar sat erect, with his tail curled around his paws, and looked down at Alderpaw. "It began many, many seasons ago, in the old forest. SkyClan lived there, too, along with the four Clans that you know."

"So there were *five* Clans?" Alderpaw breathed out.

"Yes. But SkyClan lost their territory because Twolegs took it to build their own nests. And the other four Clans refused to share the territory that was left. They drove SkyClan out of the forest."

"That's so unfair!" Alderpaw exclaimed indignantly.

Bramblestar bowed his head. "The remaining Clans were ashamed of what they had done, and afterward they never spoke of SkyClan. Eventually, all memory of them was lost."

"And what happened to SkyClan?"

"They traveled a long way and finally came to the gorge where you saw them. Their Clan thrived there for a while, but at last they were driven out and scattered."

"So what I saw was a vision from the past?" Alderpaw asked. His pelt was growing hot with anger at what SkyClan had suffered, and he dug his claws hard into the ground.

Bramblestar shook his head. "Back in the old forest—it was about the time that I became a warrior—Firestar was visited by the spirit of the SkyClan leader who had led his Clan out of the forest. He charged Firestar with a quest to find the remnants of SkyClan and restore it."

"Wow! And Firestar really did that?"

"Sandstorm went with him, and she can tell you everything that happened," Bramblestar replied. "But in the end, yes, they restored SkyClan and left the cats living by the warrior code in the gorge."

"So that's how Sandstorm recognized the cats I saw!" Alderpaw meowed. "Their leader, Leafstar, and the deputy,

Sharpclaw, and . . . what was the medicine cat's name? Oh—Echosong!"

"That's right," Bramblestar responded. "I believe that Sky-Clan may need our help again. But listen, Alderpaw. What happened to SkyClan is such a secret that only three living cats know about it: Sandstorm and me, and now you. That means we can't tell *any* cat what your quest is really about—not even Leafpool and Jayfeather."

Alderpaw stared at him, so stunned for the moment that he couldn't get any words out. "You—you mean," he stammered at last, "you mean there's a part of warrior history so secret that even the *medicine cats* don't know about it?"

Bramblestar nodded. "Only you and I and Sandstorm know the truth."

Alderpaw took a moment to think about that. "Why does it need to be a secret?" he asked. "Isn't it sort of dishonest to lie about the quest?"

"You just need to have faith in me," Bramblestar mewed gently. "Telling the truth now would do more harm than good. I know I'm trusting you with a huge responsibility," he added. "But I wouldn't be doing it if I didn't think you were up to the task."

Rising to his paws, he nuzzled the top of Alderpaw's head briefly, then padded back toward the camp. Alderpaw watched him go, a flood of emotions surging through him. The secrecy worried him, while at the same time he felt an intense curiosity to know what was going on, and whether SkyClan really needed ThunderClan's help. His anxiety that he might not be good enough to be entrusted with the task warred with the pride he felt that Bramblestar believed in him.

Maybe Sparkpaw is right, he thought. *She's always telling me that I overthink things. I'm just going to focus on my father's faith in me,* he decided at last, *and hope that all the rest will fall into place.*

CHAPTER 9

"I don't care what you say!" Sandstorm hissed. "I'm going on this quest, and that's final!"

"It's out of the question!" Bramblestar snapped back at her. "I asked you here to tell Alderpaw all you know about Sky-Clan. I never intended for you to go with him."

Alderpaw shifted nervously from paw to paw on the sandy floor of Bramblestar's den. It was the day after his father had told him that he must go on the quest, but so far no decisions had been made about which cats would accompany him.

And it doesn't look like I'll be leaving anytime soon, not if Bramblestar and Sandstorm keep on arguing. He had always believed that the two cats got along well together. Now they looked furious enough to claw each other's pelts off.

"Then you may be Clan leader, but you're acting like a mouse-brained apprentice." Sandstorm's neck fur was bristling with anger. "I'm the only—"

"Enough!" Bramblestar lashed his tail. "Sandstorm, you're an elder. You've made your contribution to our Clan, and it's been a magnificent contribution. Now you deserve to have the rest of us take care of you. I want you safe in camp, not traipsing about in unknown territory."

"That's exactly the point." Sandstorm's voice grew quieter, the words forced out through clenched teeth. Alderpaw was glad she wasn't glaring at him like she was glaring at Bramblestar. "I'm the only living cat who has any idea how to find SkyClan's camp. And I'm the only one who has met the cats of SkyClan before. They're more likely to accept me than cats they've never laid eyes on."

As she spoke, the anger in Bramblestar's face was fading, replaced with a thoughtful expression. "I understand," he began uncertainly, "but elders just don't—"

He broke off at the sound of a patter of paw steps approaching up the tumbled rocks. Alderpaw turned to see Squirrelflight at the entrance to the den. Bramblestar and Sandstorm exchanged a swift glance, and Alderpaw realized that Squirrelflight didn't know about SkyClan either.

"All the hunting patrols have gone out," she reported. "I wanted to ask which warriors you've chosen to go with Alderpaw. He'll need a strong group of cats. I don't know where his paws will lead him, but I do know there'll be danger."

"I will be going with him," Sandstorm announced, before Bramblestar could reply.

Her green eyes flashed with triumph when Bramblestar reluctantly dipped his head in agreement, but Squirrelflight's expression was horrified.

"Sandstorm, you can't!" she exclaimed. "It's bad enough having to let Alderpaw go. Do you think I want my kit *and* my mother off on a dangerous quest together? I couldn't bear it!"

Dangerous? Alderpaw thought, feeling more nervous still.

"Squirrelflight, it will be fine," Sandstorm meowed. "I may be old, but I'm still strong. And Alderpaw will be in a lot less danger if I go with him."

"I hate to admit it, but she's right," Bramblestar agreed.

Squirrelflight glanced sharply from her mother to Bramblestar and back again, her green eyes glittering. "Is there something you're not telling me?" she demanded.

"You have to trust me," Bramblestar responded.

A few tense heartbeats passed while Squirrelflight held Bramblestar's amber gaze. Then she sighed, her tail drooping. "I suppose I do."

Without further argument, Bramblestar led the way out of the den and onto the Highledge. Squirrelflight stayed by his side, while Sandstorm and Alderpaw picked their way down the tumbled rocks to the floor of the camp.

"Let all cats old enough to catch their own prey join here beneath the Highledge for a Clan meeting," Bramblestar yowled.

All the cats in the clearing turned toward the Highledge. Leafpool and Jayfeather emerged from their den and sat side by side in front of the bramble screen. Lilyheart and Daisy appeared from the nursery and settled themselves near the entrance while Lilyheart's kits play wrestled around their paws. Cloudtail, Brightheart, and Dovewing slid out from the warriors' den and took their places at the foot of the rock wall.

Purdy broke off a story he was telling to Snowbush and Ambermoon. "I'll finish the rest later," he promised as he padded off to flop down beside Graystripe and Millie near the elders' den.

Alderpaw looked around for Sparkpaw and spotted her emerging from the thorn tunnel with Cherryfall and Molewhisker. *She's hardly limping at all,* he told himself with a burst of pride. *I did a good job.* All three cats were loaded with prey; they bounded across the camp to drop it on the fresh-kill pile, then joined their Clanmates to listen to Bramblestar.

"Cats of ThunderClan," their leader began, "I have important news. Alderpaw has had a vision about the prophecy from StarClan. We think that it will help us find what will 'clear the sky,' and so he must go on a quest to find the place that he saw in his dream. Because Sandstorm knows about some of what he saw in the vision, she will be going with him."

Murmurs of amazement rose from the assembled cats at Bramblestar's words, and they exchanged glances alive with curiosity. Alderpaw thought that Graystripe and Millie looked especially shocked to hear that Sandstorm would be part of the quest.

"Why Alderpaw, and not one of the medicine cats?" Thornclaw asked, sounding faintly aggressive.

Leafpool spoke up from her place in front of her den. "Alderpaw *is* a medicine cat, Thornclaw, and you know that as well as I do. As for why StarClan chose him . . ." She shrugged. "I'm sure they knew what they were doing."

"More important, why Sandstorm?" Brightheart asked, with an affectionate glance at the ginger she-cat. "She's an elder; she's earned her rest."

"Because I was afraid she would claw my ears off if I forbade her from going," Bramblestar responded drily.

"And I would have," Sandstorm muttered.

"There are reasons why I believe Sandstorm is vital to the quest," Bramblestar went on. "Now all that's left is to choose warriors to join the group."

Several enthusiastic yowls greeted his words.

"I'll go!"

"Let me!"

Sparkpaw scampered up to Alderpaw and pressed herself against his side, her eyes shining. "I'll come and help you!" she mewed.

"Oh, thank you!" Alderpaw responded, his relief at the thought of having his sister with him flooding over him.

Then he noticed that Bramblestar and Squirrelflight, up on the Highledge, were exchanging dubious glances. Cherryfall, who had followed her apprentice, shook her head sternly. "Bramblestar decides who will go," she told Sparkpaw. "And he's not likely to choose an apprentice for a quest like this."

Shaken, Alderpaw gazed up at Bramblestar. "Please," he begged desperately, "can't Sparkpaw come?"

Bramblestar paused, clearly torn, while Squirrelflight leaned closer to him and murmured something into his ear. She looked horrified at the thought of both their kits risking themselves on this quest.

The Clan leader and his deputy spoke together quietly for a few heartbeats. Then Bramblestar turned back to the cats in the clearing. "Very well," he meowed. "Sparkpaw may go with you. And in that case," he added, raising his voice to be heard above Sparkpaw's squeals of triumph, "Cherryfall and Mole-whisker will join the group as well."

The two cats exchanged delighted glances.

"You leave at dawn tomorrow," Bramblestar finished. "And may StarClan light your path."

"Alderpaw! Come on! Wake up!"

Sparkpaw's voice seemed to come from a long way away. Alderpaw opened his eyes, blinked blearily, and made out her face right next to his, her green eyes gleaming in the shadow of their den.

"Wake up!" she repeated, prodding him hard in the side. "It's time to go. This is *your quest*, mouse-brain, and you're still asleep."

Alderpaw stretched his jaws into a massive yawn and staggered to his paws. He had lain awake for so long the night before, thinking about the quest, that it felt as if he had only been sleeping for a heartbeat.

Following Sparkpaw, he scrambled through the ferns that shaded the apprentices' den and headed out into the clearing, holding his head and tail high to hide how nervous he felt.

The dawn air was damp and chilly, striking deep into Alderpaw's fur. Above his head the sky was washed with the pale light of dawn, and a faint breeze was rustling the trees on top of the hollow.

It seemed to Alderpaw that the whole of ThunderClan was out in the clearing, most of them clustering around the medicine cats' den. Their excited murmurs sounded like the buzzing of a whole colony of bees.

Alderpaw and Sparkpaw pushed their way through the crowd to join Jayfeather and Leafpool outside their den. Cherryfall, Molewhisker, and Sandstorm were already waiting there, and Leafpool was distributing small leaf wraps of herbs to them.

"There you are!" Jayfeather mewed to the two apprentices. Alderpaw had expected to be scolded for being late, but for once Jayfeather sounded friendly. "Come and have some traveling herbs."

Leafpool set down two more leaf wraps in front of Alderpaw and Sparkpaw. Alderpaw delicately separated the herbs with one paw, studying them carefully.

"That's sorrel to quench thirst." Jayfeather identified the herbs by sniffing at each one. "Daisy to keep your joints supple, and—" He broke off, then added, "But I guess you know all this. You're really starting to learn your herbs."

"Chamomile to ease tiredness, and burnet for strength." Alderpaw identified the other two herbs in the mixture. He was happy at Jayfeather's praise. *He and Leafpool have been treating me differently since they talked to Bramblestar about my vision,* he reflected. *It's almost as if they think that there's more to the quest than they know about, and they believe I know the truth.* He suppressed a shiver. *And, of course, I do know.*

Jayfeather nodded at Alderpaw's accurate description.

"Good. We give these herbs to every cat who needs to travel. They'll help keep you going even if you don't have the chance to hunt."

"They taste weird," Sparkpaw commented as she licked up her share.

Jayfeather rolled his eyes but said nothing.

While Alderpaw was eating his share of the herbs, he noticed that Bramblestar had appeared and had drawn Sandstorm away from the other questing cats. The two of them were having a quiet conversation, their expressions serious. Alderpaw caught a few words.

"If this secret gets out, it could be devastating for the Clans," Bramblestar meowed.

"But StarClan gave Alderpaw this vision . . . ," Sandstorm began. Alderpaw lost the rest of what she said as the cats moved away.

Uneasiness stirred in Alderpaw's belly. This was his own quest, and yet there was so much about it that he didn't understand. *And suppose I give away the secret about SkyClan? I wouldn't mean to, but . . . what would happen then?* He heaved a massive sigh. *At least Sandstorm is coming with us, and she can advise me.*

At last Bramblestar stepped back from Sandstorm with a nod of agreement, and he bounded across the camp to climb up to the Highledge.

Sandstorm padded over to Alderpaw and rubbed her cheek against his, her green eyes shining with pride in him. "You look worried," she murmured.

"I heard part of what you and Bramblestar were saying,"

Alderpaw confessed. "It sounds like he doesn't trust me."

"Nonsense!" Sandstorm responded. "It's not that Bramblestar doesn't want you to know about SkyClan; he doesn't want *any* cat to know. It's not his feelings about you. It's his guilt about what the four Clans allowed to happen to SkyClan."

But that was seasons and seasons before Bramblestar was born, Alderpaw thought. *Why should he feel bad about it? It wasn't his fault.*

"I'm not sure I understand," he mewed.

"Maybe you will in time," Sandstorm responded.

Alderpaw dipped his head respectfully. "Thank you, Sandstorm. I'm glad you're coming with us."

"Cats of ThunderClan!" Bramblestar called from the Highledge. "Alderpaw has had an important vision—and this vision is to set him off on a quest that, I predict, will prove as important to our Clan as the one that Dovewing undertook as an apprentice, when the drought came and she saved our lake." Dovewing raised her tail proudly.

Alderpaw was aware of every cat turning to stare at him. He was startled to see the respect and admiration in their eyes. He ducked his head in embarrassment and stared at his paws. *I really don't deserve this.*

"The medicine cats' prophecy told us that unless we embrace what we find in the shadows, the sky will never clear. Alderpaw's vision gives us hope that the cats of ThunderClan can find what lies in the shadows, and if so, then our Clan will prosper."

The whole of ThunderClan erupted into enthusiastic yowling. "Alderpaw! Alderpaw!"

Alderpaw froze, almost wishing that a big owl would swoop down and carry him off. Then Sparkpaw gave him a nudge. "Come on, slow mole!" she meowed, giving him an affectionate glance. "It's time to go."

Alderpaw straightened, bracing himself. "I'm glad you're with me, Sparkpaw," he murmured.

To his relief, Sandstorm took the lead as he and the other questing cats headed for the thorn tunnel. The rest of ThunderClan padded along with them, calling out their good wishes.

"Best of luck, Alderpaw!"

"Keep safe!"

"May StarClan light your path!"

At the last moment, before Alderpaw and Sparkpaw stepped into the tunnel, Squirrelflight bounded up to them. Alderpaw saw fear in her eyes, but her voice was brisk as she meowed, "Don't you dare get yourselves killed! I want to hear all about it when you get back."

"We'll be careful," Alderpaw promised.

"I'll look after him," Sparkpaw added with an impudent glance at her littermate.

Squirrelflight touched noses with each of her kits, then took a pace back. Alderpaw was aware of her gaze on him until he headed into the tunnel.

This is it! The quest has really begun!

The sun was rising as Alderpaw's group headed through the forest toward the lake, strong rays of sunlight striking through the trees and making patterns on the forest floor. Alderpaw remembered how vast and frightening the territory had seemed when he first left the camp. Now he found it familiar and safe.

"How long will this quest take?" Sparkpaw asked, bouncing along at his side. "Where's the place you saw? I want to know more about your dream—no, wait, your *vision*."

"I have no idea where the place is, or how far it is," Alderpaw replied, feeling a prickle in his pelt at his littermate's questions. "And I can't really talk about it. It's medicine-cat stuff."

"Oh, come on, you can tell *me*. Were there cats in your vision? What did they look like? What did they say?" she persisted, her eyes sparkling eagerly.

Alderpaw's nervousness increased under the flood of questions, until he felt like he had rats gnawing at his belly. He wished he could tell the truth to the other cats; it felt really awkward having to lie. *Especially to Sparkpaw. I've never kept secrets from her before.*

He staggered sideways as Sparkpaw gave him a hard prod in his side. "What's wrong with you?" she asked crossly. "I'm only trying to help. I want to find what lies in the shadows and save ThunderClan. So how do you know your vision's got something to do with the prophecy? Huh?"

"Sparkpaw, stop nagging your brother," Sandstorm meowed tartly, pausing to let the younger cats come up with her. "You heard him. It's medicine-cat business."

Sparkpaw glared for a couple of heartbeats, then shrugged, relaxing. "Okay. I'll find out soon enough, anyway." She bounded over to Cherryfall, who had moved into the lead. "What do you think?" she asked. "What does Alderpaw's vision mean?"

Alderpaw let out a sigh of relief. He was secretly pleased that Sparkpaw hadn't been cowed by the rebuke. He felt bad enough for hiding things from her without getting her into trouble as well.

"I'd answer that better if I knew what the vision was," Cherryfall replied patiently.

"Wouldn't we all?" Sparkpaw responded, flicking a glance at her brother. "But you must have some ideas, Cherryfall. What do you think we'll find at the end of the quest?"

"What we need to, I guess," Cherryfall mewed.

"Something that will help clear the sky," Molewhisker added. Then he muttered, "Whatever that means."

"*I* think it might mean we find some new hunting grounds," Sparkpaw announced. "I hope it does. Then we—"

She broke off as they came to the edge of a clearing where a squirrel was sitting upright among the grass, nibbling at something held in its front paws. Instantly Sparkpaw darted off, her tail flowing out behind her.

But the squirrel was too fast even for her. Spotting her at once, it raced for the nearest tree, swarmed up the trunk, and vanished into the branches. A few leaves drifted down around Sparkpaw, who stood looking up with a frustrated expression on her face.

"We all know you're a quick learner," Cherryfall mewed teasingly as Sparkpaw returned to the group with her tail drooping. "But do you really need a *new* hunting ground already? It seems like you still have something to learn on the one we have." She suppressed a *mrrow* of laughter.

Sparkpaw didn't respond, only giving her chest fur a few furious licks to cover up her embarrassment.

For a moment Alderpaw felt bad for her. He knew exactly how it felt to lose prey.

"Well, I think we should stop and hunt for a while," Sparkpaw meowed. "There's a lot of prey here, and who knows how much there'll be once we've left our territory?"

"No, I think we should keep going and hunt later," Alderpaw objected. He guessed that Sparkpaw just wanted another chance to prove what an awesome hunter she was. "We have a long way to go."

"And Thunderpaths to cross," Sandstorm added. "Graystripe helped me work out a route so that we don't have to cross the mountains, but it means more danger from Twolegs and monsters."

"Huh, Thunderpaths!" Sparkpaw sniffed dismissively. "Purdy told me all about them. They're no big deal."

"No big deal?" Sandstorm's neck fur began to bristle. "Are you mouse-brained? Cats have *died* on Thunderpaths."

"Well, I still think we ought to hunt now," Sparkpaw retorted, bristling in turn. "Last time I checked, we can't fill up on herbs and bits of chewed-up bark!"

Alderpaw lashed his tail in frustration. *I'm supposed to be in charge, but Sparkpaw still thinks she can boss me around. And she's arguing with an elder!*

He drew his lips back in the beginning of a snarl, ready to snap at his sister. But Sandstorm forestalled him, her neck fur lying flat again and her voice calm.

"Sparkpaw, even though you're both young cats in training, this is *Alderpaw's* quest, and *his* vision. You need to listen to him. He's right. We should continue on, not stop to hunt before we've even left our own territory."

Sparkpaw ducked her head, her tail drooping. "Fine," she muttered. "Sorry."

Alderpaw puffed out his chest, pleased that Sandstorm had backed him up and announced that he was the leader. All the same, he didn't like to see his sister miserable. As they set out again, he brushed his tail along her side. "It's okay," he whispered.

They emerged from the trees on the lakeshore not far from the stream that marked the border with WindClan. Alderpaw had been this way before, when they'd gone to the Gathering, and he felt quite confident as he splashed through the shallow water and led the way alongside the lake.

With his Clanmates clustered closely around him, Alderpaw glanced up to see if any of the leggy WindClan warriors were in sight, but nothing moved on the bare hillside.

"Good," Molewhisker murmured. "I'd just as soon get away without WindClan knowing we're gone. StarClan knows what rumors would start if any cat saw us."

Sandstorm nodded. "They might even follow us. Come on, Alderpaw, pick the pace up a bit."

Alderpaw sped up into a fast lope along the pebbly

lakeshore, and his Clanmates followed him until they reached the WindClan border near the horseplace. Now and again he cast swift glances at the moor, and once he thought he saw a flicker of movement among some gorse bushes, but no cat emerged to challenge them.

When they crossed the border and stood near the horse-place, Alderpaw halted. He felt a fluttering in his belly. "You'd better lead now, Sandstorm," he meowed. "You're the only one of us who has been this way before."

Sandstorm nodded. "We have to climb the ridge," she responded, pointing upward with her tail to where a steep hill, dotted here and there with thickets of trees, led to a bare ridge many fox-lengths above their head. "I'll never forget the night we arrived here," she murmured, her green eyes deep with memory. "We climbed that ridge from the other side, and we had no idea where StarClan was leading us. Then we reached the top and saw the lake, and the spirits of our warrior ancestors reflected in the water." She sighed. "It was one of the most wonderful nights of my life."

She paused for a moment, then gave her pelt a shake. "Let's go."

Alderpaw and the others followed Sandstorm on the tough climb up to the ridge. She led them past the clustered Twoleg dens of the horseplace, then alongside a fence made of some shiny Twoleg stuff.

"Look!" Sparkpaw whispered excitedly to Alderpaw. "Horses!"

Alderpaw recognized the huge animals from how Daisy

had described them in the nursery. There were two of them—one dark brown and one mottled gray—standing together in the shade of a tree, gently whisking their tails to and fro.

"They're not dangerous unless you bother them," Sandstorm mewed briskly. "And they won't come on this side of the fence."

All the same, Alderpaw was relieved when they left the horses behind and scrambled up the last few tail-lengths to the top of the ridge. Reaching it, he halted, his paws frozen to the ground.

"Wow!" Sparkpaw breathed out, coming to stand beside him. "I didn't know the world was so big!"

Gazing out in front of him, Alderpaw saw that the ground fell away sharply, sweeping down into a wide valley with stretches of woodland and what looked like a hard black snake winding across it. Beyond it were masses of trees, the huddled dens of an enormous Twolegplace—far bigger than the one by the lake where they had gone to collect catmint—and fields and hills stretching away on every side until they became hazy with distance.

A shiver passed through Alderpaw, as if he were being stabbed by masses of icicles, all at once. Glancing back, he could still see the lake with the Clan territories around it, the only place he had known all his life. Ahead, everything was unknown. It was even more frightening than his journey to the Moonpool, because then he had been following a path the other medicine cats had traveled before him. Now he was taking his Clanmates where there were no familiar paths.

"Can you see the place in your vision?" Sparkpaw asked him. Her eyes were bright with excitement as she took in the vast landscape.

Alderpaw peered around, trying to make out the rocks of the gorge, but it was Sandstorm who replied.

"Of course not. That place is much too far away."

"Great StarClan!" Sparkpaw squeaked. "You mean there's *more* of it?"

"Much more," Sandstorm told her. "And the sooner we get going, the sooner we'll arrive. Come on: I'd like to cross the Thunderpath down there before nightfall."

Alderpaw realized she meant the black snake-thing. It was so different from the little Thunderpath that ended at the lake, separating ShadowClan territory from RiverClan. Glittering objects, which looked like tiny beetles at this distance, were speeding back and forth along its length.

"When we get there," Sandstorm went on, "you will *not* cross before I tell you to. Is that quite clear?" she added, with a hard look at Sparkpaw.

Sparkpaw nodded, as cheerful as ever after her earlier scolding. "Sure, Sandstorm."

With Sandstorm in the lead, the five cats headed down the slope and soon came to a wide stretch of woodland. Even though it wasn't as thick as the forest, Alderpaw was grateful to be back under the shade of trees, enjoying the warm scents and the long grass underpaw.

Gradually he became aware of voices from somewhere up ahead. But as they grew louder, he realized they were not the voices of cats, or of any other animal he had come across before. The hairs on his pelt began to rise.

Sandstorm halted, raising her tail as a sign for the others to do the same. "Twolegs!" she hissed.

"Really?" Sparkpaw's eyes were alight with interest. "Can we go and see?"

Sandstorm hesitated. "It's not a bad idea for you to get an idea of what they're like," she replied at last. "But we're not here to gawk at Twolegs, and don't you forget it."

More cautiously she led the way forward.

Alderpaw had to admit that he was just as curious as his sister. So far he had only glimpsed Twolegs now and again, mostly near the greenleaf Twolegplaces, and always from a distance. He had never heard their raucous voices, or gotten close enough to discover what they were really like.

Skirting a bramble thicket, Sandstorm stood screened behind a clump of ferns and beckoned with her tail. "Okay, come and look, but don't let them know you're here."

Alderpaw crept forward, with Sparkpaw by his side, and peered through the ferns. A group of five Twolegs, all different sizes, were sitting in a clearing. Just beyond them was a stretch of ground covered by the black Thunderpath stuff, with one of the glittering things—this one bright red— crouching under a tree.

"What's that?" he whispered to Sandstorm.

"A monster," Sandstorm murmured in reply. "They'll kill you if they catch you with those big black paws. But that one looks like it's asleep, so it's probably safe for now."

"And what are the Twolegs sitting on?" Sparkpaw asked. "They look like tree trunks, but sort of flat."

Alderpaw thought that was a good description. There was a bigger flat trunk, too, with big leaf wraps scattered upon it. They must have held prey, because the Twolegs were stuffing something into their mouths.

Sparkpaw passed her tongue over her jaws. "I'm hungry," she complained. "And whatever that is, it smells *good!*"

Alderpaw's pelt bristled with fear to see the Twolegs so close, to hear their harsh voices and to pick up their weird scent. But he was fascinated too.

"They have hardly any fur," he murmured. "Are they sick? I remember Leafpool telling me about a sickness that made cats lose their fur. But these Twolegs *all* seem to have it." Turning to Sandstorm, he asked, "Why don't their medicine Twolegs help them?"

Sandstorm's green eyes were gleaming with amusement. "They're not sick," she explained. "That's just what Twolegs look like."

Then they look pretty stupid, Alderpaw thought, his pelt smoothing out as he wondered why he had been scared of them at all.

Suddenly the smallest Twoleg kit leaped up from the flat tree, letting out a loud yowl. To Alderpaw's horror it set off at a stumbling run toward the cats, waving its forepaws in the air. Its round face was red, and crazy sounds were coming from its mouth.

"It's seen us!" Cherryfall gasped.

At the same moment Sandstorm snapped out a command. "Don't run! We'll get separated. Hide!"

Forcing himself to move, Alderpaw darted back to the bramble thicket and thrust his way into it, feeling the thorns rake through his pelt. He could hear Sparkpaw burrowing close by. "StarClan-forsaken thorns!" she muttered.

Molewhisker's voice came from further away. "We should have known! Twolegs are always trouble."

Alderpaw could hear the Twoleg kit's voice rising to a shriek. Then the lower-pitched, adult Twoleg voices drew closer, and the ground shook with the trampling of their huge, clumsy paws. Alderpaw crouched as small as he could and hoped that all his Clanmates were well hidden.

Finally the sounds died away and the footsteps retreated. Alderpaw worked his way backward out of the thicket and stood shaking his pelt. He felt as if every thorn in the forest were sticking into him.

Then he noticed that Sparkpaw had emerged and returned to the edge of the clearing to peer through the ferns again.

"What do you think you're doing?" he hissed, creeping up to her side. "Do you want the Twolegs to catch you?"

"It's okay; they're leaving," Sparkpaw replied. "Come and watch. It's really interesting."

Curious in spite of himself, Alderpaw parted the fern fronds so that he could see. The three Twoleg kits were climbing into the monster. The adult Twolegs were collecting the leaf wraps from the big flat tree trunk; then they crossed the clearing and dropped them into a Twoleg thing that looked like a rock with a tiny cave at the top.

"That's food!" Sparkpaw whispered. "I can smell it. But why are they putting it in there?"

"Maybe that's where Twolegs store food," Alderpaw suggested. "I expect when they're hungry they'll come back for it."

"No." Alderpaw jumped to realize that Sandstorm had padded up beside him. "That's just where Twolegs leave their extra food when they don't want it anymore."

"How could they not want it?" Sparkpaw asked. "It smells amazing!"

Alderpaw tasted the air, and his jaws began to water at the delicious scent that flooded over him. He realized how hungry he was.

"Twolegs are very strange," Molewhisker commented, as he and Cherryfall padded up to join the others.

Alderpaw watched as the two adult Twolegs also got into the monster with their kits. He started as the monster woke up with a ferocious roar, flooding the air with an acrid scent, then swiveled around and moved off, its black paws rolling faster and faster on the black Thunderpath stuff until it disappeared among the trees.

"Did the monster just *eat* them?" Sparkpaw asked, her eyes stretched wide with horror.

Sandstorm shook her head. "No, the monsters just let Twolegs ride inside them. I don't even try to understand it."

"I told you Twolegs are strange," Molewhisker mewed. "And that goes for their monsters, too. Mind you," he added after a moment, "they may be strange, but some of their food is really tasty. I'm not too keen on Twolegs, but it would be mouse-brained to let their food go to waste when it's *right there*." He waved his tail at the open-topped rock.

The cats glanced at one another.

"I'm not sure . . . ," Sandstorm murmured. "You know that warriors don't eat kittypet food."

"It's not *kittypet* food," Cherryfall argued. "It's Twoleg food."

"Well . . . okay," Sandstorm agreed reluctantly. "You see if you can get it out of there. I'll keep watch."

She stayed by the ferns at the edge of the clearing while Sparkpaw eagerly led the way over to the rock. Alderpaw looked up; there was shiny black stuff poking out of the cave at its top, and its sides were shiny silver with no paw holds.

"How are we going to get in?" Molewhisker asked, sounding as if he didn't really expect an answer.

Cherryfall tried climbing up, but her paws skidded on the smooth surface of the rock, and she slipped back before she got anywhere near the top. "Mouse dung!" she exclaimed.

"I've got an idea!" Sparkpaw's fur bristled and her tail bushed out with excitement. "Stand back, all of you."

She trotted back for several fox-lengths, then raced and took a flying leap to the top of the rock, balancing precariously on the cave's edge.

"Come down!" Cherryfall yowled. "You'll fall in, and how will we get you out?"

"I'm fine!" Sparkpaw squealed.

She swayed to and fro as she gripped the top edge of the cave with her paws. The rock tilted with her weight and suddenly tipped over. Sparkpaw leaped to safety as the rock thumped to the ground and masses of Twoleg stuff spilled out of it.

"There you go," Sparkpaw panted, a smug look on her face. "Easy."

Molewhisker put his head into the cave, Twoleg leaf wraps crackling under his paws, and emerged with a lump of something in his jaws. Alderpaw breathed in more of the enticing smell.

"What is it?" he asked.

"Dunno," Molewhisker mumbled around his prey. "Some kind of bird, I think. Go and get some. There's plenty."

Sparkpaw instantly followed, dragging out a huge piece of the bird. "This is so big it must have been an eagle," she meowed. "I'll share it with Sandstorm."

Alderpaw and then Cherryfall ventured in and collected some of the prey for themselves. "Thanks, Sparkpaw," Alderpaw murmured as he joined the group beside the ferns. "You're really good at hunting Twoleg prey, too!"

Biting into his piece of fresh-kill, Alderpaw realized that it tasted even better than it smelled. But as he gulped it down, he began to feel a prickling in his pelt, as if some creature was watching him. He tried to tell himself not to be stupid, but he couldn't shake off the feeling.

A rustling sound came from the trees. Alderpaw tensed, glancing back over his shoulder.

Maybe the crazy Twoleg kit came back? Or maybe the Twolegs weren't really done with their food after all.

But the rustling died away, and there was nothing to be seen. Alderpaw tried to pick up a scent, but the aroma of the delicious Twoleg prey swamped everything else. He turned back to finish his food, trying to tell himself that he was imagining things.

It's weird . . . I just have the feeling that we're being watched.

CHAPTER 10
❧

The sun was going down, the sky a blaze of scarlet, as the cats plodded on through the trees. Alderpaw's belly was growling with hunger; he had felt so tense since sunhigh, moving farther and farther away from his home, that he hadn't realized the pain in his belly was because he hadn't eaten. It felt like days since they had eaten the Twoleg food.

"I think we ought to stop and hunt," Molewhisker meowed. "It'll be dark soon."

Sandstorm looked undecided. "We still need to get across the Thunderpath," she responded. "I thought we might cross first, and then hunt."

Alderpaw noticed for the first time an acrid tang in the air, and a distant rumbling sound that he would have thought was thunder, except that the sky was clear. The scent reminded him of the monster that had swallowed the Twolegs, and he realized it must come from the Thunderpath.

"But I'm starving!" Sparkpaw protested to Sandstorm. "*Please* can we hunt first?"

Sandstorm twitched her whiskers. "Okay," she agreed at last. "I'm hungry myself, I admit it."

Before she had finished speaking, Sparkpaw plunged into the undergrowth and emerged a few moments later with the limp body of a vole in her jaws.

"Good job," Sandstorm commented with a nod of approval.

"I don't know how she does it," Molewhisker muttered.

At the same time as he admired Sparkpaw's skill, Alderpaw tried to subdue his feelings of envy. It was even harder when Molewhisker turned to him and mewed, "Do you want to hunt with me, Alderpaw?"

"Yeah . . . sure." Alderpaw guessed that Molewhisker didn't think he was capable of catching prey by himself. *It's like being his apprentice again,* he thought as he followed his former mentor into a clump of thickly growing hazel bushes.

"Try the way I taught you before," Molewhisker suggested. "Concentrate on one small area at a time. That seemed to be working well for you."

Not well enough, Alderpaw reflected, crouching down and focusing on the fallen leaves and twigs underneath the nearest hazel bush. Sniffing carefully, he caught the scent of mouse, and a moment later he spotted it almost hidden by a heap of dead leaves.

Trying to remember everything he had learned when he was Molewhisker's apprentice, Alderpaw crept forward. The mouse seemed unaware of him, scuffling about among the leaves. Then Alderpaw paused, his gaze flicking to a branch above his head. *Do I have room to pounce? Will I touch the branch and alert the mouse?*

While he was hesitating, the mouse suddenly froze, then

scuttled away. It would have escaped if Molewhisker hadn't leaped for it and slapped a paw down on it.

"Try again," Molewhisker suggested, clearly fed up with hunting with Alderpaw. "I'm going to see if I can find a squirrel."

He padded off, leaving the mouse for Alderpaw to collect.

Alderpaw tried again, spotting a blackbird pecking in the grass at the edge of the hazel clump. He slipped into the hunter's crouch and began to creep up on it, determined that this time he wouldn't fail. He imagined himself trotting back to meet his Clanmates with the bird clamped in his jaws. His paws began to shake with excitement as he drew closer.

But then one of his forepaws slipped to one side, and he lost his balance. The blackbird flew off with a raucous cry. "Fox dung!" Alderpaw hissed as he righted himself and realized that he had stumbled over a small hollow in the ground, screened by overhanging grass.

That could have happened to any cat, he thought, trying to defend himself, then added wretchedly, *but it had to happen to me.*

He glanced around to spot more prey, but all he saw was Molewhisker, dragging a squirrel along the ground between his forepaws.

"No luck?" his former mentor asked sympathetically. "Never mind. You can share this. Don't forget to pick up the mouse."

When he returned to the spot where he had left his Clanmates, Alderpaw saw that Sandstorm had caught a plump pigeon, while Cherryfall had two mice.

"Hey!" Sparkpaw exclaimed as Molewhisker and Alderpaw approached. "You caught a mouse!"

"No, I didn't," Alderpaw replied, dropping the prey. "Molewhisker caught it."

He felt more useless than ever as he and his Clanmates feasted on the prey.

By the time they had finished eating, the sun had gone down, and shadows were gathering under the trees. "It's getting late," Sandstorm mewed. "If we want to cross the Thunderpath tonight, we'd better get a move on."

As they set out, Alderpaw felt his pelt start to prickle again with the sensation that they were being followed. Eyeing some thick undergrowth as they padded past, he was almost sure that something was watching them from deep inside it. He wondered whether he should tell Sandstorm his suspicions, but when he tasted the air, he was so overwhelmed by his companions' scents that he couldn't make out anything strange. *They'd just think I was imagining things,* he told himself, trying to shrug off the feeling. *And maybe I am.*

The roaring sound grew louder as the cats loped on, and the acrid stench filled the air, drowning out the scents of the forest. Before they had traveled many fox-lengths, the trees came to an end, and the cats emerged onto a strip of grass that bordered the Thunderpath.

Alderpaw stared at it, his heart pounding so hard that he thought it would break out of his chest. He had never seen anything so terrifying. Monsters were racing past in both directions, so close that the wind of their passing ruffled the cats' fur. As they ran, they let out weird, high-pitched noises, as if they were talking to one another. Most of them had two blazing eyes that cut through the darkness in front of them.

Then Alderpaw spotted a monster that had only one eye. It looked even more dangerous than the others.

"A one-eyed monster!" Sparkpaw gasped, pressing close to Alderpaw and for once sounding just as scared as he was.

"You have to be brave," Sandstorm meowed, her voice steady. "We need to cross before it's completely dark. Come with me, and remember what I told you. No cat is to cross until I give the word."

Alderpaw took a deep breath and gathered all his strength. He closed his eyes and called up the memory of the cats in his vision. *I'm doing this for you.* Full of resolve, he opened his eyes again. *If we have to cross, then that's what we'll do.*

He followed Sandstorm and stood in a line with his Clanmates at the very edge of the Thunderpath. He couldn't believe how close they were to the monsters as they whizzed by. Noise and wind and harsh scents buffeted him so that he hardly knew where he was. The monsters moved so quickly that he couldn't see their paws, just a blur of black as they raced by. Their roaring was so loud it hurt his ears, and their eyes were so bright that he couldn't bear to look at them.

"Don't worry," meowed Sandstorm, standing next to him. "As long as we time our crossing right, the monsters won't get us."

Alderpaw wanted to believe her, but he couldn't help noticing the fear in her voice and in her scent.

There was no gap between the monsters where the cats could safely cross. Alderpaw imagined himself squashed beneath those massive black paws, flattened onto the black surface of the Thunderpath.

Then something flew out of one of the monsters. It glittered in the light from their eyes, heading straight for Molewhisker. Sandstorm saw it, too.

"No!" she yowled, leaping at Molewhisker and shoving him out of the way.

Both cats lost their balance and fell over in a tangle of legs and tails, while the object smashed down on the edge of the Thunderpath and shattered into pieces.

"Thanks!" Molewhisker panted, scrambling to his paws. "Sandstorm, you probably saved my—"

He broke off as another object appeared from another monster, a dark shape hurtling through the air.

"Run!" Sandstorm yowled. "Back into the trees!"

No cat waited to find out what the second object was. Alderpaw heard it thump to the ground behind him as he raced back into the woodland with Sparkpaw by his side. At first he was scared that they would lose one another in the gathering darkness, but after a moment they all came together and huddled, trembling, in the shelter of some ferns.

"That does it!" Sandstorm's voice was shaking. "I'm not trying to cross in the dark, not with monsters throwing things at us. We'll make camp here and cross in the morning."

Alderpaw felt a vast wave of relief that he didn't have to go back and face the monsters with their glowing eyes. He tried to squash down the niggling anxiety that he felt when he thought about making the crossing on the following day.

Every cat was too exhausted to think of making real nests. They crawled more deeply into the patch of ferns and curled up close together. Alderpaw was grateful for the comforting feel of his sister's fur pressed against him on one side, and Molewhisker's on the other.

But as sleep washed over him, his pelt tingled with the certainty that he could still feel their mysterious follower's eyes.

Sunlight slanting through the ferns woke Alderpaw the next morning. Scrambling up, he pushed his way out into the open to see Sandstorm grooming herself at the foot of a beech tree. There was no sign of his other Clanmates.

"It's so late!" he gasped. "Why did you let me sleep? Where are the others?"

"Keep your fur on," Sandstorm meowed, licking her paw and drawing it over one ear. "It's only just after sunrise. The others have gone hunting."

As she spoke, the fern fronds waved and Cherryfall emerged, carrying a squirrel. Molewhisker and Sparkpaw followed her, each with a vole.

"Great catch," Sandstorm commented. "Let's eat and be on our way."

It was comforting to have a full belly when he followed his Clanmates to the edge of the trees and reached the Thunderpath once more. He was still scared as he crouched at the edge of the hard black path, his fur buffeted as the monsters roared past. But it wasn't quite as terrifying as the night before.

At least we can see the monsters properly, not just their blazing eyes!

Sandstorm stood in the middle of their line, her head turning to and fro as she waited for a gap between the monsters. "When I say 'run,'" she mewed, "then run as if the whole of ShadowClan were after you, and don't stop until you get to the other side."

It seemed a long time to Alderpaw before the roaring of monsters died away and the last of them dwindled into the distance.

"Now!" Sandstorm exclaimed. "Run!"

Alderpaw leaped forward in massive bounds, his paws barely touching the hard surface of the Thunderpath as he raced toward the trees on the other side, Sparkpaw keeping pace next to him. Then the roar of a monster burst upon Alderpaw's ears, and he heard Sandstorm shriek, "Faster!"

Glancing over, Alderpaw saw the biggest monster yet bearing down on him, looming over him with its jaws gaping. All his instincts told him to freeze in terror, but Sparkpaw barreled into him, forcing him to keep running. The monster passed behind them with a blast of wind, and Alderpaw collapsed, panting, on the grass at the far side of the Thunderpath.

"Great StarClan, that was scary!" Sparkpaw exclaimed.

Alderpaw sat up, panting for breath. "Thanks, Sparkpaw. You saved—"

His sister gave him a hard nudge. "Shut up, stupid furball."

"We ought to get under cover," Molewhisker suggested.

"The monsters might start throwing things again."

"Good idea," Sandstorm agreed.

They trekked through the trees for the rest of the day, as clouds began to gather, casting a gloom over the forest. Wind rustled the upper branches, and a few drops of rain spattered down. Toward evening the sky cleared again, but the air remained chilly. Fluffing up his fur, Alderpaw wished he could look forward to his cozy nest in the apprentices' den. *At least I don't think we're being watched anymore. Maybe we lost the creature, whatever it was, back at the Thunderpath.*

Eventually they came to a hollow edged by thick holly bushes. There was a small pool of water at the bottom, and all the cats, sore-pawed by now, limped down the slope and lapped gratefully at the water.

"This is as good a place as any to make camp," Sandstorm meowed. "Alderpaw, you and I will collect bedding while the rest of you hunt."

Alderpaw felt a pang of regret that he would never be chosen to join the hunters, but quickly set to work collecting leaves, moss, and ferns to make a nest for his Clanmates to share in the shelter of a bush. It was ready, soft and comfortable, by the time the moon had risen and the others returned with a couple of thrushes and several shrews.

"Good night," Sparkpaw yawned when she had gulped down her share of the prey. "Maybe we'll find this shadowy thing tomorrow."

"Oh, no," Sandstorm responded sleepily. "There's a long way to go yet."

Alderpaw burrowed down into the nest with Sparkpaw by his side.

He was almost asleep when he heard the crunching of leaves coming from somewhere among the bushes. He sat up, instantly alert, to see that Sandstorm had heard it, too, while the other three cats were still struggling to their paws. As the crunching sound continued, Alderpaw thought that he could distinguish paw steps.

Sandstorm signaled with her tail for the others to stay where they were. "I'll check it out," she whispered.

As cautiously as if she were stalking a mouse, Sandstorm crept out of the nest and headed toward the bushes. She had almost reached them when the night air was split by a ferocious growl.

A strong reek flooded over Alderpaw, and he let out a yowl of fear as a shape hurtled out of the bushes and lunged at Sandstorm. Alderpaw caught the flash of teeth and claws, the gleam of malignant eyes.

"StarClan, no!" Sparkpaw wailed. "I think that's a fox!"

CHAPTER 11

Alderpaw couldn't believe how fast the fox was. He watched, stunned, as its wiry body leaped through the air and landed on Sandstorm, its pointed snout burying itself in her fur as its gnashing teeth sank into her shoulder. Sandstorm let out a shrill yowl of pain.

Shaking off his shock, Alderpaw raced forward and flung himself on top of the fox. Snarling, it turned and reared up, throwing Alderpaw off its back. Free of its jaws, Sandstorm rolled away, looking dazed. Blood was pouring from the wound in her shoulder.

"Get out of this!" Alderpaw called to her. "It's too dangerous—you're hurt!"

Sandstorm hesitated, sliding out her claws, then reluctantly started dragging herself off to one side.

Alderpaw darted toward the fox again, scoring his claws down its side, then leaping back out of range as it snapped at him. *Where are the others?* he thought. He gazed around, and his heart pounded even harder as he saw a second fox attacking his other Clanmates, who were defending themselves desperately. *They won't be able to help me,* Alderpaw realized, his terror mounting. The night air was full of snarls and yowling and the reek of blood.

Alderpaw's fox swiped at his face, and he barely managed to duck in time to avoid the blow. The fox lunged at him again; leaping backward, Alderpaw crashed into something hard, and he realized that he was trapped against the trunk of a tree.

The fox growled, claws raking at the ground in front of it. Alderpaw tried to hiss at it in defiance, but the sound came out weak and unthreatening. *I wouldn't even frighten a kit!*

Alderpaw braced himself as the fox crouched to spring. But before it could move, a high-pitched cry rang out. In the moonlight Alderpaw saw a whirlwind of fur fly out of the bushes and land right on the fox's back.

The fox let out a fearsome screech and thrashed back and forth, trying to dislodge the ball of fur from its back. But the furball had dug its claws in and managed to cling on.

It's a she-cat, Alderpaw realized. *Great StarClan, she's brave! But she's no match for a fox.*

There was no time to wonder who the strange cat was. Throwing himself back into the fight, Alderpaw tried to get his claws into the fox's throat, but his grip gave way as it shook its head violently. Then he realized that Sparkpaw had joined him, fighting fiercely by his side, slashing at the fox's shoulder, then darting back out of range.

"Swipe at its eye!" the cat on the fox's back called out. "Go for its hind leg!"

The strange cat's voice sounded oddly familiar to Alderpaw,

but he had no time to think about that, and in the fitful moonlight he couldn't see her clearly.

"Whatever you do, don't let go!" Sparkpaw gasped to her.

"I wasn't planning to!" The strange cat raked her claws along the fox's back, while Alderpaw and Sparkpaw kept on attacking from the side, trying to throw the fox off balance.

At last the creature screeched and, with a massive shake, hurled the strange cat off; she went sprawling in a patch of fern. Alderpaw dashed between her and the fox, ready to defend her, but the fox had clearly had enough. It turned tail and ran, while Cherryfall and Molewhisker drove the second fox after it.

For a few heartbeats all the cats stood still, their chests heaving as they fought for breath. Sandstorm was the first to speak. "Is every cat okay?"

"I'm fine," Alderpaw responded.

"I banged my shoulder on the ground," Molewhisker mewed. "I think it'll be stiff tomorrow, but it's not serious."

"I've just lost a bit of fur," Cherryfall added.

Alderpaw began sniffing Sparkpaw all over to make sure she was unhurt, though she wriggled under his questing nose. "Honestly, Alderpaw, I'm okay."

"So am I." The voice of the strange cat came from behind Alderpaw, and he turned to see her emerging from the clump of ferns where she had fallen.

"Thanks for your help," he meowed, and the other cats joined in a chorus of agreement. "I think the fox would have gotten me if it weren't for—"

Just then the moon came out from behind a cloud, and Alderpaw got a good look at the strange cat for the first time. "Needlepaw!" he gasped. "What are you doing here?"

Needlepaw strolled into the midst of the group of cats and gazed around at them calmly. "Saving you from foxes," she replied.

"But . . . aren't you a ShadowClan apprentice?" Cherryfall asked. "Where's your mentor? What are you doing so far away from home?"

Clearly annoyed at being questioned, Needlepaw gave a defiant flick of her tail. "I was exploring on WindClan territory when I saw you all heading out," she replied. "I was sure it had something to do with the prophecy, so I followed you."

"You're not supposed to be wandering around without your mentor," Sandstorm scolded her. Her voice was tight with pain from her wound, and Alderpaw knew she needed rest and treatment, not an argument with this ShadowClan cat. "And you're not supposed to be exploring on WindClan territory."

"I wasn't hunting!" Needlepaw retorted. "And I . . ."

Her voice faded to silence at Sandstorm's green glare. "You're certainly not supposed to leave Clan territory by yourself, without permission from your Clan leader," Sandstorm went on. "Don't you realize how dangerous it is, being out here alone? You're going to be in a lot of trouble with Rowanstar when you get back."

Needlepaw returned her glare defiantly but kept her jaws clamped shut.

"Did you really follow us across the Thunderpath?" Mole-whisker asked curiously. "It's very dangerous."

"Of course I did." Needlepaw's voice was scornful. "Thunderpaths are no big deal. I'm not afraid of monsters!"

Alderpaw wondered whether she really meant that, or whether she was just saying it to make herself look tough. *Thunderpaths are terrifying!*

"Then you're a mouse-brain," Molewhisker told her caustically.

"I can take care of myself," Needlepaw retorted. "Which is more than I can say for the rest of you. Obviously you need my help. I just saved you!"

"You maybe *helped* save us," Sparkpaw pointed out, her tail-tip flicking to and fro in irritation. "But you only *helped*."

Needlepaw ignored her. "I'm coming with you now," she announced.

Cherryfall and Molewhisker exchanged an incredulous glance. "No way!" Cherryfall exclaimed.

"Exactly." Sandstorm's voice was brusque. "You should go back to your own territory."

"I'm staying, and you can't stop me," Needlepaw meowed, quite undeterred. "I know you're going to look for the thing in the shadows that the prophecy spoke about. And there's no way I'm going to let you find it just for ThunderClan. Who's to say ShadowClan can't have some of that destiny, too?" Her gaze traveled around the group of cats, and her voice grew urgent; Alderpaw sensed that her desperation was about more than seeking what lies in the shadows. "If I can do anything to help the sky clear for my Clan, then I have to do it."

Alderpaw felt a pang of sympathy for Needlepaw. *If I were in her place, I'd want to make sure the sky cleared for ThunderClan, too.* But he was taken aback when Needlepaw swung around and spoke to him directly.

"Alderpaw, you're a medicine cat. You know about this stuff. What do you think?" Her voice softened into a persuasive purr. "*Please* let me come."

Alderpaw felt good to be asked, to know he had this cat's respect. He knew he shouldn't like Needlepaw as much as he did. *She's from another Clan, and she breaks rules all the time, and she's rude about senior warriors . . . but she's fun, and different, and she's really good at hunting and fighting. And she always says exactly what she thinks.*

"I . . . uh . . . I don't know," he stammered uncomfortably. "I'm not sure I—"

"This *is* Alderpaw's quest," Sandstorm broke in, to Alderpaw's relief. "But even so, he cannot make this decision alone. We must discuss it . . . in private," she finished with a stern glare at Needlepaw.

"Sure," Needlepaw mewed, pausing before she gave one paw a nonchalant lick.

She's not really casual about this, Alderpaw realized. *She'd never admit it, but she's worried about what we'll decide.*

The ThunderClan cats padded off into the shelter of a clump of trees at the edge of the hollow. Alderpaw noticed that Sandstorm was limping, and the wound in her shoulder was still bleeding.

"Are you okay, Sandstorm?" he asked. "I ought to take a look at that wound."

"I'll be fine," Sandstorm responded with a dismissive twitch of her whiskers.

But Alderpaw wasn't satisfied. "Give the wound a good lick to clean it," he told Sandstorm as soon as they were settled under the trees. "Sparkpaw, find me some cobweb."

"Ooh, bossy medicine cat!" Sparkpaw exclaimed. "Have you been taking politeness lessons from Jayfeather?" But she started sniffing around in the undergrowth and soon came back with a pawful of cobweb.

By this time Sandstorm had cleaned her wound. Alderpaw examined it thoroughly, glad to see that the bleeding had slowed to a trickle.

"This is all very well," Sandstorm meowed as Alderpaw fixed the cobweb in place, "but what are we going to do about Needlepaw? I don't like the thought of her tagging along with us, but she's too young to be out on her own, and we can't just send her back to her own territory without any cat to look after her. It's not safe!"

"I think you're right," Cherryfall agreed.

Molewhisker lashed his tail angrily. "The nosy little cat got herself into this mess," he growled, "and she should get herself out of it! Cheeky ShadowClan apprentices are *not* our problem!"

"Well," Alderpaw began, feeling shy about contradicting a senior warrior, "her nosiness *did* come in handy when the foxes attacked us."

Molewhisker grunted. "I suppose so."

"We would have fought the foxes off eventually," Sparkpaw meowed. "We don't need Needlepaw."

"This is getting us nowhere," Sandstorm sighed. "Alderpaw, Needlepaw was right about one thing: it's your quest. What do you think?"

"I don't agree with Molewhisker and Sparkpaw," Alderpaw admitted, even though he was reluctant to go against his former mentor, and his sister. "I think Needlepaw should come with us. If we try to send her back," he added, "she's just going to ignore us and follow us anyway."

"Maybe," Molewhisker snorted, "but that's no reason to *welcome* her."

"Okay," Sandstorm mewed, "since we can't agree, I'll make the final decision. Needlepaw will come with us."

Sparkpaw and Molewhisker exchanged a disappointed look.

"Fine!" Sparkpaw snapped. "But there's no way we're telling her what this quest is *really* about, right?"

Alderpaw couldn't meet his littermate's gaze. *Even my own Clanmates don't know what the quest is* really *about!*

Sandstorm caught his eye. "No, we won't tell her that," she murmured.

Rising to their paws, the ThunderClan cats padded back into the hollow to tell Needlepaw their decision. On the way, Alderpaw could hear Cherryfall and Molewhisker muttering just behind him.

"That cat is going to be in a *lot* of trouble once she gets back to her own territory," Molewhisker grumbled.

"But that's not our problem," Cherryfall responded. "It's hers!"

While they were away, Needlepaw had obviously been grooming herself, and her sleek silver pelt shone in the growing light of dawn. Alderpaw, still covered in dust and bits of debris from the fox fight, felt very scruffy by contrast.

"We've decided to let you join us," Sandstorm announced.

Needlepaw raised one paw and examined her claws. "Well, of course you have," she mewed coolly. "It's not like you could stop me, anyway."

Alderpaw's pelt prickled with irritation at her rudeness, and yet he sensed that Needlepaw was much happier than she was prepared to admit. *There's something sort of . . . lonely about her,* he thought.

As the sky began to flush red where the sun would rise, Alderpaw saw Needlepaw's face more clearly. And he thought he could see in her eyes how pleased she was to be included.

CHAPTER 12

❧

"Sandstorm," Alderpaw meowed, *"now that the* sun is up, I want to have a better look at your shoulder."

The old she-cat sighed. "I was expecting you to say that."

She stayed still while Alderpaw peeled off the cobweb he had applied the night before. A small amount of blood was still oozing from the wound.

"What can we do to help?" Sparkpaw asked, peering anxiously over his shoulder.

Alderpaw was pleased and relieved that he knew exactly what was needed. *Leafpool and Jayfeather would be proud of me.*

"Comfrey root," he replied. "Cherryfall, Molewhisker, could you go and find some? It has large, long leaves. The root is black, and it has a tangy smell."

"The stuff you put on my pad, right?" Cherryfall asked. "I know exactly what to look for. Come on, Molewhisker."

"Honestly, it's not that serious," Sandstorm protested as the two warriors disappeared into the undergrowth. "I'll be fine."

"You still need to let me treat the wound," Alderpaw responded. "It's important."

It felt weird to be telling an elder what to do, and he was

glad when Sandstorm gave a reluctant nod. "Meanwhile, give it another good lick," Alderpaw added. "Then it'll be ready for the poultice."

The sun had not risen much farther up the sky by the time Cherryfall and Molewhisker returned, carrying plenty of comfrey. Alderpaw set to work at once, chewing up the root, and once it was a fine enough paste he applied it to Sandstorm's wound. Sandstorm relaxed, letting out a long sigh, as the juices sank in.

"That feels so much better," she murmured.

"Now the rest of you," Alderpaw meowed.

"We're fine, honestly," Sparkpaw protested.

"You're fine when I say you are," Alderpaw retorted, remembering what Jayfeather liked to say to cats who didn't want to be fussed over.

Sparkpaw twitched her whiskers but stood still while Alderpaw examined her. In the clear light of morning he spotted a scratch on her foreleg that he had missed the night before, and he patted some of the comfrey poultice onto it.

"Thanks, that's great," Sparkpaw mewed. "Hey, do you know your ear's been bleeding?"

Alderpaw hadn't realized his ear was stinging, distracted first by the stress of the fight and then by the discussion about Needlepaw and the need to treat his Clanmates.

"Daft furball!" Sparkpaw gave him a nudge. "Hold still, and I'll give it a lick." Her tongue rasped swiftly over his ear. "Now I'll dab a bit of that root on it," she continued. "There! All done. Do you think I'd make a good medicine cat?"

"No way!" Alderpaw gave a purr of amusement. "But you're going to be a sensational warrior!"

When he checked his other Clanmates, Alderpaw was pleased to find that although the fox had clawed out some of Cherryfall's fur, she wasn't actually injured.

"My shoulder still aches a bit," Molewhisker told him, "but it's not so bad. I think it'll be fine once we get moving."

"I can see a scratch on your back," Alderpaw meowed, turning to Needlepaw. He felt slightly shy at offering help to a cat from another Clan. "Do you want me to look at it?"

"Please," Needlepaw replied with an uncomfortable wriggle. "That mange-pelted fox threw me into a gorse bush, and it *hurts*."

Examining her more closely, Alderpaw saw that a couple of thorns were sticking into Needlepaw's back, and she had a nasty scrape clotted with dried blood.

"You've picked up some thorns," Alderpaw mewed. "Crouch down and I'll get them out."

Needlepaw flattened herself, and Alderpaw managed to get his teeth into the shanks of the thorns and yank them out, then spit them onto the ground. A trace of blood welled up where they had been.

"Now comfrey root," Alderpaw continued. "This will take the pain away."

She stretched and relaxed as the comfrey juices soaked into her back. "Thanks, Alderpaw. You must be a really good medicine cat, because I feel better already. And *hungry*!"

Alderpaw's pelt grew hot with embarrassment at

Needlepaw's praise, and he was glad to step back as Cherryfall organized a hunting patrol. She and Molewhisker, Sparkpaw, and Needlepaw headed off into the trees, while Alderpaw stayed with Sandstorm.

"You're doing a good job, Alderpaw," Sandstorm murmured when the others had gone.

Alderpaw ducked his head. "Thanks, Sandstorm." He wasn't sure he deserved the compliment, but he felt himself filling up with happiness like a hollow filling up with rain.

Sunhigh was still some way off when the hunting patrol returned. Molewhisker and Sparkpaw were each carrying mice, while Cherryfall had a vole. Alderpaw's eyes stretched wide with amazement when he spotted Needlepaw with her prey. She was dragging along a pigeon and a squirrel, both of them so big that she could hardly manage them. She picked up her pace to stride ahead to the bottom of the hollow, where Alderpaw and Sandstorm were sunning themselves beside the pool, and dropped her catch at their paws.

Alderpaw tried hard to hide how impressed he was, but he was sure that Needlepaw could tell.

"Not bad, huh?" she meowed. "You don't regret having me around now, do you? And I got even more than that!"

Sparkpaw and the others caught up and put down their own prey. Alderpaw could see that his sister looked a bit annoyed to be outdone by Needlepaw, and kept casting sidelong glances at her.

"It's true," she meowed to Sandstorm. "Needlepaw did

catch more than the squirrel and the pigeon. She caught a big, fat rat."

"So where is it?" Sandstorm asked.

"Needlepaw already ate it!" Sparkpaw sounded outraged. "She ate it herself! That's against the warrior code."

Alderpaw would never have said so out loud, but he felt that it wasn't their place to teach Needlepaw about the warrior code. *She's not part of our Clan, and even if she did eat the rat, she still brought back more prey than the other three put together!*

"Let's all just eat and relax a bit," Sandstorm responded to Sparkpaw; her voice sounded weary. "We've had an exhausting time, and we could all do with a good meal and some rest."

Sparkpaw said no more, though she ruffled up her fur indignantly and glared at Needlepaw, who seemed quite untroubled by her complaints.

"Let's eat," Needlepaw mewed. "Come on, Alderpaw, you can share my squirrel."

Sharp pangs of hunger were clawing through Alderpaw's belly, and every mouthful of the squirrel seemed like the best prey he had ever tasted. But as he sat up again and used one paw to clean his whiskers, he noticed that his sister had disappeared.

"Where's Sparkpaw?" he asked, an uneasy feeling prickling his pads. *Suppose those foxes came back . . . but then there would have been a fight. She wouldn't just vanish!*

The ThunderClan cats scattered around the hollow, looking for Sparkpaw, crying out her name. There was no response, but then Sandstorm called to them from the bush where she and Alderpaw had made the nest the night before.

"She's here!"

Alderpaw bounded up to see his sister cozily curled up among the ferns, her tail wrapped over her nose. She was snoring softly.

"Should we wake her up?" Cherryfall asked, as his Clanmates clustered around.

"I think she's got the right idea," Molewhisker commented, stretching his jaws into an enormous yawn.

"Yes, let's let her sleep," Sandstorm agreed. "In fact, I think we should all sleep for a while."

Alderpaw thought that Sandstorm looked particularly exhausted. Though he said nothing, he was beginning to realize that this journey, especially with her injury, was taking more out of her than she was willing to admit.

"Who will keep watch?" he asked as the others were settling down in the nest. "We know there are foxes around."

I should volunteer, he thought, trying to ignore the weariness weighing down his limbs. *This is my quest, after all. We wouldn't be on this trip if it weren't for my vision, and even though I didn't ask for it, I'm responsible for them all.*

"I'll do it." Needlepaw, who had taken no part in the search, strolled up from the pool, flicking drops of water off her whiskers. "I don't need much sleep anyway, and now that my belly's full, I could go on for days."

Thanking Needlepaw, Alderpaw curled up in the nest and

closed his eyes with a sigh of relief.

But instead of sinking into a refreshing sleep, he found himself standing on a bleak moorland hillside with tendrils of white mist wreathing around him. The sky glittered with stars, and somewhere in the distance shrieks of distress split the silence of the night.

His pelt tingling with fear, Alderpaw padded in the direction of the cries. Dark shapes began to appear through the mist, and as he drew closer, he realized that they were cats, standing in a circle and crying out their anguish to the stars.

"Help us! Oh, help us!"

Alderpaw's chest heaved and his breath came faster; he felt the cats' suffering as if it were his own. *I know these cats!* He recognized Leafstar, the SkyClan leader from his previous vision, and the big ginger tom, her deputy, Sharpclaw. Farther around the circle was the small silver tabby Echosong, the Clan medicine cat, and beside her was the young black-and-white cat he had seen made into a warrior. And there were many, many more, all raising their voices in fear and pain.

"Help us! Help us!"

"I'm here!" Alderpaw gasped out, bounding forward until he stood just outside the circle. "I'll help you! Tell me what to do."

But the cats seemed not to hear him. Not even Echosong turned in his direction. Their terrible wailing continued as if they had no idea he was there.

"I'm doing my best!" Alderpaw tried to draw closer still,

but something held him back from touching any cat or entering their circle. "Look, I'm here! I'll do anything you need me to do."

Still the cats couldn't hear him. Their cries grew more and more frantic until, with a jolt, Alderpaw woke.

For a couple of heartbeats he lay trembling among the moss and ferns. *Another vision . . . what did it mean?* he wondered. *Those cats must really be in trouble!*

As he sat up, Alderpaw realized that his Clanmates had vanished. Scrambling out of the nest, he spotted them lounging by the pool, nibbling on the leftover fresh-kill. The sun had dipped low over the trees, filling the hollow with golden light.

Alderpaw dashed down to join them. "We need to get moving as soon as we can!" he exclaimed.

Cherryfall blinked lazily at him. "What's the rush?" she asked. "It's not like the place you saw is going to disappear."

Alderpaw couldn't explain his sense of urgency. *Only Sandstorm will understand. I've got to talk to her.* "Sandstorm," he meowed, "come over here and let me check your wound again before we move off."

With a twitch of her ears Sandstorm got up and padded beside Alderpaw where he had left the remains of the comfrey root. He glanced back swiftly to make sure that they were out of earshot of the other cats.

"What's the matter?" she asked, her brief irritation vanishing. "I can see this isn't just about my wound."

"I had another vision," Alderpaw told her. "I saw the

SkyClan cats in a circle, wailing and wailing as if they were in terrible pain. They sounded so frightened! And they didn't hear me when I spoke to them and offered to help."

Sandstorm nodded understandingly. "Now I see why you're so keen to get going," she meowed. "That's all we can do, Alderpaw. Just get to the place you saw as soon as we can."

Thank StarClan some cat gets it! Alderpaw thought. But in spite of his urgency, he reached out a paw to stop Sandstorm as she turned to rejoin the others. "I meant it about looking at your wound."

Sandstorm sat down with a grunt of annoyance. "If you must."

Alderpaw's belly lurched as he scraped away the comfrey root poultice from Sandstorm's injured shoulder. The wound was slightly red and swollen, and when he laid his paw gently on it, he could feel heat rising from it.

"This could be the beginning of an infection," he told Sandstorm, trying not to let his voice shake. "You really shouldn't be traveling until it's healed. Or at the very least," he added, as Sandstorm opened her jaws to protest, "you should rest a bit more while I go and look for some horsetail or marigold to treat the infection. Honey would help, too."

"You sure have learned a lot," Sandstorm meowed, her approving gaze showing how impressed she was. "But we can't hang around here while you go looking for horsetail. If we pass some on the way, then you can gather some."

"But—" Alderpaw began.

"Until then, you have to trust me," Sandstorm interrupted.

"I'm *fine*. You may be a medicine cat, but I've been around a long time. I've had a lot of wounds in my day, and this one isn't so bad." Briefly she touched Alderpaw's shoulder with her tail-tip. "It's certainly not worth turning aside from our quest, especially after that terrible vision you just had."

Once again Alderpaw struggled to protest. "But your wound—"

"You have to trust me," Sandstorm repeated. "This is your quest, but I am your elder."

Although he still was uneasy, Alderpaw didn't feel that he could argue with Sandstorm anymore. He dipped his head in acceptance; then Sandstorm rose, and the two cats began to walk back toward their Clanmates, side by side.

But before they reached them, Alderpaw spotted sleek silver fur in the midst of a clump of long grass. He realized that Needlepaw was crouched only a couple of tail-lengths away from where he and Sandstorm had been talking. Her gaze locked with Alderpaw's, but he couldn't interpret her expression.

How much did she overhear?

CHAPTER 13

❧

The cats trekked on through the woods as the sun sank lower in the sky. Sandstorm had taken the lead again, with Alderpaw just behind her, Needlepaw stalking along a little way away from the others, and the rest of the ThunderClan cats bringing up the rear.

Alderpaw still felt tired, and he guessed the others did too. Their paws were dragging, and although no cat was talking much, he picked up occasional snatches of complaints from the cats behind him.

"I don't see why we had to leave so quickly," Molewhisker grumbled. "What's the rush?"

"Yeah, we could have stayed the night there," Sparkpaw added.

Glancing back, Alderpaw wished he could tell them the truth. "I just wanted to get going," he explained.

Sparkpaw snorted but made no reply in words.

Before long the trees thinned out, and Alderpaw could see open country ahead. In the distance he spotted a huge Twoleg structure built of some kind of yellow stone. *I wonder what that is.*

As they set out across the open ground, Needlepaw came

sidling over to Alderpaw until she was padding close by his side. Alderpaw felt uncomfortable having a cat from another Clan so close to him, even though she seemed to be losing her harsh ShadowClan scent.

"You know when you were talking to Sandstorm back there?" she murmured, leaning close to speak into Alderpaw's ear. "Well, I overheard *everything!*"

Alderpaw started, and his neck fur bristled with anxiety and dismay. *Oh, no! Now she knows the real reason we're on this quest. After Bramblestar told me no other cats should know. And she isn't even a ThunderClan cat.* Then, as he met Needlepaw's green gaze, he realized that she didn't look altogether confident. Could she be bluffing? *Well, two can play at that game.*

"Oh, really?" he responded, trying to keep his voice casual and forcing his neck fur to lie flat. "Well, it can't have done you much good, unless you want to know more about comfrey root."

"Comfrey root!" Needlepaw let out a *mrrow* of laughter. "Oh yes, and the rest!"

"What 'rest'?" Alderpaw asked. "It's not like we were discussing anything important."

Needlepaw cast a quick glance around to make sure they were out of earshot of the other cats. "It wouldn't have been anything about your *vision*, would it?"

"What are you meowing about?" Alderpaw was getting flustered, wondering how much Needlepaw had worked out for herself, and how much she could only have learned if she had heard the whole of his conversation with Sandstorm. "If you must know, we were talking about cats who might need our help."

"How noble of you," Needlepaw purred. "Which cats would they be?"

"Well . . . any cats. I'm a medicine cat. Helping is what I do."

"Hmm . . ." Needlepaw twitched her whiskers thoughtfully. "Cats who need help . . . and your vision . . . and this quest for what will clear the sky. It's all starting to add up, isn't it?"

Alderpaw felt cold from his ears to his tail-tip. Guiltily he realized that if Needlepaw was only pretending to have overheard, he had given away more than he should have.

However much she knows, he thought with a shiver, *it's enough to cause a problem. And that gives her power. She'll have to stay with us now, whether we want her or not.*

"Hey, look at that." Cherryfall's mew cut into Alderpaw's thoughts. He looked up ahead and saw that the group was now very close to the big yellow Twoleg den he had seen in the distance.

"Let's go explore it!" Sparkpaw suggested with a bounce of excitement.

Molewhisker shook his head. "It's a Twoleg thing, and it's better to stay away from Twolegs."

"I'm guessing that it's a barn like the one at the horseplace," Sandstorm told them. "This must be a farm—look, you can see more Twoleg dens just beyond it. My advice would be to keep well away from it."

Alderpaw agreed, but before the cats had gone much

farther, their path was blocked by a tall fence. It was made of interlinked tendrils of some hard, shiny stuff, topped by fearsome-looking spikes.

"*Now* what do we do?" Cherryfall asked, dismayed.

The fence stretched into the distance on either side; Alderpaw realized it would take far too long to go around it. While he was hesitating, Sparkpaw stepped forward and sniffed at the bottom of the fence.

"Maybe we could try going under it," she suggested.

"What are we, rabbits?" Needlepaw muttered, while Sparkpaw scraped experimentally at the earth where the fence disappeared into the grass.

"No," she reported, with a discouraged shake of her head. "It seems to go a long way down into the ground."

"Then maybe there's a hole that we can fit through," Molewhisker mewed.

Alderpaw led the way along the fence for a few fox-lengths, but everywhere it was strong and intact. Only a mouse could have slipped through the gaps between the tendrils.

"There's only one thing to do," Needlepaw announced at last. "We'll have to go over it."

"You've grown wings, have you?" Sparkpaw muttered sarcastically.

Needlepaw ignored her. "I'll go first," she meowed. "It doesn't look that hard. Watch."

Every cat watched nervously as she began to climb, fitting her paws into the narrow spaces between the shiny tendrils. The fence bobbed and swayed alarmingly, but Needlepaw kept going until she reached the very top, her paws balancing between the spikes.

"Be careful!" Sandstorm called out.

For a moment Alderpaw was certain that Needlepaw would impale herself on the sharp spikes. But then, bunching and stretching her muscles, she flung herself off the top of the bobbing fence and landed neatly on the other side.

"Easy!" she called out, giving her shoulder a smug lick.

"If she can do it, so can I," Sparkpaw mewed, swarming up the fence the same way Needlepaw had, then leaping gracefully down on the far side.

Cherryfall went next, more slowly but without mishap, and Molewhisker followed her.

"Your turn now, Alderpaw," Sandstorm told him. "I'll go last."

Alderpaw's belly squirmed as he approached the fence. He tried not to think of the spikes tearing into him, or of looking a fool in front of his Clanmates—and Needlepaw.

To begin with he climbed slowly, but he made himself think of the cats in his vision, crying out in anguish and far more terrified than he was now. *I have to do this. They need me.*

More determined, he managed to pick up the pace, and he found it wasn't as hard as it looked to haul himself upward with his paws slotting into the narrow gaps. The only really frightening moment was when he clung to the top of the swaying fence. For a moment his belly felt queasy; then he launched himself into the air and thumped down beside his sister.

I did it!

Sandstorm had already begun to climb. She made it quickly to the top, but clinging between the spikes, she hesitated. Her paws slipped, and she fell, crashing down to the ground and rolling over.

"Sandstorm!" Molewhisker's yowl was full of panic as he lurched forward, dropping to his belly to stop her momentum.

The older cat fell against him and then lay still, panting. Alderpaw rushed over to her, with his other Clanmates hard on his paws. "Are you okay?" he asked anxiously.

Sandstorm sat up. "I'm fine," she rasped, as if for a moment she had trouble breathing. "I just felt like being a bird."

"Well, don't try it again," Alderpaw responded.

Sandstorm rested for a little while, and then the cats set out again, still heading for the big Twoleg den. Walking beside Sandstorm, Alderpaw noticed that her wound looked bigger, and drops of blood were oozing out of it.

"Did you catch your shoulder on one of the spikes?" he asked her.

Sandstorm shrugged. "I might have scraped it. Don't fuss, Alderpaw; it's fine. If you want to worry," she added, "you might worry about that enormous beast up ahead!"

Alderpaw had been so concerned about Sandstorm that he hadn't noticed what lay in front of them. Now he looked up to see that the other cats had stopped and were uneasily eyeing a huge creature that stood a few fox-lengths away. Even Needlepaw looked scared.

It was smaller than the horses Alderpaw had seen as they left Clan territory, but still big enough to be frightening. Its lumpy body was covered in black-and-white fur; its legs were spindly with hard, sharp paws. Its tail, ending in a tuft of hair, swung to and fro. Enormous eyes in a square face gazed expressionlessly at the cats.

"What is it?" Sparkpaw gasped.

"Nothing to be afraid of," Sandstorm mewed calmly. "I've seen them before, and they're not unfriendly. Mostly they just ignore cats."

"Mostly?" Alderpaw asked nervously.

"They're okay unless something scares them into running. Then they're big enough to trample us underpaw. So we need to be careful not to scare this one."

"You've no idea how good that makes me feel," Molewhisker muttered.

Alderpaw forced his paws into motion, heading in a wide circle around the strange animal, never taking his eyes off it. His friends followed him. The creature swung its head around to track their progress, still gazing at them with those large, incurious eyes. Then without warning it opened its jaws and let out a deep-throated bellow.

Thoroughly spooked, Alderpaw gave a yowl of terror and raced for the big Twoleg den. He could hear caterwauling from behind him as the others pelted after him.

Have we scared it? Will it run?

But when he halted and looked back, panting, the huge animal hadn't stirred. It just stood there, still staring at them. Its jaws moved rhythmically as it chewed.

"Great StarClan!" Cherryfall exclaimed. "What *is* that?"

After a moment Sandstorm let out a *mrrow* of laughter, and the others joined in, beginning to relax. Alderpaw suddenly felt ashamed of his nervousness, and he could see from his friends' faces that they felt the same.

"Let's move on," he meowed.

Skirting the big yellow den and the cluster of smaller dens, the cats headed away at a brisk lope. Alderpaw hoped they were leaving the Twoleg stuff behind them, until he spotted a smaller wooden den, with birds pecking at the earth around it and straying into the cats' path.

"What are those?" he asked curiously.

The birds were bigger than pigeons, with reddish-brown feathers and scaly yellow legs. They didn't pay much attention as the cats approached.

"They're birds, mouse-brain," Sparkpaw replied to Alderpaw. "And that means they're prey."

Crouching down, she began to creep up on the nearest bird. But there was no cover, and the bird spotted her as she pounced. It spun around to face her, flapping its wings and letting out a series of harsh squawks.

The rest of the birds scattered, running across the grass as if they didn't know how to fly. But the bird Sparkpaw had tried to hunt stretched its neck out and attacked her with furious pecks. Sparkpaw leaped backward, hissing defiantly.

"It looks like you're the prey," Needlepaw meowed, her voice full of laughter and her eyes gleaming.

"Leave them," Sandstorm ordered, gesturing with her tail for Sparkpaw to rejoin the group. "It's not worth risking injury. We'll hunt when we get past this place."

"Yes, we need to keep going," Alderpaw added, urgency pricking his paws as he remembered the desperate cries of the SkyClan cats.

Looking sulky, Sparkpaw obeyed. She glared at Needlepaw as the ShadowClan cat let out a stream of squawks in imitation of the weird birds. "Stop messing around, you crazy furball," she muttered.

But Needlepaw seemed not to understand the need to move on quickly. Alderpaw's irritation with her rose as she poked her nose into every hole and clump of long grass. She halted at the sight of another strange creature, smaller than the first, but with the same hard, pointed paws. It had curving horns and a long wisp of hair dangling from its chin. Alderpaw shivered at the sight of its eerie eyes.

It let out a high-pitched, drawn-out cry, and Needlepaw at once tried to imitate it, snorting with laughter at her own weird meows.

"Whenever you've finished. . . ," Alderpaw snarled, giving her a hard shove.

"Keep your fur on!" Needlepaw retorted.

She was still bouncing around like a kit on its first day out of the nursery when the cats approached a hedge. Beyond it, rows of tall, yellow-brown plants stretched into the distance. Alderpaw could hear a faint rumbling and noticed a haze hanging in the air.

"There may be a Thunderpath on the other side of this," he mewed.

Sandstorm nodded. "I still think this is the way we should go."

Without hesitating, Alderpaw began to push his way through the hedge; fortunately the bushes weren't too thick. "Sandstorm, watch out for your shoulder," he warned her.

Sandstorm brushed through without mishap, while Cherryfall and Molewhisker followed. Sparkpaw pushed Needlepaw ahead of her and brought up the rear. "I swear by StarClan," Sparkpaw hissed as she emerged, "if you behave like this for much longer, I'm going to claw your ears off."

Needlepaw swiped playfully at her. "You can always try."

"Let's go," Alderpaw mewed curtly.

He headed out into the stretch of yellow-brown plants. Their stalks were hard and scratchy, and the ground underpaw was hard, bare earth. At least Needlepaw seemed to have calmed down as she slid through the gaps between the plants.

The rumbling sound Alderpaw could hear grew louder, and he guessed that they might be coming to the Thunderpath. Then he realized that the plants on one side were thinning. Veering in that direction, he poked his head out of cover. His companions clustered around him, peering over his shoulder.

There was no Thunderpath. Instead Alderpaw saw a stretch of ground where the plants had been cut down, leaving only stubble behind. Now he discovered where the rumbling came from: a huge monster with spinning jaws was moving straight toward them, slicing off the next swath of plants and tossing them into its belly! All around it the air was full of dust.

Alderpaw felt as if his whole body had been suddenly drenched in icy water. "It's eating the field!" he gasped out.

"And it'll eat us!" Sandstorm meowed. "It could gulp down all six of us at once. Run!"

Alderpaw whipped around and began to race through the plants, bobbing and weaving as gaps opened up. Behind him he heard Cherryfall yowl, "Stay together!"

Glancing over his shoulder, Alderpaw could spot all the other cats racing along with him. The tall plants blocked his view of the monster, but he knew it was close—the noise it made seemed loud enough to rattle the air. *We have to keep running!*

As he fled, Alderpaw realized that the hard ground had given way to soft mud that clung to his paws and gave off a terrible smell. He was too scared to wonder what it was, or to do anything except keep on pelting away from the monster.

Alderpaw was glancing behind him again when he suddenly crashed into something hard but springy that bounced him back a tail-length into the plants. Regaining his balance, he looked up and let out a groan.

"No! I don't believe it!"

He was facing another fence made out of the shiny tendrils with the spikes along the top. His companions gathered around him.

"We'll have to climb it," Molewhisker meowed, "or the monster will get us."

"Right." Sparkpaw took the lead, climbing rapidly up the fence and hurling herself down on the other side into soft grass. "Hurry!" she urged the others.

Needlepaw went next. While Alderpaw was waiting for his turn, he noticed that some of the foul-smelling mud had got into Sandstorm's wound, which was red and swollen now. Alderpaw was certain that it was infected. And Sandstorm was standing with her head lowered and her chest heaving; she was clearly exhausted, much more so than her age and the race through the plants would explain.

It must be her wound, Alderpaw told himself. *I can just feel it.* With an inward start of surprise he realized that this must be part of what being a good medicine cat was all about. *I can't just see that she should probably rest; I can tell that she needs to.*

"You ought to rest," he mewed to Sandstorm.

Sandstorm raised her head and gave him an annoyed look. "I'm an elder," she retorted. "I've been around for a long time. I *know* I'm okay."

Alderpaw had heard that argument before, and this time he wasn't about to accept it. "No!" he meowed sharply.

Sandstorm's eyes stretched wide in outrage. "What do you mean, no?"

"Sorry," Alderpaw responded. "It's just that I can tell how tired you are. I'm your medicine cat, and I'm saying you *need* to rest."

The ginger she-cat hesitated for a moment. "Maybe you're right. But let's get across this StarClan-cursed fence first."

She began to climb without waiting for a reply. Alderpaw could see how hard it was for her to haul herself upward. When she reached the top, she toppled rather than jumped onto the far side, letting out a screech as she fell.

Alderpaw scrambled over the fence without even thinking about it, and ran to Sandstorm. His eyes widened with horror as he saw her wound pooling with blood. *She must have torn it on one of those spikes!*

"That does it," he growled. "We rest *now*." Turning to the others, he added, "Find me some cobwebs."

The cats scattered to search among the bushes that were dotted here and there across the grassland. While he waited for them to return, Alderpaw licked the clinging mud out of Sandstorm's wound. The old cat just lay on her side, panting.

When his companions returned, Alderpaw packed the wound with cobwebs, but blood still kept oozing out of it. He gazed down at Sandstorm, trying to ignore his rising panic.

Her wound is worse now, and she's weaker. How will she fight off the infection?

Cherryfall touched him on the shoulder. "It's getting late," she meowed. "Should we hunt?"

Alderpaw looked up, startled. In his anxiety he hadn't noticed that the sun had gone down and the shadows of night were gathering.

"Please," he responded. "I'll stay with Sandstorm and fix up some nests."

He found a gentle hollow sheltered by elder bushes and heaped dead leaves into it before helping Sandstorm across to it. The old cat had stopped insisting that she was fine, and she leaned heavily on his shoulder as she staggered across to her nest.

Cherryfall came back with a mouse as Alderpaw was getting

Sandstorm settled. "Thanks," Alderpaw mewed. "Sandstorm, eat this. And then you can go to sleep."

"Bossy furball," Sandstorm muttered, but she ate the mouse and curled up without protest.

Watching her, Alderpaw was relieved to see that the bleeding had almost stopped. At the same moment he realized how bone-weary he was. He could hardly keep awake until the other hunters returned, and he managed just a few mouthfuls of thrush before he too sank into sleep.

The patter of raindrops on the bushes above his head woke Alderpaw to the light of a chilly morning. Fortunately the bushes were so thick that very little rain penetrated to his nest.

Raising his head, Alderpaw saw that Sandstorm was still sleeping beside him. All the other cats were gone, except for Cherryfall, who crouched with her back to him at the top of the hollow, peering out through the branches. As Alderpaw sat up, the dead leaves crackling under his paws, she turned around.

"The others have gone hunting," she mewed. "I stayed to keep watch. How is Sandstorm?"

Alderpaw examined the old she-cat. She was muttering in her sleep, shifting restlessly in her nest. Her wound had stopped bleeding, but it was more swollen than ever, red and hot to the touch.

Sandstorm's green eyes blinked open as Alderpaw bent over her. "Hi," she murmured. "Have you come to do my ticks?"

Alderpaw realized that Sandstorm thought she was back in

the ThunderClan camp. "No, we're on our quest, remember?" he replied. "Is there anything I can do for you? How are you feeling?"

"I'm perfectly okay," Sandstorm told him, her voice a little stronger. She winced, gasping in pain, as she tried to sit up, and let herself flop back into the nest. "Don't worry about me."

But Alderpaw couldn't help worrying. Sandstorm's green eyes looked glassy, and he guessed that she was just trying to put on a brave front. When he stroked her pelt, she felt warm all over, and already she was drifting back into sleep.

She roused again a few moments later as the hunters returned, dragging a rabbit and a couple of blackbirds into the shelter of the bushes.

"It's horrible out there," Needlepaw complained, shaking her pelt so that the drops spattered Alderpaw. "Most of the prey is in hiding."

"You did well, though," Alderpaw praised her. "Come on, Sandstorm, do you want one of these blackbirds?"

His misgivings increased as Sandstorm struggled to stay awake enough to eat, and after a few mouthfuls she turned her head away. "I'm full," she mewed. "You finish it, Alderpaw."

When the other cats had settled down at the top of the hollow to eat their prey, Alderpaw rose to his paws to talk to them. "Sandstorm is sick," he announced. "We can't start traveling again until she's fit to move."

"I'm fit now," Sandstorm protested, though any cat could see she was lying. "Don't listen to this stupid furball."

Clearly all the others understood how serious the situation

was; they gazed down silently at Sandstorm, their eyes somber. Even mischievous Needlepaw had stopped joking around.

"What can we do?" Cherryfall asked.

"You know we'll do everything we can," Molewhisker added, and Sparkpaw nodded eagerly.

"I need marigold, horsetail, or honey," Alderpaw told them. "They'll help Sandstorm's infection. I don't know what kinds of herbs grow around here, but hopefully you'll be able to find at least one."

When his companions had gone, Alderpaw sat beside Sandstorm, gently licking her ears as she drifted in and out of sleep. He hardly noticed when the rain eased off, until a weak ray of sunshine sliced through the bushes. It brought Alderpaw a slight glimmer of hope.

Sparkpaw was the first cat to return, and relief flooded over Alderpaw as he saw that she was carrying a few stalks of marigold. "Good job!" he told her. "Now I can make a poultice. Can you get the cobweb off Sandstorm's wound? Very carefully, please."

Sparkpaw sat beside Sandstorm and began to ease the wad of cobweb away. Sandstorm twitched and grunted in her sleep, as if she was in pain, but when Sparkpaw hesitated, Alderpaw just nodded to her to keep going.

While he was chewing up the marigold, Needlepaw pushed her way through the bushes with a dripping ball of moss in her jaws. "I couldn't find any herbs," she meowed, setting the moss down beside Sandstorm, "but I brought this. I thought she might be thirsty."

"That was a really good idea," Alderpaw told her, feeling warmer toward the ShadowClan cat than ever before. Needlepaw ducked her head to lick her chest fur, embarrassed at his praise.

"Sandstorm." Alderpaw gently stroked the old cat's head. "Wake up and have a drink."

Sandstorm's green eyes blinked open. "Oh, that's good," she breathed out, lapping at the moss.

While she drank, Alderpaw plastered the marigold poultice to her wound. *I just hope it's enough,* he thought. *I wouldn't worry so much about the infection if she weren't so weak from the bleeding.* He let out a long sigh. *Oh, I wish Leafpool or Jayfeather were here to help me!*

Sandstorm reached out her tail to touch him briefly on his shoulder. "Don't worry, Alderpaw," she rasped. "I'm going to be fine, and we must set out again soon. The . . ." For a heartbeat she hesitated. "The *others* need us," she finished.

"Which others?" Sparkpaw asked curiously.

Alderpaw's belly lurched. "Oh, she's feverish," he mewed quickly. "She doesn't know what she's talking about." But inwardly he felt worse than ever. *Sandstorm must be losing her sharpness, to mention the secret.*

"You have to rest," he told her. "You have to get better. We can't finish this quest without you!"

But he was not even sure if Sandstorm had heard him. When he looked down at her, he saw that she had drifted back into a fevered sleep.

CHAPTER 14

❦

Alderpaw stood on the grass outside the sheltering elder bushes. Above his head the sky blazed with stars. Although the night wasn't cold, he was shivering as though he had just clambered out of icy water.

Just ahead, a cat was walking away from him, toward the fence they had crossed the day before. Her head and tail were proudly raised, and she moved with a strong, purposeful gait. Starlight glimmered at her paws and around her ears.

"But that's—" Alderpaw cut off his words with a gasp, and he spun around to check on the nest beneath the elder bushes.

But the elder bushes were no longer there. When Alderpaw turned back, the fence had vanished, too. He stood in the middle of a stretch of lush grass, with whispering groves of trees all around. The starry cat was facing him now, and he saw clearly that it was Sandstorm.

"Oh, no, no . . . ," he whispered.

The ginger she-cat looked taller and stronger than he had ever seen her, and her infected wound had disappeared. Her pelt was thick and sleek, and her green eyes gleamed with love for him.

"It is my time to leave you," she meowed, with no pain or confusion in her voice. "But don't worry, Alderpaw. StarClan is where I belong now."

"No!" Alderpaw protested with all the strength that was in him. "You can't leave us now. We need you!"

"This is my destiny," Sandstorm responded. "And you do not need me anymore. You are stronger than you know. Listen." She took a pace toward him. "You must lead the others now. Continue heading toward the rising sun. It is many days' journey, and you will have to cross a very big and busy Thunderpath. After that, you will come to a river. Follow it upstream, and you will find the gorge where SkyClan has their camp."

Alderpaw tried to memorize what Sandstorm was telling him. *The rising sun . . . a big Thunderpath . . . then the river.* At the same time, he felt hot with shame that she wouldn't be there to guide him. He turned his gaze away, unable to go on looking at her.

"I failed you," he muttered.

"No," Sandstorm murmured gently. "No cat could have done more to help me. I doubt that even Jayfeather or Leafpool could have kept me alive so long. I knew the risks when I chose to come on this quest," she reminded him. "I know how important your visions are."

"But you could have lived for many seasons in ThunderClan," Alderpaw mewed wretchedly.

"And now I will live for many more in StarClan," Sandstorm pointed out. "I will get to see Firestar again, and all the cats I have loved and lost. Alderpaw, this is how it was meant to be. You have nothing to feel ashamed of, or guilty about."

Alderpaw turned in an anxious circle, unable to believe what Sandstorm was telling him. *What will I do without her? How will I lead this quest?*

"This *isn't* a vision!" he insisted, fear overwhelming him. "It's just a dream. I'm going to wake up, and you'll be sleeping beside me, just like always. You're going to be all right."

Sandstorm's eyes glowed with a mixture of pity and affection. "I was dying," she reminded Alderpaw. "You knew that, didn't you?"

"No—you're going to get better!" Alderpaw retorted, even though deep within him was the cold certainty that she was right. "I'm going to make sure of it!"

Sandstorm gave a sad shake of her head. "There was nothing you could have done to save me. It was my time to die. No cat lives forever. This is one of the most important lessons that you—or any medicine cat—will ever learn."

On the last few words her voice began to fade, while the starry light around her blazed brighter and brighter, until Alderpaw couldn't go on looking at the dazzling glory. A moment later he jerked awake in his nest under the elder bushes.

Thank StarClan! It was only a dream. Sandstorm is right here beside me.

Scrambling to his paws, Alderpaw turned to nudge Sandstorm awake. But as soon as his pads touched her fur, he knew that he hadn't been dreaming. Sandstorm's fur was limp, the body beneath it cold, and her ribs weren't rising and falling with her breath.

It was a vision. Sandstorm is dead.

Alderpaw backed away in horror, his fur pricking up and his belly clenching. He couldn't keep back a wail of distress. "No! *No!* It *wasn't* her time!"

Cherryfall's head popped up from her nest. "Alderpaw? What's happening?"

The other cats were waking, too, confused and questioning. A shocked silence fell over them as Alderpaw pointed to Sandstorm's body with his tail. Slowly they all padded over to Sandstorm and stood looking down, a tail-length away from the huddle of cold fur.

Sparkpaw was the first to break the silence. "She's . . . she's dead, isn't she? Now what do we do?"

"Sandstorm was the only one who knew the route," Molewhisker pointed out gloomily. "We were relying on her to help us complete the journey. Is her death telling us that the quest is doomed?"

Murmurs of agreement, with a note of fear, came from the other cats.

In spite of his grief, Alderpaw felt a surge of purpose flooding through him from ears to tail-tip. "Sandstorm wouldn't want us to stand around like this, wondering what to do," he told the sad and confused cats in front of him. "She would want us to sit vigil with her, and then bury her, before we decide what to do next."

"You're right," Cherryfall meowed. "Let's do that."

Together the ThunderClan cats dragged Sandstorm out of the nest and laid her on the grass, gently stroking her fur and fluffing up her tail. It was dark; the sky was studded with stars, as if all the spirits of their warrior ancestors were waiting to welcome Sandstorm and to honor her.

As they began to settle down around her, Needlepaw padded up to Alderpaw. "I know Sandstorm wasn't my Clanmate," she murmured; to Alderpaw's surprise she sounded almost shy. "But I traveled with her long enough to know what a great cat she was. May I keep vigil with you?"

"Sure," Alderpaw replied, warming once again to the silver she-cat. "Come and sit by me."

Sparkpaw crouched down beside Sandstorm's head, and gave her ears a lick. "We've come all this way," she mewed sorrowfully. "We've come so close to being killed by monsters or foxes; we've fought so hard to survive. . . . It doesn't seem fair that Sandstorm died anyway."

"I know," Cherryfall sighed. "She deserved so much more than this."

"What do you think, Alderpaw?" Molewhisker asked, turning to him. "Do you still want to go on?"

Alderpaw bit back a sharp retort. *I just told them they could agonize after we laid Sandstorm to rest.* "I'll think about it during the vigil," he replied.

"Maybe StarClan will send you a sign," Cherryfall suggested.

The questing cats gathered around Sandstorm's body, staying there throughout the night. Sustained by the day spent drowsing in the den, Alderpaw didn't find it hard to keep awake. He tried to focus on the future, but he couldn't help wondering if there was anything he could have done to keep Sandstorm alive.

She told me in my vision that it was her destiny to die now, he thought. *So why does my heart still ache? And if every cat is going to die eventually, why bother trying so hard to stay alive?*

Eventually he dozed, and he roused to hear the voices of the other cats. Blinking his eyes open, he found himself surrounded by the gray light of dawn.

"Back in camp," Cherryfall was mewing, "the elders bury our dead Clanmates. Molewhisker and I are the oldest cats here, so we ought to do it."

"But I want to help," Sparkpaw protested, raw grief in her voice. "She was my mother's mother."

"Okay, you can," Molewhisker told her comfortingly.

Alderpaw staggered to his paws, his legs stiff after the night spent in vigil. "Let me say the proper farewell to her." He took a deep breath, looking up at the sky where a few warriors of StarClan still lingered. "May StarClan light your path, Sandstorm," he meowed, speaking the words used by medicine cats for season upon season. "May you find good hunting, swift running, and shelter when you sleep."

All the cats bowed their heads for a moment.

"We need to find a good spot for her burial," Molewhisker mewed after a moment. "What about under these bushes where she died?"

Cherryfall shook her head. "She'd be hidden from the stars

there. Just beside the bushes would be better."

Molewhisker nodded agreement. As he and Cherryfall were preparing to move Sandstorm's body, he said quietly, "I think we should consider turning around and going home. This quest might be doomed."

"What?" It was Needlepaw who spoke, her neck fur bristling. "Sandstorm died trying to help us complete this quest. If we stop now, won't she have died in vain?"

Molewhisker swung around on her. "It's not your decision," he spat, his voice sharp as a claw. "In case it escaped your notice, you're not a ThunderClan cat."

Alderpaw felt his whole pelt quiver as he listened to the quarrel breaking out. Not waiting for Needlepaw's response, he turned and padded away, keeping to the line of the fence they had crossed two days before. He just wanted to get out of earshot, to find a little peace and quiet where he could think.

His chest fur burned with grief for Sandstorm, and his head swam with indecision. *Should we even go on? Sandstorm so wanted to see SkyClan again, and that made me feel that we were meant to be on this quest. But now that she's gone, do I even believe that these strange cats could be what StarClan says will solve our problems? Not even* Bramblestar *seemed certain of it.* Sighing, he remembered his last vision of the SkyClan cats, when they were shrieking for help. *Why do they need me?* he asked himself. *What can I do for them?*

Looking up, he saw that the last starry spirits had vanished and the sky was brightening toward sunrise. *I wonder if Sandstorm can see me now. Can she hear my thoughts? I really wish I could ask her for guidance.*

Letting out another long sigh, he spoke aloud. "What am I going to do?"

"Tell them the truth," a voice replied.

Alderpaw started and swung around, arching his back, even while he recognized the voice as Needlepaw's. The Shadow-Clan cat showed none of her usual mischief as she approached him.

"The others have come this far," she began, "and they won't turn away from you now. You must go on. But first you must tell the others the truth about why you're on this journey."

"Do *you* even know why?" Alderpaw asked tartly.

"No, I don't. I only heard a little bit of what you and Sandstorm said," Needlepaw admitted, her eyes serious. "But I know there's more behind it than you've told us, and I think it's time every cat knew the truth. If you don't tell them, I will." As Alderpaw opened his jaws to protest, she added, "Or I'll tell them what I know, and that will force you to tell the rest."

Alderpaw stared at her in outrage. "I didn't think you would betray me like that!"

Needlepaw flinched as if he had struck her a blow. "It's not a betrayal," she said, defending herself. "I've seen how you think things over—and over and over and over again. I know you'd never tell the others the truth on your own, but I think it's important for them to know."

"Why?" Alderpaw challenged her.

"It will help bind them together after losing Sandstorm," Needlepaw explained; Alderpaw realized she must have thought long and hard about this. "And it will help every cat recognize how important the quest is. I saw how you and Sandstorm looked at each other when you talked about it; I know how serious it is."

Alderpaw thought about that, then gave a nod, trying to hide his surprise. *I can't believe it's Needlepaw of all cats giving me such wise advice.* "I'll do as you suggest," he meowed.

The gleam returned to Needlepaw's eyes. "First, let's go hunting," she suggested. "Full bellies will help the truth go down easier!"

Alderpaw was about to argue when he felt a gnawing in his belly and realized that no cat had hunted since the previous morning. "You're right," he responded. "I'll hunt with you." *Not that I'm likely to be much use,* he added to himself.

Alderpaw crept across the grassland, trying to pick out prey-scent over the stink of farm animals that the breeze was carrying toward them. Just ahead of him, Needlepaw padded forward, slowly but decisively.

She must have found a scent, but I can't smell anything except those weird creatures back there.

Suddenly Needlepaw halted, raising her tail to signal that she had spotted prey. Half turning toward Alderpaw, she jerked her head to one side, telling him to go that way.

Alderpaw obeyed, putting on speed as he wove his way through the long grass. *I hope I'm not getting this totally wrong!* Finally he caught the scent that Needlepaw must have picked up long before. *Rabbit!* At the same moment he spotted the creature a couple of fox-lengths in front of him, nibbling at some low-growing plant. Its ears shot up as Alderpaw tried to slide soundlessly around it, and it took off, its white tail bobbing as it raced away. With rising excitement Alderpaw gave chase.

Needlepaw appeared from nowhere, right in the rabbit's path. She lashed out with one paw, and the rabbit's shriek was cut off abruptly as it fell limply to the ground. "Thank you, StarClan, for this prey," she meowed.

Then Needlepaw looked up, her eyes alight with the thrill of the hunt. "Wow, you're fast!" she exclaimed. "You drove it right toward me. That's pretty impressive."

Alderpaw turned away, embarrassed, though his chest was swelling with happiness. *I was useful on a hunt! I wish Sparkpaw had been here to see that!*

Padding over to Needlepaw, he nuzzled her head with his nose. "Thanks for your help," he mewed. "We may be from different Clans, but I'm glad you stayed with us."

When he and Needlepaw returned to the elder bushes with the rabbit, Alderpaw found his three companions cleaning earth from their paws. They sounded more cheerful as they greeted him and settled down to feast on the rabbit.

When they had finished eating, Alderpaw rose to his paws, clearing his throat nervously. "I have something to tell you," he began.

He paused, looking for the right words, and Molewhisker twitched one ear impatiently. "Spit it out, then," he meowed.

"It's about the vision that sent us on this journey," Alderpaw responded. "It's more complicated than you know. I saw a group of cats—the cats of SkyClan—and I believe they need help."

"SkyClan? Who are they?" Sparkpaw asked.

"I've never heard of them," mewed Cherryfall.

"I don't know much about them," Alderpaw explained. "Only what Bramblestar and Sandstorm told me. Long ago, back in the old forest, there were five Clans, not four. But Twolegs took SkyClan's territory, and the other four Clans drove them out. They made camp in a gorge, beside a river, but eventually their Clan withered and died."

"And that could happen to *us*, if we don't find what lies in the shadows," Sparkpaw pointed out. "Firestar said a time of great change is coming. It doesn't sound like *good* change."

"That's true," Alderpaw meowed, struck by the balance. *I wonder if SkyClan is what lies in the shadows,* he mused.

"If SkyClan died out, who were the cats you saw?" Molewhisker asked.

"Firestar restored their Clan. He and Sandstorm went on a quest, long ago, and they brought cats together—descendants of the old SkyClan—and established the Clan again. When I told Sandstorm what I saw in my vision, she recognized some of the cats."

"So that's how Sandstorm knew the way!" Cherryfall exclaimed. "But how can we get to SkyClan, now that she's dead?"

"Because she told me where to go," Alderpaw replied. "If

we head toward the rising sun, eventually we'll come to a river, and if we travel upstream, we'll find SkyClan's camp in the gorge."

His Clanmates exchanged uncertain glances; Alderpaw wasn't sure that they believed him.

"Why did the other Clans drive SkyClan away and let them die out?" Molewhisker asked eventually.

"It's a very shameful part of warrior history," Alderpaw replied. "No cat knows the whole story, and the only living cat—apart from us—who knows anything is Bramblestar. I shouldn't even be telling you, but I thought it was important for you to know the truth."

After a few moments' silence, while the cats were clearly thinking over what they had heard, Cherryfall got up and rubbed her cheek against Alderpaw's. "That was brave of you," she meowed. "Your first act as our leader."

Alderpaw was touched, especially by her admission that they would follow him now.

"It will take us a few days to get used to all this," Cherryfall went on, "but I'm glad you told us the truth."

"So am I," Needlepaw agreed.

Molewhisker rose to his paws and glanced around at his Clanmates. "I think I speak for all of us," he mewed, "when I tell you that we pledge ourselves to do whatever it takes to find SkyClan and complete the quest."

As his friends murmured their agreement, Alderpaw thought that his heart would burst with pride.

CHAPTER 15
♣

Alderpaw led the way cautiously along the cliff edge, his belly fur brushing the dusty ground. On one side, rough grass stretched into the distance, dotted here and there with scrubby trees and bushes. On the other, the ground fell away into a precipice; at the bottom a river tumbled along between sandy rocks.

We're almost there! he thought, exultation breaking through his weariness. *This must be close to the place where SkyClan made their camp.*

Many sunrises had passed since Alderpaw had told his friends the truth about their quest. Afterward they had hardly stopped to rest. Following Sandstorm's directions, they had passed through more farms, crossed busy Thunderpaths, and skirted Twolegplaces until they reached the river and turned upstream.

I never knew the world was so big! Alderpaw reflected, wincing as his sore paws padded over the gritty earth. *I can't believe how far we've had to travel!* Casting a glance back at his companions, he could see that they were all as tired as he was, limping onward with tails drooping.

An unexpected gust of wind drove sand into Alderpaw's

eyes and brought the sound of cats' voices drifting up from the gorge below. Strong but unfamiliar cat scent came with it. Blinking fiercely, Alderpaw raised his tail to warn the others to be silent, and he crept forward to crouch at the very edge of the cliff.

When his vision cleared, he made out paths and jutting outcrops in the rock face and, far below, a pile of reddish boulders blocking the way ahead. The river poured out of a gaping black hole in the rock and dropped into a pool before flowing away down the gorge.

"This is where the river begins!" Alderpaw breathed out. "It must be where SkyClan's camp is."

It was a weird place for a camp, he thought. He couldn't see any dens, or any fresh-kill pile, just the heaps of red stone with the river cutting its way through. *Cats live here?* he asked himself, bewildered. Yet, as he looked more closely, he could see cats slipping between the boulders, pausing to talk to one another, sunning themselves, just as his own Clanmates did in their camp.

"Are these the cats from your dreams?"

Alderpaw realized that Needlepaw had crept up beside him and was peering over his shoulder. "They're too far away for me to be sure," he responded. "But the red rock seems familiar."

"Hmm . . ." Needlepaw edged up beside him to give the scene a closer scrutiny. "They might be far away," she continued, "but they don't look like cats in need of help to me."

Realizing she was right, Alderpaw let out a sigh. "Maybe

I misinterpreted my vision."

"What?" Sparkpaw, craning her neck to gaze down on Alderpaw's other side, began to bristle with outrage. "You led us all this way for nothing?" she hissed.

"We can't know Alderpaw is wrong," Needlepaw retorted. "Not from this distance. Maybe we should get closer."

Alderpaw was grateful for her defense, for how she always had the spirit to adapt to setbacks, but at the same time he worried that Sparkpaw had a point. *What if this journey has been wasted?*

"Okay, what are we waiting for?" Needlepaw asked, springing to her paws. "Let's find a way down."

Instantly Molewhisker moved to block her. "Are you mouse-brained?" he demanded. "We can't just stroll into their camp. None of us know much about SkyClan, and they don't know much about us, either. There's no way of being sure we can trust them." He gave his tail an irritable twitch. "Sandstorm was the only one who had met the SkyClan cats, and she's dead now."

Needlepaw shrugged, unmoved by the older cat's argument. "We can only find answers by getting closer. Alderpaw wouldn't have dreamed of these cats if they weren't important, right?"

Alderpaw swallowed nervousness. "That's true," he meowed, trying to sound strong and decisive. "Lead on, Needlepaw."

After a moment's searching, Needlepaw found the beginning of a path that led down into the gorge, winding to and fro across the rock face. Alderpaw followed hard on her paw steps, hugging the cliff wall to stay well away from the drop at the edge of the path and feeling the heat of the sun-warmed rocks striking up through his pads.

To his relief the others headed down after them.

"Alderpaw must have bees in his brain," he heard Sparkpaw mutter. "Following this stupid ShadowClan furball!"

Before they had descended more than a few fox-lengths into the gorge, Alderpaw heard a loud yowl coming from below. Turning toward the sound, he spotted a long-furred gray tom staring straight at him. The yowl had attracted three of the other SkyClan cats, who raced toward him; then all four began to climb the rocks, with the gray tom in the lead.

"Uh-oh!" Needlepaw murmured.

"Well, we had to meet them sometime," Alderpaw responded. He slid past Needlepaw to take the lead and padded down a couple of tail-lengths, as far as a wide ledge. "We'll wait for them here—and for StarClan's sake, remember that we're here to help. We're not looking for a fight."

He had hardly finished speaking when the SkyClan cats came into sight, springing confidently up the narrow path until they faced the questing cats on the ledge.

The gray tom took another pace forward until he stood nose to nose with Alderpaw, who tried not to flinch as the SkyClan cat's cold green gaze raked over him. This was a powerful cat, his shoulder fur bristling and his tail bushed up.

"If you've come for the territory," he snarled, "you can think again. You're way outnumbered."

Alderpaw hesitated, wondering if he should respond. Although it was his quest, Molewhisker and Cherryfall were the senior cats now that Sandstorm wasn't with them anymore. *Maybe they should be the ones to speak.*

But when Alderpaw glanced back at Molewhisker and Cherryfall, neither of them moved. *It's up to me, then,* he thought, turning back toward the hostile long-furred tom.

"We don't want your territory," he explained, his voice quiet and calm. "But we've traveled a long way to meet you—the cats of SkyClan who live in this gorge."

The gray tom tilted his head to one side, a glint in his green eyes. "What do cats from far away know about SkyClan?" he asked.

"Not much," Alderpaw admitted, "but we're here to learn more."

The tom let out a disdainful snort. "Then you'd better come and speak to our leader." He jerked his head to indicate that they should follow him, then turned and padded back down the path.

Alderpaw had only taken a single paw step to follow him when Sparkpaw pushed forward to his side. "Are you sure this is a good idea?" she whispered.

Would you be so doubtful if another cat were leading us, and not me? Alderpaw wanted to hiss the words at his sister, but he bit them back with clenched jaws. "Bramblestar sent us on this journey," he murmured. "Wherever it leads *must* be right."

The three cats who had accompanied the gray tom parted to let the traveling cats pass, then closed in around them. As he got a closer look, Alderpaw saw that one was a black tom, and the others were she-cats: one tabby and one with white fur stained with dirt and dust. In fact, all four cats looked as if they could do with a good grooming.

Don't SkyClan cats ever wash? Alderpaw asked himself. He could just imagine what any ThunderClan mentor would say to an apprentice who went around looking like that.

Then he reminded himself that SkyClan had been driven out of their original territory and exiled to this gorge. They had lived separately from the other Clans for so long, maybe it wasn't surprising they had slightly different customs.

As they padded down the path, Needlepaw sidled past Alderpaw and caught up the gray tom in the lead. "What's your name?" she asked.

The gray tom's ears flicked in surprise—Alderpaw guessed at the ShadowClan apprentice's confident tone. "I'm called Rain," he replied.

Just Rain? Alderpaw wondered why Needlepaw didn't ask that question. *They probably do things differently,* he told himself again. *Even names.* But he was sure he remembered Sandstorm mentioning SkyClan cats called Leafstar, Sharpclaw, and Echosong. *Those are proper warrior names. But then, Sandstorm was here so long ago . . .*

By now Needlepaw was walking beside Rain, chatting without a trace of apprehension. Thinking that perhaps she had the right idea, Alderpaw turned toward the tabby she-cat, who was the closest to him of their escort.

"Hi, my name's Alderpaw," he began.

The tabby she-cat ignored him, except for one glance from baleful yellow eyes.

Okay, be like that, Alderpaw thought. He was disappointed that the SkyClan cats didn't seem more welcoming, but he told himself that perhaps they would open up once they knew him and his companions better and discovered why they were there.

The long-furred tom led Alderpaw and his companions up to the pile of rocks where the river gushed out. Sitting at the base of the rock pile was a strong, muscular tom, his white fur broken up by black spots around his eyes and his long, black tail. Sunlight gleamed on his glossy pelt, and his blue eyes shone as he surveyed the newcomers.

Alderpaw could imagine this cat perched up on the rocks to call a Clan meeting. *But no!* His belly lurched suddenly. *This isn't the Clan leader I saw in my vision, making a new warrior.* Glancing around, trying to push down fear, he saw more and more of the SkyClan cats slipping out of the shadows, or from cracks in the surrounding rocks, slowly encircling him and his little group. He examined each one of them, hoping to recognize at least one cat from his vision, but none of them looked at all familiar. *Why?*

The white tom rose to his paws, a sneering look on his face. "Who are these?" he asked Rain. "Lost kitties?"

Alderpaw saw his Clanmates begin to bristle at the insult. "Steady," he whispered. "Don't provoke them. We need to know more."

"Greetings, Darktail." Rain dipped his head. "These are

strangers from far away, looking for SkyClan."

*So they call their leader Dark*tail, Alderpaw thought, growing even more bewildered. *Why not Darkstar? Or is this just another way these weird cats are different from us?*

Darktail turned an unblinking gaze on Alderpaw. "What do you want with SkyClan?"

Staring into the leader's eerie blue eyes, Alderpaw felt his fur prickle with apprehension. He wished that either Mole-whisker or Cherryfall would speak up rather than leave him to take the lead.

"I'm from ThunderClan," he replied, choking back his uneasiness. "I've been sent to find the cats of SkyClan."

"Why?" Darktail asked.

Alderpaw wasn't sure how to answer that. *I thought we'd find out more when we arrived.* "Every Clan's survival depends on us all working together," he mewed uncertainly, and was relieved to see Cherryfall and Molewhisker dipping their heads in assent.

Darktail narrowed his eyes. "Are you asking me and my cats to go with you to this . . . ThunderClan?"

Feeling like a kit before its eyes opened, groping around in the dark, Alderpaw nodded. But he still didn't know whether SkyClan was really was what StarClan meant for them to "embrace." *If I convince them to journey back with us to the lake, what will Bramblestar think? How would we cope with all these extra cats?*

"Do you need our *help?*" Darktail pressed him.

"No!" Alderpaw blurted. "We're not asking for help with a fight or anything. The Clans are all settled in their own ter-ritories, and there aren't many disagreements, because there's plenty of prey for every cat." *Do you need our help?* he added silently to himself. *Or have I completely misunderstood my vision? Oh, Sandstorm, I wish you were here to help me figure this out!*

Darktail seemed to think for a moment, then inclined his head politely to Alderpaw. "I'm impressed," he purred. "I appreciate that you have made a long journey to find SkyClan. But I hope you understand, we can't just abandon our territory at the urging of strangers."

Alderpaw felt some of his tension ease. *At least Darktail sounds reasonable.* But he hadn't expected the meeting with SkyClan to go this way at all, and part of him would have liked to leave and pretend that none of this had ever happened. These cats didn't seem to be in any need of help.

Then he remembered his vision, especially his dream of the cats shrieking in anguish on the bleak moor. *I can't just turn around and go home,* he thought, wishing once again that Sandstorm were with him.

"Why don't we stick around for a bit?" It was Needlepaw who spoke, her head and tail raised fearlessly as she addressed Darktail. "We could join in with some hunts and patrols. It wouldn't take long for you SkyClan cats to see that we can be trusted."

Alderpaw wasn't sure whether he liked that suggestion or not. But he couldn't think of a better idea, so he supposed he would have to go along with it.

Darktail remained quiet for a moment, his blue gaze resting on each cat for a heartbeat before returning to Alderpaw. "Very well," he meowed at last. "Rain, show our guests where they can sleep. And yes," he added to Alderpaw, "there's probably quite a bit that we can learn from one another."

Alderpaw nodded in reluctant agreement, though his pelt still prickled and a shiver ran through him from ears to tailtip. *Why does this feel so wrong?*

The sun was warm on Alderpaw's pelt as he bent his head to lap from the stream. Gazing down into the water, he wished he could wash his paws, but he knew that would only make it easier for dust and grit to stick to them.

How can the SkyClan cats bear to live in such a filthy place? he asked himself. *Maybe if they do return with us to the forest, the ways of the other Clans will rub off on them.*

The evening before, when Rain had taken him and his friends to a den—a bare cave in the side of the gorge with nothing on the floor but sand—Alderpaw had settled to sleep in the hope that StarClan would send another vision to guide him. But now he couldn't even remember whether he had dreamed at all.

A pang of homesickness pierced him, sharp as a thorn, and he longed to feel cool grass beneath his pads, and to hear the gentle rustling of leaves as branches swayed above his head. *I hope SkyClan will decide to come with us, just so we can head home soon. My Clan doesn't even know that Sandstorm is dead.*

Grief tugged at Alderpaw's belly as he remembered the wise old she-cat. She would have known what to do, and helped him figure out why none of the cats here looked like the cats from his vision. She would have worked out why they didn't seem to be looking for help.

Is my timing wrong? Was I dreaming of past SkyClan cats?

A yowl from a little way downstream distracted Alderpaw from his thoughts. Turning, he spotted Needlepaw, who was perched on a boulder a few tail-lengths away.

"The hunters are back!" she announced. "And they're bringing prey."

Alderpaw left the waterside and bounded back to the center of the camp to meet the hunting patrols. His belly rumbled when he saw the quantities of prey that lay around Darktail as if presented for his approval. The hunters stood around the prey in a wide half circle, with Rain closest to their leader.

The rest of the questing cats clustered around Alderpaw and watched as Darktail chose a plump pigeon and tore mouthfuls of flesh from it. Then the SkyClan leader nodded to Rain, who stepped forward and chose a squirrel for himself.

"This is weird," Sparkpaw muttered into Alderpaw's ear. "Where's their fresh-kill pile? Who takes food to the elders and the nursing queens?"

Before Alderpaw could even try to answer her question, Rain stepped back with the squirrel in his jaws. As if at a signal, the hunters closed in, butting heads and hissing as they tried to grab the juiciest pieces of fresh-kill.

At the edges of the circle Alderpaw spotted two or three skinny elders, who tried to join in the fight for food, only to be shoved back by the stronger cats, who crouched over their prey, glaring around as they ripped flesh from the bones. A she-cat, with three tiny kits mewling around her, darted in and grabbed a vole, but a huge tabby tom tore it out of her jaws and thrust her away with a powerful stroke of his hind legs.

The questing cats shared glances of horror and confusion. "What do they think they're doing?" Cherryfall breathed out.

Beside Alderpaw, Needlepaw shrugged. "Maybe they've never been taught the warrior code."

"I'm surprised *you've* even heard of it," Sparkpaw muttered.

Needlepaw gave her a sly, sideways glance. "Just because I don't always follow stupid rules doesn't mean I don't know they exist," she retorted.

Then without hesitation she dived into the midst of the chaos of butting heads and swiping claws, easily batting two or three of the younger cats aside. Heartbeats later she emerged from the skirmish with a mouse, and crouched down in the shade of a rock to gulp it down.

Alderpaw spotted Darktail strolling back to the pile of rocks, with a casual glance over his shoulder at the fighting cats. He curled up beneath an overhang and watched the scene with slitted eyes.

Alderpaw's belly was growling, but he couldn't bring himself to join in the melee. *I'm not going to battle elders or kits for food!*

Beside him he heard Sparkpaw stifling a growl. "This isn't fair," she murmured. "Some of these SkyClan cats must go hungry day after day. That's why so many of them look thin and ragged."

As she finished speaking, she bounded forward, skirting the scrimmage, and marched boldly up to Darktail.

"Sparkpaw, no!" Alderpaw exclaimed, hurrying after her. To his relief he realized that Molewhisker and Cherryfall were following too.

"Why do you eat like this?" Sparkpaw piped up in a challenging tone as she planted herself in front of Darktail.

Alderpaw wasn't sure whether to be impressed by her courage or embarrassed by her manners. *We are SkyClan's guests, after all.*

"What do you mean?" Darktail asked, lashing his tail.

"In the Clans," Sparkpaw explained, "we bring all the prey back to camp and make a fresh-kill pile. Some cat will take food to the elders and the nursing queens, and to any cats who are sick, and then the warriors and apprentices are allowed to help themselves. We don't fight like *that*," she finished with a disdainful flick of her ears.

Darktail's only response was to narrow his eyes. Alderpaw stepped up to his sister's side, ready to defend her if the Sky-Clan leader struck at her.

"It's only fair," Sparkpaw went on. "You must have eaten like that in the past, since you're warriors too, and you're supposed to follow the warrior code."

Alderpaw noticed a glint of amusement in Darktail's eyes at the words *warrior code*.

"We have developed our *own* code," the leader told Sparkpaw. "After we left the other Clans, SkyClan realized our members were becoming weak, and we decided to make up some new rules. *SkyClan* rules reward the strong and aggressive—the cats who will best defend the Clan."

Sparkpaw looked confused. "What about sick cats, then, or elders?"

Darktail shrugged. "They learn to take care of themselves."

Alderpaw winced as he saw Sparkpaw's neck fur beginning to bristle in anger. "Then why do you even bother living in a Clan? It's *rogues* who are out for themselves!"

A low growl of anger rose from deep in Darktail's chest, and he slid out his claws. Hastily Molewhisker stepped forward, thrusting himself between Darktail and Sparkpaw.

"She's young and curious, that's all," he meowed. "But that's enough for now. Come on." He gave Sparkpaw a shove, back in the direction of their den.

Sparkpaw was clearly upset as they headed away. By now the fighting was over. The hunters were relaxing in the sun, lazily grooming themselves; Alderpaw spotted Needlepaw with them. Meanwhile the elders and the she-cat with the kits were picking over the remains of the prey, searching out any morsels the hunters had missed. The kits were wailing with hunger.

"We should go home," Sparkpaw whispered as they settled themselves in their den. "These weird cats don't need our help, and I'm not even sure that they *are* Clan cats anymore."

Alderpaw found that he agreed with her about the way the SkyClan cats were behaving. What Darktail had told them just now about the way SkyClan had changed the rules didn't seem to fit with Bramblestar's story of how Firestar and Sandstorm had traveled upriver to restore the Clan. "It's all so confusing—" he began.

"What are you talking about?" Needlepaw interrupted as she strolled into the den.

"I said we should go home," Sparkpaw repeated. "These cats don't need us."

"What?" Needlepaw sounded scornful. "We're here to find what lies in the shadows, right? And we've found it. These cats are *really* . . . well, dark. We can't turn away now."

"I think Sparkpaw is right." Cherryfall gave Alderpaw a serious look. "Something is . . . *off* about these cats. I think they're beyond our help. Is all this really what you saw in your dream?"

Alderpaw glanced around at his cats, sensing that they were really doubting him now. "I'm not sure," he confessed. "But I can't believe that Bramblestar got it so wrong, or that Sandstorm died for nothing. I don't know the reason, but I *do* know that this is where we are meant to be."

He waited tensely as the other cats exchanged doubtful glances. At last Cherryfall gave a nod.

"Very well, then," she meowed. "We'll stay and try to figure it out."

Alderpaw let out a sigh of relief. "Thank you."

I hope StarClan sends me another vision soon, he added to himself. *Because I really don't know what we're doing here.*

CHAPTER 16

When the last scraps of prey had been picked over, the rest of the SkyClan cats drifted away. Only one of them—a young orange she-cat—stayed close to their leader; she was coughing so hard she could barely stay on her paws.

Alderpaw watched in shock as Darktail swung one huge paw and thumped the young she-cat hard on her back.

"Stop that racket *now*!" he growled.

The she-cat gave him a scared look. She wasn't coughing anymore, though Alderpaw didn't think that the swat on her back had done her any good. She was obviously struggling to suppress her coughs.

Alderpaw padded up and dipped his head politely to Darktail. "It sounds as though she's suffering from whitecough," he mewed, indicating the she-cat with a wave of his tail. "She should see your medicine cat."

Both SkyClan cats gave him a blank look. Alderpaw felt as though he had missed his footing and plunged down into dark, icy water. *They don't have a medicine cat?*

Struggling to control his shock, he continued, "Whitecough isn't a big deal. Some tansy should help."

Darktail still looked blank, as if he wanted to ask what tansy was. Alderpaw's confusion deepened. *Sandstorm mentioned that Echosong was SkyClan's medicine cat. So what happened to her? And why has their leader never heard of a basic herb like tansy?*

Meanwhile the young she-cat had started coughing again, backing away from Darktail as if she was afraid of making him angry again.

"I'll be back soon," Alderpaw mewed. "I'm going to find some tansy."

He headed for the path that would take him to the cliff top, meaning to search for herbs among the rough grass and bushes there. But before he reached it, he spotted a den low down in the cliff wall. Because of the jutting line of the rocks, it was very close to the water, and a few wilting plants grew close beside it.

Alderpaw bounded up to the den and gave the plants a sniff. At once he recognized tansy, along with sorrel, yarrow, and chervil. Some cat had planted them, he realized, just as Leafpool and Jayfeather planted herbs near the old Twoleg nest, but clearly no cat was taking care of them now.

This has to be where the medicine cat stayed, Alderpaw thought. *But why would they have such a perfect medicine cat's den and no medicine cat? Maybe Echosong died without training an apprentice.*

The tansy leaves were limp, and the scent wasn't as strong as Alderpaw was used to in the forest, but he knew it was better than nothing. Tearing off a few stems, he padded back toward the rock pile.

When he returned, he discovered the orange she-cat lying

on her side, revealing a shock of white belly fur. The other SkyClan cats were keeping their distance, going about their business without even looking at their sick Clanmate, who was rasping and spluttering. *Her cough is even worse than I thought at first,* Alderpaw realized with a stab of anxiety.

Alderpaw dropped the tansy in front of the orange cat. "Eat that," he told her.

The she-cat looked up at him, her green eyes widening in confusion and a trace of fear. "I will get better, won't I?" she wheezed. "I don't want to be exiled."

Horror touched Alderpaw like a frozen claw. Gently he laid one forepaw on the she-cat's flank. "What's your name?" he asked.

"Flame," the she-cat choked out, before giving way to another spasm of coughing.

"I'm Alderpaw. I'm learning to be a medicine cat in my own Clan. I promise you, the tansy will help."

As Flame began to chew the tansy leaves, Alderpaw stepped back to give her a little breathing space.

"Will that work?" a rough voice rasped into his ear.

Startled, Alderpaw turned to see Darktail, glaring sternly at him. "Tansy usually clears up whitecough quite quickly," he replied, trying to sound reassuring. "But if whitecough is left too long, it can turn into greencough—and then Flame would have been in real trouble."

Darktail began to look interested; Alderpaw guessed he had never heard the names of these sicknesses before. *Maybe in SkyClan they're called something different.*

"So what cures greencough?" the white-and-black tom asked, not sounding as if he was much concerned about Flame.

"You can still use tansy," Alderpaw told him, "but catmint is much better, if you can get it."

"Hmm . . ." Darktail riffled his whiskers. "And what about wounds? Will catmint cure those as well?"

"No." *Doesn't this cat know anything?* "For wounds you would use cobweb to stop the bleeding, and comfrey root for the pain. Marigold or horsetail if the wound gets infected."

Darktail nodded. "And for fever?"

"Er . . ." For a moment Alderpaw couldn't remember. *This is worse than being tested by Jayfeather. I wish he were here!* "Borage leaves," he mewed at last. "And dandelion to help the feverish cat sleep. But Darktail . . ." He couldn't resist asking the question. "Don't you treat your sick cats?"

For a heartbeat Darktail looked confused. "Of course we do," he replied with a flick of his tail. "We just do it . . . differently. Why should all Clans behave the same?"

Because we all came from the same place, Alderpaw thought, but he couldn't bring himself to say the words aloud. He hadn't mentioned anything to Darktail about how the SkyClan cats had been driven from the forest, and he was reluctant to say anything now.

Bramblestar told me how terrible it was for SkyClan. The other Clans were wrong not to share their territory. SkyClan might blame us for it, even though it was so long ago.

But Alderpaw still couldn't understand why Darktail seemed so unfamiliar with the way the Clans lived. *Have they really wandered so far away from the warrior code?*

Then understanding started to grow inside Alderpaw, like a flower unfolding from a bud. Perhaps the prophecy meant something different from what he had thought at first. Maybe SkyClan was "in shadow" not just because they lived in a distant and forgotten place, but because they had lost their connection to the warrior code, and everything that made Clan cats different from rogues.

So it must be my task to guide them back again, and clear the sky!

Alderpaw's whiskers twitched happily. "If you like," he meowed to Darktail, "I'll take some of your cats on a tour of your territory to see what herbs we can find, and show them what they're used for. Of course," he added modestly, "I'm only an apprentice."

Darktail seemed unconcerned by Alderpaw's inexperience. He gave an approving nod. "Hey, Rain!" he yowled.

The long-furred gray tom sprang up from where he sat at the edge of the river, talking to Needlepaw, and bounded over to his leader. "What do you want, Darktail?" he asked, with a respectful dip of his head to his leader.

"Go with this cat," Darktail ordered, indicating Alderpaw with a flick of his tail. "He's going to look for herbs and tell you what to do with them. Listen to him—he's an apprentice."

"Okay," Rain responded, though he looked as confused as Alderpaw felt. Darktail said *apprentice* like it was . . . important.

"I'll come too," Needlepaw added, sidling up to them. "I'd like to get a better look at the gorge."

Alderpaw couldn't imagine why Needlepaw would want to

see any more of such a barren, dirty place, but there was no point in objecting. *Needlepaw is weird anyway. Nothing she does makes sense!*

Rain took the lead as the three cats headed downstream, passing the den that Alderpaw was sure must have been Echosong's at one time.

With every paw step Alderpaw began to feel more optimistic. If he could teach these cats how to treat illness, they might start to show more compassion for one another, instead of heartlessly ignoring sick cats like Flame. They would start to feel and behave more like a real Clan. And then they could return to the forest as real allies.

This is the first stage of completing the quest—to help SkyClan find the way back to Clan life.

Alderpaw shifted restlessly in his den, unable to sleep. He kept thinking about the tour of the territory he had taken with Needlepaw and Rain, and how much Rain needed to be taught. They had found yarrow and more tansy, and Rain had seemed to think that these two herbs could cure everything.

"You'll need to search for herbs on either side of the gorge," Alderpaw had pointed out. "And maybe even travel farther than your usual hunting territory. There are lots of different diseases that can strike a cat, and they need different herbs and different kinds of treatment."

Rain had shrugged, seeming okay with that. "It might make more sense for Darktail to lead us to new territory soon," he had meowed.

Now Alderpaw curled up more tightly and tried to will himself into sleep. He was desperate for another vision, perhaps a visit from Sandstorm to reassure him that everything was happening how it was supposed to. He knew deep within himself that there was something not right about SkyClan. However hard he tried to tell himself that it was only because they had lived apart from other Clans for so long, he couldn't shake the feeling that all this was somehow *wrong*. Was there a reason why he hadn't had any visions since they arrived in the gorge?

Then a reason occurred to him, and he shivered all over, wanting to mewl in terror like a tiny lost kit. *Suppose StarClan can't reach me in this place!*

As Alderpaw's shuddering died away, he was distracted by the sound of voices. He had already discovered how the walls of the gorge trapped sound, so it was useless trying to have a quiet conversation, or say anything they didn't want the SkyClan cats to hear. He wrapped his tail over his ears to blot out the sound, only to raise his head alertly as he heard Darktail's voice.

"It will be easy."

As silently as he could, Alderpaw edged toward the entrance to the den and peered out into the darkness. There was just enough light from the moon for him to make out Darktail and Rain a few tail-lengths away, along with a long-furred black she-cat named Raven.

"I don't know . . . ," Raven mewed doubtfully. "The journey will be long and hard. I've heard stories about huge

Thunderpaths out there, and how many cats lose their lives on them."

"Thunderpaths hold no fear for us," Darktail responded with a dismissive wave of his tail.

Hope thrilled through Alderpaw. *Maybe the SkyClan cats are deciding to leave tomorrow, to journey with us to the lake and reunite with the other Clans!*

He rose to his paws, intending to join them and tell them how happy he was about their plan, but before he could leave the den, the SkyClan cats split up, padding off in three different directions.

Movement in the shadows caught Alderpaw's eye, and to his astonishment he spotted Needlepaw, emerging from the shelter of a boulder and padding up to Rain. Until then he hadn't realized that she wasn't asleep in the den with him and his Clanmates.

"It sounds like you're close to making your minds up," Needlepaw purred to Rain.

The big gray tom loomed over her. "It's rude to eavesdrop," he hissed.

"I hardly had a choice." Needlepaw was not at all intimidated; her voice was even playful. "You're not exactly subtle in how you go about your plotting."

Rain muttered something in reply, but because he turned to walk away, Alderpaw couldn't make out the words.

Needlepaw pattered alongside the SkyClan cat, and without knowing why, Alderpaw emerged from the den and followed them as they headed upstream toward the rock pile.

Although he kept his distance, he could still hear Needlepaw's teasing purr.

"Life in the other Clans is different, Rain. There are . . . rules. You and Darktail and the others will have to learn them if you want to fit in."

"Everything will work out," Rain responded. "Just the way it's meant to."

Alderpaw couldn't decide whether the big tom's voice was hopeful or amused, but either way, he wasn't sure he liked it. *I've heard enough,* he thought, turning back toward the den.

But as he turned, his paw dislodged a pebble that clinked against another. Needlepaw and Rain both swiveled around to stare at him.

"Who's that?" Rain asked sharply.

"Only me," Alderpaw mumbled. "I . . . er . . . I just came out to make dirt."

Not waiting for any comment, he scampered off into the darkness, panting hard as he reached the den where his Clanmates still slept peacefully. His hopeful feelings had evaporated, the flutter in his chest replaced by a heavy weight that seemed to be pushing from the inside, trying to force him to the ground.

CHAPTER 17

❦

Alderpaw crawled out of the den the next morning feeling so exhausted that he could hardly put one paw in front of another. Pondering how he could return the SkyClan cats to Clan life, when they obviously had no idea what it meant to be a warrior, had kept him awake all night, and so had the ache in his chest after he'd heard Needlepaw talking to Rain.

"I think we should hunt," Molewhisker announced when all the questing cats had emerged from the den and sat grooming themselves at the waterside. "It's no use expecting to eat with the SkyClan cats."

"Let's do that," Cherryfall agreed. "I can't wait to get out of this StarClan-forsaken gorge."

"Oh, I don't know." Needlepaw yawned, showing a mouthful of spiky teeth. "It's not so bad when you get used to it."

"You stay, then," Sparkpaw snapped, and added under her breath, "No cat asked you to come with us anyway."

"That's enough," Molewhisker meowed, rising to his paws and speaking with authority. "Needlepaw, you can do what you want. The rest of us are going to hunt."

"It looks like there's thicker forest on the other side of the river," Cherryfall pointed out. "Let's go that way."

Few of the SkyClan cats were around, and none of them tried to stop the ThunderClan cats as Molewhisker led the way across the pile of rocks. Alderpaw stumbled along in the rear, convinced that he would be even worse at hunting when he could scarcely keep his eyes open.

But when he found himself under the trees, Alderpaw revived a little. It felt good to have damp earth and leaf mold beneath his paws again, and to catch glimpses of sky between crisscrossing branches. The leaves were beginning to turn brown and gold, and for the first time Alderpaw realized that leaf-fall was almost upon them.

Cherryfall and Sparkpaw headed off together, while Molewhisker turned to Alderpaw. "Do you want to hunt with me?" he asked.

Alderpaw shook his head. "Er . . . no, thanks." He couldn't bear having his former mentor watch him fail again. "I'll just practice on my own."

"Okay. I'll see you back in camp." Molewhisker pushed his way through a clump of bracken and vanished.

Once his sound and scent had died away, Alderpaw slid deeper into the forest, his ears pricked and his jaws parted to pick up the first traces of prey. Soon he heard a chirping sound from above, along with the rustling of leaves and the flutter of wings. Looking up, he spotted a thrush perched on the branch of a nearby tree.

Alderpaw's belly rumbled, and he realized how hungry he was. He had barely eaten anything since he and his friends had arrived in the gorge two days before. He wondered if he would be in trouble if he caught the bird for himself instead of taking it back to camp, then reminded himself that he wasn't in ThunderClan now. *I'm not going to eat with SkyClan, the way they shove the kits and elders around.*

He stalked the thrush as it fluttered deeper into the forest; then, keeping two trees back, he scrambled up the trunk of a beech tree and out onto a branch. He tried to remember everything he had been taught before he'd been told he was a terrible hunter and would be much better off as a medicine cat.

Best not to think about that, he decided. *It's just a small bird. I can do this.*

Creeping forward stealthily, Alderpaw managed to cross into the tree where the thrush was perching. It seemed to be unaware of him. He was bunching his muscles to pounce when another cat exploded upward from the forest floor in a massive leap. Its forepaws were outstretched to grab the bird, but it missed by a mouse-length. With a yowl of rage the cat fell backward, tumbling back to the ground. The thrush, startled, flew away.

"Fox dung!" Alderpaw hissed.

The strange cat—a ragged, skinny gray tom—scrambled to his paws and glared up at Alderpaw. "It's your fault I missed it!" he snarled. "Didn't you see I was already stalking it? You made me rush."

But Alderpaw had forgotten all about the thrush. Now that he got a clear sight of the newcomer, he was too stunned to do anything but stare. *This is one of the cats from my vision!*

He remembered seeing the gray tom in the circle of cats who had watched the ceremony when Leafstar had made a new warrior. But then he had been a healthy Clan cat with a glossy pelt. Now he looked just like a mangy rogue, all his ribs showing through matted fur.

"Who are you?" he asked.

"My name's Mistfeather," the cat replied roughly. "What's it to you?"

Cautiously, never taking his gaze from the gray tom, Alderpaw climbed down the tree trunk. Keeping his distance so that Mistfeather wouldn't think he was looking for a fight, he dipped his head politely.

"Greetings," he mewed. "I'm sorry about the thrush. My name is Alderpaw, and I come from ThunderClan."

The gray tom's eyes widened in a mixture of wonder and disbelief. "ThunderClan!" he exclaimed. "Then you must know Firestar. I wasn't born when he came to restore my Clan, but his story was told at every full moon upon the Sky-rock. We honored him above all cats."

Alderpaw felt as if every hair on his pelt was rising in excitement. He opened his jaws to tell Mistfeather that Firestar was dead, then decided this wasn't the moment. Instead he asked, "Were you exiled from your Clan?"

The gray tom stared back at him. "Was I exiled?" he asked, bitterness invading his tone. "No, I wasn't. It was the whole Clan!"

"What do you mean?" Alderpaw asked, staring at him incredulously.

Mistfeather beckoned him nearer with a twitch of his tail. Alderpaw sat among the roots of the tree where he had stalked the thrush, and the gray tom crouched close beside him.

"You've met those cats in the gorge, right?" Mistfeather began. "I bet they let you think they were SkyClan, but they're not. They're vicious rogues who attacked the real SkyClan and took our territory for themselves."

Alderpaw's first reaction was a profound relief. *I knew there was something wrong about those cats. They're not a Clan at all! No wonder they don't know how to behave!* But he was also surprised to hear that such a terrible fate had come to SkyClan. *Is this what my visions were trying to tell me? That SkyClan has been exiled and needs my help?*

"Where did the rogues come from?" he asked.

"I have no idea," Mistfeather replied. "And I have no idea what rules they follow—if they follow any at all. They're evil!"

In the wake of his relief, doubts began to creep into Alderpaw's mind. "Surely a whole Clan should have been able to fight them off?"

Mistfeather couldn't meet his gaze; his whiskers drooped in shame. "Times had been hard for us, and to tell you the truth, we had as many daylight-warriors as we did cats who lived all the time in the gorge."

"Daylight-warriors?" Alderpaw asked, mystified.

"Cats who came to hunt and train with us warriors during the day," Mistfeather explained. "Then at night they would go back to their Twolegs."

"You mean they were *kittypets*?" Alderpaw was so outraged

that he could hardly get the words out. "You let *kittypets* into your Clan?"

"It worked for us," Mistfeather mewed defensively. "And the daylight-warriors were brave and worthy Clanmates, but the rogues attacked at night when they were with their house-folk, so we were terribly outnumbered."

"And the rogues won."

Mistfeather nodded. "We were trying to protect one another, not kill our enemies, and it's easy to defeat cats who do that."

"So where did the rest of your Clan go?" Alderpaw asked, glancing around as if he expected more cats to emerge from the undergrowth.

"I don't know," Mistfeather told him. "We all scattered. I'm the only one left here, and I have no idea how many of the others survived, or where they might be."

"Why did you stay?"

Deep grief flooded into Mistfeather's amber eyes. "My mate was killed in the battle. I decided that I'd rather live as a loner in the place where she died than leave to look for new territory."

Alderpaw's heart clenched with pity and fury. *Everything makes sense now!* Guilt tore at him like a fox's fangs as he realized that his vision had been real. SkyClan had needed help, but he and his friends had come too late.

"That's why the cats in the gorge don't act like a Clan," he murmured half to himself. "It's because they're *not* a Clan. They're just rogues who pounced on a group of cats when they were vulnerable. They're no better than thieves."

"What do you know about it?"

The harsh voice came from behind Alderpaw; he sprang up and whirled around to see Darktail standing a fox-length away, a sneer on his face. His unsettling blue gaze showed almost no emotion as he regarded Alderpaw and Mistfeather.

"It seems you've met one of the dregs of the gorge," he meowed to Alderpaw. "Somehow he's still alive! And it sounds like you're plotting against *my* cats."

Alderpaw backed away until he had the trunk of the tree behind him. His gaze flickered to and fro, hoping that some of his Clanmates might be nearby. But there was no sound or scent of them. In the dark shadows cast by the trees, Darktail seemed to be twice his size. *I'll have to think fast to get out of this.*

But weariness and hunger seemed to have made Mistfeather mouse-brained. Lurching to his paws, he arched his back and hissed at Darktail. "You're a filthy rogue who stole territory!"

"Territory belongs to those strong enough to defend it— or to *take* it," Darktail pointed out, unmoved. "If SkyClan couldn't dig their claws into the land they claimed as theirs, they have nothing to complain about. And if you want to stake your claim, Mistfeather, do you want to fight me for the territory right here, right now?"

Alderpaw's outrage almost choked him. *Can't Darktail see that Mistfeather is in no state to fight any cat?*

But the exiled cat puffed up his fur and slid out his claws, drawing his lips back in a snarl. "Do your worst, Darktail!"

Alderpaw started forward to place himself between the two cats, but Mistfeather waved him back with a sweep of his tail.

"Stay back!" he hissed. "A fight is a fight."

No, it'll be a slaughter, Alderpaw thought, as reluctantly he stepped back.

Mistfeather lunged forward, aiming a blow at Darktail, but the rogue leader slipped aside easily and raked his claws down the back of Mistfeather's head.

"You'll need to be faster than that!" he taunted the gray tom.

Undaunted, Mistfeather spun around and launched himself at the rogue leader again, but Darktail avoided the second blow as easily as the first. Mistfeather's breath was already coming in ragged, wheezing gasps. He staggered and almost fell as Darktail thrust him off contemptuously with one paw.

Alderpaw couldn't help admiring Mistfeather's courage. As he watched the one-sided fight, he recognized some skillful fighting moves, and he realized that the SkyClan cat would have been a formidable opponent if only he'd had the strength.

Mistfeather scrabbled around and charged at Darktail again and again, but each time the rogue sidestepped clear of his feeble swipes and landed a strike of his own. Soon blood was trickling down Mistfeather's sides, and tufts of his fur littered the forest floor.

At last Mistfeather was completely spent, his chest heaving as he gasped for breath. Darktail padded slowly up to him and stood over him. Mistfeather raised one forepaw to strike at him, but the movement was slow and listless. Darktail easily swatted the paw aside. Alderpaw's muscles tightened with foreboding as he saw the real SkyClan cat sink to the ground, exhausted and defenseless.

"Stupid mange-pelt," Darktail growled. "You should have stayed away."

"Stop!" Alderpaw said, trying to move forward to protect the defeated cat, but he was too slow.

Darktail reared up and swept one forepaw around in a slashing blow. His claws ripped into Mistfeather's throat, opening it up so that blood gushed out in arcing spurts. Mistfeather's whole body spasmed, then went limp.

Alderpaw gazed in horror at the dead SkyClan warrior.

CHAPTER 18

🍀

Alderpaw winced as Darktail's claws dug into his haunches. Only moments had passed since the slaughter of Mistfeather, and his killer was driving Alderpaw back to the camp.

"Keep moving," the rogue leader rasped.

Stumbling onward, Alderpaw could still picture Mistfeather's body, the gush of blood as Darktail's claws slashed open his throat. "You didn't have to kill Mistfeather," he meowed, struggling to master his fear of the rogue leader. "He was already weak and defenseless. What harm could he have done to you? And you didn't even bury him!" he added.

Darktail stabbed his claws once more into Alderpaw's haunches. "There's no way I would bury such a devious cat!" he snarled. "And when you and your companions are dead, I'll leave your bodies to rot, too."

Dismayed, Alderpaw half turned to confront Darktail, who simply gave him a hard shove to keep him moving. *Is this the end of my quest?* he wondered in despair. *Maybe I should have listened to the others and left!*

"We've done nothing to you or your cats to deserve being killed!" he protested.

"Don't lie, flea-pelt!" Darktail hissed. "It's obvious you're allies of SkyClan. You've come as spies to unsettle my group, so the weak Clan with their daylight-warriors could come back. But my cats and I claimed this territory honorably, and we mean to keep it. Your plan has fallen apart!"

Alderpaw didn't know how to reply to such false accusations; he knew that nothing he said would change Darktail's mind.

Every cat stood up and stared as Darktail shoved Alderpaw across the pile of rocks to return to the camp. Alderpaw saw with relief that his Clanmates had returned. They padded to his side as Darktail pushed him into the middle of the circle of rogues.

"What's going on?" Molewhisker asked.

Darktail stood at the bottom of the rocks, his gaze sweeping across the crowd of his followers as he prepared to address them.

Of course! Alderpaw thought. *He always sits beside the rocks. A real Clan leader would speak to his cats from the top. We shouldn't have believed Darktail was a Clan cat. He's never behaved like one.*

"I found this pathetic excuse for a cat"—Darktail gave Alderpaw a contemptuous prod—"talking to a SkyClan cat in the forest. It's obvious that these cats have lied to us. They're not friendly visitors. They're working with SkyClan to steal this territory back from us, after we fought for it so bravely! This has been a conspiracy from the beginning."

Angry murmurs arose from the rogues. Alderpaw saw their neck fur beginning to bristle, their tails lashing as they closed in around the questing cats. His friends scarcely resisted, bewildered by the news and the accusation.

"They're *not* SkyClan?" Cherryfall meowed.

"We should have known!" Molewhisker hissed. "A lot of things are making sense now."

"Is this true?" Rain asked Needlepaw, thrusting his face up against hers until their noses almost touched. "Are you plotting with SkyClan?" Alderpaw could see his anger as Rain's claws flexed in and out, but he could sense something else beneath it. *Does he feel hurt?* Alderpaw wondered, the odd ache swelling in his chest again.

Needlepaw remained calm as she met Rain's furious green gaze. "Of course it's not true," she replied. "We live far away from here, and when we set out, we weren't even sure that SkyClan existed. So how could we have been conspiring with them?"

An angry yowl from Darktail followed her words. "Are you calling me a liar?"

"Certainly not." Needlepaw's voice was still even, and she raised one paw to smooth her whiskers. Alderpaw admired how she showed not the least trace of fear. "I'm not calling any cat a liar." She turned to look at Alderpaw, her face as annoyed as Molewhisker's had been sometimes when he was Alderpaw's mentor. "My medicine-cat friend might have been spending time with the wrong cat, but I'm sure he didn't mean anything by it."

Darktail seemed to be considering her words. In the brief silence the black she-cat, Raven, sidled up to him.

"Better safe than sorry," she mewed. "We don't know for sure that we can trust these cats. After all, they did turn up out of the blue. And does any cat really believe what they told us?"

Alderpaw felt as though his windpipe was swelling, cutting off his breath. *Is every cat here ruthless and nasty?*

Darktail went on thinking for a moment longer, then fixed an unblinking blue gaze on Needlepaw. "You know I can't just let you go. Not after everything that has happened."

Instantly Molewhisker and Cherryfall stepped forward, their backs arching and their shoulder fur bristling. "You can't keep us here if we don't want to stay," Molewhisker snarled.

"Right," Cherryfall agreed. "If we say we're leaving, we'll leave."

Alderpaw realized in despair that Darktail had no need to respond. Without a word from him, the rogues tightened the circle around them, their tails raised and their claws flexing, ready to fight.

We're outnumbered, Alderpaw thought. *They can keep us here. They can do what they like with us.*

"It's nothing personal," Darktail meowed smoothly. "Already one enemy has trespassed in the forest. I'm just making sure that no more danger is brought here to the gorge. Once I'm convinced that the danger has passed, I'll let you go." He licked one paw and drew it over his ear. "I promise . . ."

But how can we believe your promises? Alderpaw added silently.

The sun had gone down, and deep shadows lay over the gorge. After the earlier confrontation, Alderpaw and the others had been escorted to a different den, no more than a jagged crack in the rock, where they huddled together tightly. The rough walls pressed into their fur, and it was impossible to get comfortable.

Just outside, Raven was sitting on guard, her back to the den. Seeing her ears pricked alertly, none of the questing cats had felt able to discuss plans for what they might do next.

"So what happened to the real SkyClan?" Cherryfall asked Alderpaw at last, her voice a low murmur. "Did you find out?"

Alderpaw nodded. "Mistfeather—the cat I met in the forest—told me that the rogues attacked SkyClan and drove them out of the gorge. After that, the SkyClan cats scattered. Mistfeather didn't know where they went. And then Darktail killed him."

Sparkpaw let out a horrified gasp, and dug her claws hard into the sandy floor of the den.

"Darktail is evil," Molewhisker mewed. Turning to Needlepaw, he added, "What were you thinking this morning? We shouldn't have tried to explain to him. We should have walked out of our own accord."

"And don't you think the rogues would have followed us?" Needlepaw retorted. "We would have led them straight to our own Clans."

Her voice rose as she spoke. Alderpaw and the others all turned to look at Raven, but if the black she-cat had heard them, she was giving nothing away.

The Clan cats settled once more into an uneasy silence, nestling down into the uncomfortable new den. Alderpaw felt the dust sticking to his pelt, the sharp stones and pebbles jabbing at his flesh, and he began to wonder where this quest had gone so wrong.

We found what's left of SkyClan . . . but will we share their fate?

CHAPTER 19

Alderpaw dozed uneasily, only to rouse again as he felt a paw prodding him gently in the shoulder. He opened his eyes; there was just enough light for him to see Sparkpaw staring down at him.

"Shh!" she whispered. "We need to go—now."

Alderpaw blinked at her. "What are you talking about?"

"The rogues are asleep," Sparkpaw murmured, "but who knows for how long? The sun will be up soon. This is the best chance we'll have."

Alderpaw staggered to his paws, stretching his jaws in a massive yawn. As he arched his back, stretching his cramped body, he saw Molewhisker and Cherryfall standing just behind his sister. Needlepaw, looking unusually hesitant, was waiting near the entrance to the den.

"I think this is a bad idea," she mumbled. "If they catch us—"

Molewhisker brushed his tail across her shoulder. "We'll just have to make sure they don't," he said.

Needlepaw's head drooped in reluctant agreement as Molewhisker turned to the others and jerked his head to signal they should move. He led the way out into the open. A couple of tail-lengths away, Raven was sleeping with her tail curled over her nose. Alderpaw guessed she would be in trouble with Darktail when he woke up.

Silently the questing cats wove their way among the rocks, heading toward the water's edge. Alderpaw's pelt prickled as he imagined rogue cats looking out from the dens in the cliff face and spotting their stealthy movement. But no warning yowls split the dawn silence.

Eventually they reached the river and turned downstream. Molewhisker picked up the pace until they were loping swiftly over the rocks. Alderpaw shivered in the damp, chilly air; the sky was covered with cloud, and there was no sign of where the sun would rise.

Before they had gone very far, they came to a spot where a spur of rock jutted out from the cliff. The river curled around it, running fast and deep.

"Mouse dung!" Molewhisker muttered as he scrambled up to the top of the rock. "Can't we ever get out of this filthy place?"

Alderpaw struggled up after him, driving his claws into tiny cracks and feeling the grit digging into his pads. To his relief, the rock sloped down more gently on the other side, and he was able to slide down easily to stand beside Molewhisker.

"At least now we can't be seen from the camp," Cherryfall mewed as the others joined them.

"We still have to get a move on," Molewhisker commented. "Don't forget that the rogues can follow our scent."

"Then maybe we should cross the river," Alderpaw suggested. "That would break our scent and make it harder for Darktail and the rest to follow us. It would give us a better chance of getting clear."

"Good idea," Cherryfall responded. "Let's look for a place to cross."

But as Molewhisker swung into motion again, Sparkpaw hung back.

"What's the matter?" Molewhisker asked, a trace of irritation in his voice.

"I'm wondering if we *should* leave," Sparkpaw replied hesitantly. "StarClan sent us here, and we haven't found SkyClan. Maybe we should stay close by and look for them."

"We can't help SkyClan now," Alderpaw responded grimly, even though he admired his littermate for her courage in making the suggestion. "We have no idea where they've gone. And if we try to stay in the woods, Darktail and his rogues will surely find us. Maybe when we get home, Bramblestar will have some idea of what we can do to help SkyClan, but this quest . . ." He paused, willing his voice not to shake. "This quest is a *failure*. The best we can do is get home safely."

"He's right," Cherryfall meowed, touching her apprentice sympathetically on her shoulder. "We did everything we could, but we can't save SkyClan right now."

Sparkpaw sighed, nodding. "I guess so."

Molewhisker took the lead again, padding along at the edge of the river. Alderpaw looked out for a place where it would be safe to cross, but it was still too dark to tell how deep the water was, and it was rushing past quickly, a tumbling current that could easily sweep a cat away.

RiverClan cats swim, he thought with a shudder. *But we're not RiverClan cats, and I don't want to try it.*

"There are trees farther downstream," Sparkpaw pointed out, as if she shared her brother's thoughts. "Maybe there'll be a way to cross there."

Cherryfall gave a brisk nod. "Good idea. Let's hurry. The sun will be up soon, and the rogues will be waking."

She set off, bounding toward the trees, and the others followed. The first trees they reached were small and spindly, and too far away from the water to be any help in crossing. Alderpaw had hoped for a fallen tree trunk, like the one that the Clans used to cross the lake for Gatherings, but the only log he spotted was wedged at an angle into the bank, the far end jutting out into the current.

A little farther on, bigger trees began to appear, interspersed by bushes. "This would be a good place to hunt," Sparkpaw panted as she hurried along beside her brother.

"No time," Alderpaw gasped in response.

"My belly feels so empty!" Sparkpaw complained. "I wish—"

"Look! Over there!" Cherryfall's voice interrupted Sparkpaw. She ran up to a tree that was leaning toward the river; its long branches hung over the water, stretching almost as far as the opposite side. "This is perfect!"

As he bounded closer, Alderpaw thought the tree looked dangerous, but he didn't object. Crossing here was obviously their best chance of avoiding the rogues.

"Hmm . . . ," Molewhisker murmured, sizing up the tree with an intent gaze. "Those branches might be long enough. And if our scent disappears here, Darktail might think that we fell into the river and got swept away."

"It's worth a try," Alderpaw agreed, though his belly was churning with apprehension.

"I'll go first," Sparkpaw volunteered, climbing swiftly up the slanting trunk of the tree, then edging out onto one of the longest branches. "Come on—it's okay!"

As Sparkpaw ventured farther out over the river, Molewhisker followed her up the trunk, with Cherryfall hard on his paws. Alderpaw managed to tear his gaze away from his sister's progress to peer upstream and check that none of the rogues had appeared in pursuit. Although the dawn light was gradually strengthening, there was no sign of movement.

I suppose it's too much to hope that they won't come. . . .

"You next!" Needlepaw's voice drew Alderpaw's attention back to the tree.

By now Sparkpaw had almost reached the point where she would have to leap from the branch to the far bank of the river. Molewhisker and Cherryfall were close behind her. Alderpaw hardly dared watch as they balanced precariously on the narrow branch.

"No, you go first," he mewed to Needlepaw. "I'll keep lookout."

Needlepaw looked reluctant, but after a moment's hesitation she shrugged. "If you say so." She scrambled up the tree trunk with a whisk of her tail and headed out along the branch.

With no reason to delay any longer, Alderpaw followed. It was easy to clamber up the leaning trunk, and when he crept out onto the branch, it felt sturdy enough under his paws. But the weight of the cats up ahead made it dip low, toward the water.

It would have been smarter to go one by one, Alderpaw thought, digging his claws in hard, *but we don't have time for that.*

His belly lurched as he saw Sparkpaw crouch and bunch her muscles, ready for the leap onto the bank. The branch bounced wildly as she took off, and Alderpaw let out a yelp of fear as he almost lost his grip. A moment later he drew in a long breath of relief as he saw his littermate land safely on the opposite bank. Within the next few heartbeats Molewhisker and Cherryfall joined her.

Just ahead of Alderpaw, Needlepaw edged forward, a mouse-length at a time, then halted, gripping the branch grimly with her claws. The branch was dipping and bending dangerously under her weight.

"Keep going!" Alderpaw urged her.

Needlepaw glanced back over her shoulder. "I'm scared of falling into the water," she hissed. "Okay?"

"You'll be fine," Alderpaw meowed. "Better than if the rogues catch up with us!"

But as soon as Needlepaw started edging forward again, the branch started to groan and creak. So frozen by fear that he could hardly move, Alderpaw started to back up. But he was too late. He heard a tearing sound as the branch gave way, and a screech of terror from Needlepaw, abruptly cut off as the two cats plunged into the freezing cold stream.

Alderpaw flailed his legs in the surging water, terrified as the cold, unfamiliar touch enfolded him. The current was so fast that he was swept away, not knowing which way was up. A heavy, rushing pressure filled his ears, and when he tried to open his eyes, he was blinded by dark water. Desperately he kicked and kicked, pain growing in his chest until he thought he would lose consciousness.

Then his head broke the surface. Gratefully he took a gulp of air and thrashed his legs with the flow of the current to keep himself afloat. He glanced around to see if he could spot Needlepaw, but there was no sign of her.

It's still too dark to see much, he thought, hoping that she was somewhere near him in this chaos of water.

He strained his ears to catch her cries, or calls from his Clanmates on the bank, but the river rushing in his ears cut off all other sounds.

The current seemed to be moving faster than ever. Looking ahead, Alderpaw saw the tumbled surface abruptly come to an end, with nothing but gloomy sky beyond. The roaring in his ears grew louder.

A waterfall!

Alderpaw knew that he had to reach the bank. He kicked out across the current, struggling to drag himself to safety, but the force of the water was too strong.

I'm not going to make it. This is where I'm going to die.

Then Alderpaw felt his forepaw snag on something jutting out of the water. Somehow the contact pulled him toward the bank, and as the surge lifted him for a heartbeat, he realized he was clinging to Needlepaw.

The sight of the bank so close gave Alderpaw fresh hope. "Keep going!" he gasped to Needlepaw. "We can do it!"

But however hard the two cats fought, the river was stronger. Alderpaw glimpsed the smooth curve of the water as it reached the falls and let out a yelp of alarm as he realized he was going over.

He found himself falling, torn away from Needlepaw, his body tossed and thrown about by the waterfall. His panic-stricken yowl was cut off as he slammed down onto the surface below and all the breath was driven out of his body.

Everything went black as Alderpaw sank deep into the water. Then light seared his eyes as he bobbed back up to the surface, dazed and struggling feebly, surprised that he was still alive. Something shoved him hard at the back of his neck, propelling him toward the bank. Soon he felt his paws touch mud, and he hauled himself upward, clambering clear of the water. Turning, he saw Needlepaw dragging herself out after him, her fur plastered to her body.

Alderpaw collapsed onto his belly, his flanks heaving and shivering with cold, and with relief at having survived. Needlepaw sank down beside him.

Catching his breath at last, Alderpaw strained to catch any sight or sound of their companions. "I can't hear the others," he mewed. "Can you?"

Needlepaw just shook out her wet fur. "No!" she yowled. "I

don't hear them—I can't hear anything over the water. I *told you* I didn't like it!"

Alderpaw turned an anxious circle, but all he could see were trees and sky. All he could hear was the running water. All he could smell was the wet dirt beneath him, and the fear wafting off both him and Needlepaw.

What do we do now? he wondered.

CHAPTER 20

At first Alderpaw lay in an exhausted stupor with Needlepaw by his side, but the thought of his Clanmates soon roused him. "We should get up," he panted. "Try to figure out a way to get back to the others."

Needlepaw gave her shoulder fur a couple of feeble licks. "I don't know about you," she meowed, "but I need to rest."

"But we don't know what happened to them!" Alderpaw asked, with a fretful look upstream. "We need to find them!"

And how are we going to find SkyClan now?

Needlepaw snorted. "*You* need to quit worrying about the others so much and start worrying about yourself. Let *them* find *us*. Meanwhile, we need to rest."

Alderpaw realized that Needlepaw was right. Staggering to his paws, he gazed around, only to see monsters dashing to and fro on a Thunderpath a few fox-lengths away, with a row of Twoleg dens on the far side. The air was filled with the reek of monsters and Twolegs.

"I don't believe it!" he groaned. "Twolegs everywhere!"

"It's fine," Needlepaw responded, waving her tail toward a tangle of elder bushes growing between the water's edge and the Thunderpath. "We can make a nest here. The Twolegs won't find us."

Hoping she was right, Alderpaw followed her as she thrust her way deep into the bushes and flattened a clump of long grass for a makeshift nest. His legs aching with weariness, Alderpaw curled up beside her.

Soon Needlepaw's snores echoed around their den. But in spite of his exhaustion, Alderpaw found it hard to sleep. The sound and stink of the monsters was too close, and the events of their desperate escape from the rogues kept flickering through his mind. Snuggling up to Needlepaw, Alderpaw filled his nose with her scent, trying to imagine that he was back in camp, snoozing in the apprentices' den with Sparkpaw. Finally he slept.

When Alderpaw awoke, bright sunlight was filtering through the branches of the elder bushes. Anxiety stabbed at him as he saw that Needlepaw had vanished. The sound of Twoleg voices drifted into Alderpaw's ears, and when he crept cautiously out of the bushes he spotted several Twoleg kits playing beside the nests, tossing something brightly colored to each other.

A wave of homesickness for the lake and the forest flooded over Alderpaw. *Those kits are so noisy! When will we ever get a bit of peace?*

Then the grass parted to reveal Needlepaw, trotting up to him with a plump sparrow clamped in her jaws. "Fresh-kill!" she announced, dropping it at Alderpaw's paws.

"Thank StarClan you're back!" Alderpaw exclaimed. "I was worried about you."

Needlepaw flicked her tail. "No need. Come on, eat."

"What do you think we ought to do next?" Alderpaw asked, his jaws watering as he gulped down warm bites of the sparrow. It was good to sit in the shelter of the bushes and let the sun warm his damp fur, but he knew they shouldn't stay there any longer.

"Look for the others, I guess," Needlepaw replied with her mouth full.

Alderpaw was glad that he didn't have to argue with her. He couldn't imagine turning for home without at least trying to find his Clanmates.

When they had finished eating, he and Needlepaw headed back upstream as far as the waterfall. "I guess we have to go this way," he muttered, gazing up at the moss-covered rocks that jutted from the cliff face beside the cascading water.

"It doesn't look too hard," Needlepaw meowed, springing up onto the first of the rocks.

Not sure he agreed, Alderpaw followed. The river thundered down beside him, and his legs began to shake as he remembered how he had been swept away and almost drowned. The rocks were slippery from spray, and if he sank his claws into the moss, it pulled away and almost made him lose his balance. Needlepaw was climbing determinedly ahead of him, showering him with grit and drops of water.

Alderpaw was panting hard by the time he reached the top. He would have liked to rest again, but urgency gave strength to his paws as he thought about his Clanmates.

He and Needlepaw trudged on beside the stream, now and again calling out to their friends and casting back and forth as they tried to pick up their scent. Alderpaw began to grow discouraged as they drew closer to the gorge again. *Maybe the rogues recaptured them. They could all be dead by now!*

"Hey!" Needlepaw exclaimed at last, pausing to taste the air among the roots of an elm tree that grew close to the waterside. "Over here!"

Alderpaw padded over to join her and sniffed into the leaf-lined hollow made by the roots. He could discern the scents of all three of his Clanmates.

"They must have stopped here to rest," he mewed, his voice shaking with relief. "Sparkpaw! Molewhisker! Cherryfall!" he called, hoping that they might still be within earshot. But no cat replied.

"I'll tell you something," Needlepaw murmured, concentrating hard as she followed the scent away from the tree. "They were traveling downstream. I'll bet you a moon of dawn patrols they were looking for us."

Alderpaw's heart began to thump with excitement. "Then did we pass them on the way?"

"I don't see how we could have." Needlepaw looked puzzled for a moment.

"Anyway," Alderpaw went on, energy surging back into his paws, "all we have to do is follow their scent. Come on!"

"And climb back down that StarClan-cursed waterfall!" Needlepaw groaned as she followed him.

The scent trail led downstream, sometimes by the waterside, sometimes ranging farther away. Now and again individual scents split off from the main trail, but they always joined it again.

"They're searching for us," Needlepaw mewed. "I can't think how we missed them."

But when they reached the bushes near the Twoleg dens where they had curled up to rest, they found that the scent trail led onward, past their makeshift den and along the grass between the river and the Thunderpath.

"I don't believe it!" Needlepaw snarled with a lash of her tail. "*They* missed *us*! They must have walked straight past while we were asleep."

Alderpaw bit back a growl of frustration. "We were so wet, the water would have washed out our scent," he meowed. "And all these Twoleg scents don't help. But it's not so bad. At least we know that they're alive, and they haven't been recaptured by Darktail. All we have to do is follow them."

But when he and Needlepaw headed downstream, they found it wasn't as easy as that. There were so many conflicting reeks of Twolegs and monsters covering the scent trail. Finally they came to a place where Alderpaw guessed that a monster must have stopped, leaving splashes of something dark and foul-smelling on the grass. The cat scent was completely swamped, and they couldn't pick it up again on the other side.

"We've lost them," Alderpaw mewed.

"They probably think we drowned," Needlepaw responded in a tiny voice. "Who knows where they went after this?"

"They must still be following the river," Alderpaw pointed out. "Where else is there for them to go? There's no way of crossing here."

"Maybe." Needlepaw seemed unusually despondent. "But what if we're wrong? What if we never find them?"

Alderpaw swallowed hard. "Then we have to find our own way back to camp from here," he stated, trying to sound confident. "If they give up looking for us, that's where they'll go."

Glancing around, Alderpaw realized that he had no idea where they were. They had approached the gorge from the opposite bank, and everything looked different from where he was standing now. He wasn't even certain if they had been swept past the point where they had first come upon the river.

"We have to cross back to the other side," he meowed, "and then head toward the setting sun."

"That's a bit vague," Needlepaw pointed out with a sniff. "We could completely miss the lake and the Clan territory. And don't even think about swimming across the river, because I'm not going to."

"No cat asked you to," Alderpaw meowed mildly. "We'll head downstream on this side to start with, and maybe there'll be a fallen tree or something where we can cross. We might even catch up with the others, if we're lucky."

Needlepaw let out a snort. "We could use a bit of luck!"

By this time the sun was starting to go down, casting scarlet light over the river. Alderpaw realized they would soon have to look for somewhere to spend the night. *At least we're far from those Twoleg dens,* he thought.

Soon the Thunderpath veered away from the river, so that a grassy stretch of ground opened up, dotted here and there with clumps of bushes.

"This would be a good place to rest," Alderpaw meowed, stretching his jaws in a yawn. "Any chance of prey?"

Needlepaw perked up at the thought of hunting. "Just watch me!"

She disappeared into the nearest bushes and returned a few moments later with the limp body of a blackbird dangling from her jaws. Meanwhile Alderpaw found a sheltered hollow underneath the branches of a hazel bush and scraped together some dead leaves to make a nest. As he ate his share of the fresh-kill, he realized how exhausted he was. Not even his worries about finding his way home were enough to keep him from falling into a deep sleep. But StarClan still did not visit him in his dreams.

For three more sunrises Alderpaw and Needlepaw trekked along the river. Their hopes revived when now and again they picked up traces of their friends' scents and knew that they were still following in their paw steps. The river rolled on, wider and stronger now; there was nowhere safe for the cats to cross.

During the third day Alderpaw began to pick up the reek of monsters again, and there was a haze in the air ahead of them. Shortly after sunhigh more Twoleg dens loomed on the horizon.

"That's a really big Twolegplace," Alderpaw meowed, stifling a groan. "And I know we never passed it on the way to the gorge. We've come too far downriver."

Needlepaw shrugged. "We didn't have much choice."

"And we still don't." Alderpaw cast a glance at the surging river, the far bank looking impossibly far away. "We're going to have to travel through the filthy place."

"You know, that might not be a bad thing," Needlepaw mused as the two cats padded on side by side and the first of the Twoleg dens grew closer and closer.

Alderpaw was already feeling oppressed by the stinks and noises of the Twolegplace. "Not funny, Needlepaw," he snapped.

"I'm not joking." Needlepaw halted and turned to face him. Amusement was glimmering in her green eyes, but her tone was serious as she added, "We need to find a kittypet."

"A *kittypet*?" Alderpaw was outraged. "Are you feeling okay? I don't think there's an herb for a cat with bees in her brain."

"No, listen, idiot." Needlepaw gave her ears and impatient flick. "A kittypet might be able to tell us where we can cross the river."

Alderpaw snorted. "What makes you think that?"

"A kittypet would know this area well," Needlepaw replied, "which we do not. And maybe they would even give us some kittypet food."

Alderpaw wanted to retch with disgust. "You're joking now, right?"

"No. We still have a long journey ahead," Needlepaw meowed. "It makes sense to fill up while we can."

"I'm not filling up on that stuff," Alderpaw muttered as

they set off again. "It's totally against the warrior code to eat kittypet food. And they say it looks like mouse droppings!"

Alderpaw knew there was no point in protesting any more as he followed Needlepaw toward the Twolegplace. She kept marching on determinedly until they reached a Thunderpath that ran alongside the nearest dens. Needlepaw halted, glancing up and down for monsters, then stretched out a paw and rested it gently on the hard black surface of the Thunderpath.

"What are you doing?" Alderpaw asked.

"Feeling for vibrations," Needlepaw replied. "Monsters are so huge, you can feel them coming before you can see them."

"That's useful," Alderpaw murmured. He had never seen Needlepaw do that before, but then, Sandstorm, and then Molewhisker and Cherryfall, had taken the lead when they'd crossed Thunderpaths on the outward journey.

I wonder how much wandering Needlepaw has done on her own before this.

Needlepaw's prodding him in the side roused Alderpaw from his thoughts. "Come on! It's safe to cross."

Alderpaw felt more and more uneasy as he bounded across the Thunderpath behind Needlepaw and followed her as she plunged deep into the network of Twoleg dens. *It's like she owns the place,* he thought. *How can she stand getting so close to Twolegs? They might even pick us up and stroke us!*

His whole body thrilled with tension as Needlepaw trotted up to a male Twoleg who was bathing a bright blue monster outside his den. Showing no fear at all, she rubbed up against the Twoleg's legs and let out a friendly little trill.

Before the Twoleg could make a grab, Alderpaw dashed up and gave Needlepaw a shove, pushing her until they were well away. "What are you *doing*? Do you want him to feed you to his monster?"

"Don't be stupid!" Needlepaw retorted. "Don't you know that if you cozy up to Twolegs they'll often give you a piece of meat or something else tasty? I do it all the time at the greenleaf Twolegplace on ShadowClan territory. Of course, it wouldn't work for *you*," she added, looking Alderpaw up and down. "It only works for cute cats."

"You've got bees in your brain," Alderpaw growled. "Just keep moving."

Looking smug, Needlepaw strode on again, her tail waving high in the air.

To Alderpaw's relief, as soon as they rounded the next corner, they spotted a kittypet: a large ginger tom stretched out lazily on top of a wall. "Hi! Hi there!" Needlepaw yowled as she charged up to him.

"Hi," the kittypet responded, startled out of his doze. "How can I help you?"

"We're Clan cats, and we're lost," Needlepaw explained. "We need to get back to our territories, and to do that we have to cross the river. Do you know the way?"

Alderpaw was surprised, and a little disturbed, that Needlepaw was giving the kittypet so much information. *We don't know this cat. But then,* he reassured himself, *he probably has no idea what she's meowing about.*

The ginger tom stretched his jaws in a huge yawn. "Do you

have anything to do with those three cats who were here at sunrise?" he asked.

"Three cats?" Alderpaw pressed forward urgently. "A cream-and-brown tom, a ginger she-cat, and a younger orange tabby?"

The kittypet nodded. "That's them. They were really upset. They said they'd lost two young cats."

Wonderful relief surged over Alderpaw. "Did they say where they were going?"

"You're the cats they lost, right?" The kittypet's eyes were full of sympathetic interest. "They were looking for a place to cross the river, too."

"And did you tell them?" Needlepaw asked.

"Right down there." The ginger tom pointed with his tail down a narrow alley that led between two rows of Twoleg dens. "That brings you back to the river. A little way downstream there's a bridge."

"A Twoleg bridge?" Alderpaw asked doubtfully.

"Of course a Twoleg bridge, mouse-brain!" Needlepaw gave Alderpaw an irritated shove. "We've dealt with those before. Thanks," she added, looking up at the kittypet again.

"Anytime," the kittypet responded with another yawn.

Alderpaw was beginning to turn away when another thought struck him. "You haven't seen another, bigger group of cats traveling through here?" he asked the kittypet. "It would have been a while ago now."

The kittypet shook his head. "Sorry, no."

So SkyClan didn't come this way. "Thanks anyway," Alderpaw mewed, his last hope dying of finding the lost Clan.

Again he was turning to leave, but Needlepaw didn't seem keen to follow. "Before we go," she began, "could you help us out with some food? We're really hungry."

"Sure." The ginger tom rose to his paws and stretched. "Follow the wall along to the opening. I'll meet you there." With that he leaped down from his perch and disappeared.

Needlepaw bounded eagerly alongside the wall, and Alderpaw followed reluctantly. The kittypet was waiting for them beside a piece of fence made of something shiny and hard, with wide gaps between the bars. Needlepaw and Alderpaw slipped through.

In front of them was a rough, pebbly surface, and beyond it a stretch of grass surrounded by bushes and bright Twoleg flowers. Beyond that rose the walls of the Twoleg den. Alderpaw's fur began to bristle at the thought of actually standing on Twoleg territory.

"The food's in here," the kittypet meowed, pointing with his tail.

Turning in that direction, Alderpaw's pelt bushed up in horror. The kittypet was pointing to a small den at the end of the pebbly path; a monster was crouching in the opening.

"You can't go in there!" he gasped to Needlepaw, who was already heading for the small den with the kittypet at her side.

"The monster's asleep," Needlepaw replied nonchalantly. "And to be honest—don't tell them back in camp—I'm kind of curious to taste kittypet food."

"But what if—" Alderpaw broke off as Needlepaw, ignoring him, disappeared into the monster's den with the kittypet.

He didn't attempt to follow. *No cat is going to catch me eating kittypet food!* Instead he kept watch, in case Twolegs appeared from the den or the monster showed signs of waking up. All the while he was tearing at the grass with his front claws, flexing them in and out with impatience. With every heartbeat they delayed here, his Clanmates were getting farther and farther away.

At last Needlepaw and the kittypet reappeared from the monster's den. Needlepaw was swiping her tongue around her jaws with satisfaction. "That was great!" she mewed. "Thanks, Bob."

Bob? Alderpaw thought. *The kittypet's name is Bob? Weird!*

"Yeah, thanks, Bob," he repeated. "You've been really helpful."

"Glad to," Bob responded, touching noses with Needlepaw. "Good luck on your journey."

Alderpaw headed off down the alley Bob had shown them earlier, and Needlepaw pattered along by his side. "You can thank me later," she mewed. "My idea totally worked! Now we know how to cross the river, and we can make our way back home." She paused for a moment, then added, "What's the matter with you now? Why don't you look happier?"

Alderpaw hoped he had managed to conceal the heavy weight that had been gathering inside him ever since Bob had told them that he hadn't seen any sign of SkyClan. But clearly it was impossible to hide anything from Needlepaw.

Halting, he turned toward her. "Don't you get it?" he asked bitterly. "It's because I've *failed*. What kind of a medicine cat am I?"

❧

CHAPTER 21

Needlepaw looked puzzled. "What do you mean?" she asked.

"You know what I mean!" Alderpaw tried to choke back his anger at Needlepaw's obtuseness. "SkyClan left the gorge after the rogues attacked them, and no cat seems to know where they went. We were supposed to save them! We just got there way too late!"

"How can you be sure?" Needlepaw asked, tilting her head to one side.

"Because the other Clans—our Clans—drove SkyClan out of the forest. That was so shameful, it's been kept a secret ever since. My visions were telling me to go to SkyClan and bring them back to share our territory by the lake—to *clear the sky*, like in the prophecy." Alderpaw's voice began to shake as he realized the depth of his failure. "I messed up! I didn't understand the first vision right away, and then Sandstorm died. . . . We got to the gorge too late. We couldn't find what lay in the shadows, because SkyClan had already left. Now the sky will never clear! Who *knows* what will happen to the Clans? And it's all because I'm a terrible medicine cat!"

He crouched down on the hard Twoleg path and rested his

nose on his paws, letting out a desolate whimper. It seemed there was nothing but darkness ahead of him.

Needlepaw said nothing, and when Alderpaw at last looked up again, she was sitting watching him with her tail curled neatly around her forepaws and a skeptical look on her face. "Are you done?" she asked.

Alderpaw flicked an ear, annoyed with Needlepaw and with himself for breaking down in front of her. "I guess so."

"You're being stupid and self-pitying." Needlepaw's tone was harsh. "It would have taken the rogues a long time to set up in SkyClan's old camp. And from the way you described Mistfeather, all ragged and skinny, the attack didn't happen just yesterday. With the timing of your visions, there's no way we could have made it to the gorge in time to save SkyClan."

Alderpaw took all that in, beginning to feel a tiny bit better. "So?" he mewed at last.

"So," Needlepaw responded, rising to her paws and heading off down the alley, "your visions must mean something else."

Alderpaw was silent for a moment, thinking everything over. At the end of the alley they spotted the bridge a little way downstream, where Bob had told them it was. To his relief, it wasn't a huge Thunderpath carrying monsters across the river, but a narrow, wooden structure, a bit like the half-bridges that jutted out into the lake. With no Twolegs in sight, it took only a couple of heartbeats for Alderpaw and Needlepaw to dart across.

On the opposite side of the river, a small stream trickled into the main current, tracking through long grasses with a belt of woodland beyond. Alderpaw's spirits rose as they headed into the trees, but he still couldn't stop worrying over the meaning of his quest.

He had to admit that what Needlepaw had said made sense. *But if my visions weren't leading me to SkyClan so I could save them, what were they doing?* It was hard for him to feel that anything had been accomplished on the journey. *We haven't saved any cats. We haven't embraced what we found in the shadows. We barely managed to survive ourselves. And we lost Sandstorm. Is there something else I should have done?*

Without guidance from StarClan, Alderpaw felt as helpless as a kit.

Together Alderpaw and Needlepaw trekked across open country for several sunrises, heading toward the setting sun. They crossed Thunderpaths, skirted Twolegplaces, and found their way through fields where strange animals cropped the grass and watched them curiously. Now, toward the end of another tough day, Alderpaw was weary and cold, tired of sleeping under bushes or in drafty hollows in the ground. He longed for his comfortable nest in the stone hollow.

At least my hunting skills have improved, he thought grimly. *It seems like all I needed was to go hungry a few times, to concentrate my mind on the prey just like Molewhisker wanted me to.*

From time to time, he and Needlepaw had picked up the scent of the other questing cats, which reassured them that they were going in the right direction. But each time they found the traces, they were fainter and staler, as if the others were moving faster and drawing farther ahead.

The daylight was dying, and gray clouds were massing overhead. A chilly wind blew across the grass, ruffling the cats' fur. Now and again Alderpaw felt the sharp sting of rain, and he guessed that a storm was coming.

That's all we need! he groaned inwardly.

Suddenly Needlepaw, a little way ahead, let out an excited cry and began racing forward.

"Wait! What's the matter?" Alderpaw called after her.

"It's the farm!" Needlepaw tossed the words over her shoulder. "The one we passed through on the way!"

Bounding after Needlepaw, Alderpaw spotted the shiny fence and the field where the tall, yellow-brown plants had grown. Now only spiky stubble remained, and there was no sign of the monster with the spinning jaws.

Needlepaw reached the fence and easily scrambled over it, then pelted onward toward the cluster of Twoleg dens.

"Wait! Come back!" Alderpaw yowled, but Needlepaw ignored him.

At the same moment the skies opened and rain cascaded down, drenching Alderpaw within heartbeats. He could barely see Needlepaw ahead of him through the driving screen of raindrops. When he reached the fence, the shiny strands were already so wet and slippery that it took all his concentration to clamber over.

A sharp pang stabbed through Alderpaw as he remembered Sandstorm. *This is where everything went wrong. This terrible sharp fence, and the sticky mud that made her wound worse. We must have passed her grave on the way without even realizing it. Oh, Sandstorm, I'm sorry. . . .*

Landing awkwardly on the other side, Alderpaw pushed aside his memories and managed to spot Needlepaw, still heading toward the center of the farm. "Stop! Come back!" he called again, but if she heard him, she paid no attention.

"Fox dung!" Alderpaw snarled. He knew that the sensible thing to do was to leave the farm, shelter under some trees until the storm was over, and then work out the best way to go. But he felt he had no choice now but to follow Needlepaw.

She ran past the cluster of Twoleg dens and headed into the field with the big yellow barn. Wide wooden doors barred the entrance, but there was a gap at the bottom, and Needlepaw managed to squeeze through. Growling with annoyance, Alderpaw flattened himself to the muddy ground and dragged himself through after her, the bottom of the door scraping his back fur.

Staggering to his paws, Alderpaw looked around. The huge barn was divided into sections by wooden barriers, and he stiffened when he saw that horses were standing in two of them.

"Needlepaw, watch out!" he called, then realized that long tendrils were tethering the horses in place. *Thank StarClan! There's no way they can get at us!*

Needlepaw ran into one of the empty sections, then popped her head out and beckoned Alderpaw with a flick of her ears. "Come on, mouse-brain!"

Alderpaw followed her. Inside the section, the barn floor

was covered by dry stalks that reminded him of the yellow-brown plants in the field. A warm animal smell filled the air; the scent of horses was strongest, but Alderpaw detected mice too.

"Why did you come in here?" he asked Needlepaw, anger still surging inside him. "Haven't you learned anything? Twolegs are dangerous!"

Needlepaw settled down among the spiky stalks and began to groom herself. "I'd never want to live with Twolegs," she mewed between strokes of her tongue, "but they do have nice warm dens, and loads of food. Would you *really* rather be outside in the rain right now?"

Listening to the rain battering down on the roof, Alderpaw had to admit that the annoying she-cat had a point. Letting out a sigh, he sank down into the stalks beside her.

"We can leave when the rain stops," Needlepaw pointed out. "For now, we've got a safe place to rest and plenty of mice to eat."

Abandoning her grooming, she sprang to her paws and dived into a heap of stalks. Heartbeats later she emerged again with bits of the stalks all over her fur and the body of a plump mouse gripped firmly in her jaws.

"This is for you," she meowed, dropping the prey in front of Alderpaw. "Just to say sorry for not listening to you out in the rain."

When did Needlepaw ever listen to any cat? Alderpaw reflected, shaking his head. "Thanks," he told her, and sank his teeth into the warm prey.

Needlepaw caught another mouse for herself and settled down to eat it beside Alderpaw. Gradually Alderpaw managed to relax. The warmth, his full belly, and the repetitive sound of the rain outside soon lulled him into sleep.

"It's good to see you."

Alderpaw opened his eyes, aware at first of the glimmer of starlight on the surface of a pool and the soft plashing of water. Leaping to his paws, his heart beating wildly, he realized that he was standing beside the Moonpool. Sandstorm stood beside him, her pale ginger pelt glowing with a frosty light and the sparkle of stars at her paws. She was purring, and her green eyes shone with love for Alderpaw.

"Sandstorm!" Alderpaw breathed out. "I'm so happy to see you."

As Sandstorm bent her head to touch her nose to his ear, Alderpaw couldn't help turning away.

"It wasn't your fault," Sandstorm told him gently, as if she could hear his thoughts. "It was my time to go. I sensed when I decided to go with you to search for SkyClan that I might not survive the journey. You know," she added, her voice growing softer, "I never wanted to spend my last days as an elder, sitting around in camp. I wanted to die doing something important . . . and your quest gave me the chance to relive a special memory with Firestar."

"Are you and Firestar together now, in StarClan?" Alderpaw asked.

"Yes, we are," Sandstorm purred. She sat down at the edge

of the Moonpool and beckoned with her tail for Alderpaw to join her. "Now," she continued, "tell me how your journey has gone. What have you learned?"

Frustration welled up inside Alderpaw. "It's been terrible!" he burst out. "I don't think I've learned anything at all."

When Sandstorm only waited, her green gaze fixed on him, he began to pour out the story of everything that had happened since she died: finding Darktail and his cats in the gorge; discovering that they weren't the real SkyClan, and that SkyClan had been driven out; trying to decide what to do, then escaping from the camp and being washed downriver with Needlepaw. "Please tell me what to do now!" he finished.

When Sandstorm did not respond, Alderpaw let his head droop wretchedly. "I know I've made a complete mess of everything."

"How?" Sandstorm asked.

Alderpaw thought that was obvious. "I didn't get there in time! If we were meant to save SkyClan to 'clear the sky,' now no cat can do that. I led every cat on this quest into great danger, and what have we accomplished? Nothing! I've failed."

Unable even to look at Sandstorm anymore, he let out a despairing whimper. A moment later, he felt her nuzzle his neck, and a sense of comfort spread through his whole body. He managed to look up.

"Do you know the difference between you and Sparkpaw?" Sandstorm asked.

Alderpaw couldn't see the point of the question. "What?"

"Sparkpaw believes she's solved every problem," Sandstorm

replied, affection glimmering in her eyes. "And you believe you've caused every problem. You're two sides of the same leaf. But you haven't caused this problem," she went on. "You have not failed. And it is not too late to fulfill the quest. It will merely require a different path."

"What do you mean?" Alderpaw asked, but even as he spoke the words, he felt himself being shaken. The starshine on the surface of the Moonpool began to fade, and Sandstorm's shape faded with it. "Wait!" Alderpaw exclaimed in alarm. "What different path?"

But he was already waking, to find Needlepaw shaking his shoulder. "It's stopped raining," she meowed. "I thought you'd want to know, since you're so eager to get home."

Groggily Alderpaw sat up. "Yes, let's go home," he murmured. *But,* he added silently to himself, *we'll need to follow a different path.* . . .

CHAPTER 22

♣

Alderpaw and Needlepaw were approaching the first Thunderpath they had crossed after they left their territories so many days ago. Tired and sore-pawed, Alderpaw was struggling with mixed feelings at the thought of being so close to home.

"I can't wait to get back to ShadowClan territory," Needlepaw mewed as she trotted along at his side. "I've missed my den so much, and—"

"Won't you be in trouble with your Clan?" Alderpaw asked. "What's your mentor going to say? Apprentices aren't supposed to leave without permission."

"I left *in service* of my Clan, remember?" Needlepaw replied. "Because I knew you sneaky ThunderClan cats were going in search of *what you find in the shadows*. Besides," she added airily, "no cat ever *really* gets in trouble in ShadowClan. Sure, the older cats will yowl and stomp a bit, but what can they . . ."

Her voice trailed off as they drew close to the Thunderpath and halted at the sight of glittering monsters flashing past in both directions.

Alderpaw wasn't really listening to her anymore. He stood still, staring thoughtfully into the distance.

After a moment Needlepaw prodded him. "What are you doing?"

"Thinking."

Needlepaw gave an exasperated snort. "Thinking about *what*?"

"I'm *not* looking forward to getting home," Alderpaw replied with a sigh. "Because that means the quest will be over. And I still don't know what it was about."

"It was about embracing what you find in the shadows, right? And we didn't find it, but we found out a lot about it. You don't have to stand here moping over it. Why can't we just go?"

"Because I feel there's more I should be doing." Reluctantly Alderpaw admitted to himself that he would have to tell Needlepaw about Sandstorm visiting him when he was sleeping in the Twoleg barn. He had tried hard to work out what the starry warrior had meant by "a different path," but with the last paw steps of their quest ahead of him he had still not found understanding. "I had a dream . . . ," he began.

Needlepaw's eyes widened as he revealed to her what Sandstorm had said. "Why didn't you tell me earlier?" she asked.

Alderpaw shrugged awkwardly. "It was *my* vision. I wanted to figure it out by myself."

"After all we've been through," Needlepaw responded with an exaggerated sigh, "you should realize that you need me! Hmm . . . ," she mused, glancing around her. "A different path . . ."

"I don't think Sandstorm meant a *literal* different path,"

Alderpaw meowed. "Just a different way of thinking. Like—"

But Needlepaw wasn't paying attention. "Look!" she cried, dodging away from the Thunderpath.

Alderpaw watched as she bounded down a dip in the grass beside the edge of the black surface. It led to a tunnel opening, its mouth covered by bars of hard Twoleg stuff that were set wide enough for a cat to slip between them. A musty, damp scent flowed out of the opening.

"What are you doing?" Alderpaw demanded as he trailed after Needlepaw. "That looks dangerous."

Needlepaw turned back to him, rolling her eyes. "Have you got bees in your brain, or what? Look, we came *over* the Thunderpath, and now here's a 'different path' that leads *under* it. Plus it's all in shadow! We can go this way!"

"You're the one with bees in your brain!" Alderpaw retorted. "I doubt StarClan just wanted us to go through a tunnel! It's dark in there, and it smells weird. There could be anything lurking inside. *And* I can see water in the bottom of it."

But there was no point in arguing. Needlepaw was already wriggling through the bars. "You *never* listen to me!" Alderpaw groaned, but the she-cat took no notice.

Alderpaw sighed, glancing from the Thunderpath to the tunnel and back again. The Thunderpath wasn't as crowded with monsters as when they had crossed it before. He could ignore Needlepaw, head over the Thunderpath, and let her fend for herself. *After all, she's not a part of my Clan. She's not even supposed to be on this quest.* But even while the arguments passed through his head, he knew there was no point to them. He was following Needlepaw into the tunnel.

The stench caught him in the throat as he squeezed through the bars, and it was hard to stop himself from retching. Alderpaw picked his way carefully through the water, then realized that there was a higher area to one side, where he could scramble up and keep his paws dry.

The tunnel was full of shadows, but once Alderpaw's eyes adjusted to it, he realized there was a little light filtering in from the entrance behind him, and the glow of the gap on the other side. He could see Needlepaw's figure, dark against the distant outlet, bounding along ahead of him.

"I wonder where Sandstorm would want us to go next," she meowed, her voice echoing strangely in the tunnel. "What's most *different*? Maybe we shouldn't even head back the way we came anymore. What if we went in another direction?" she continued, halting and half turning back toward Alderpaw. "We could loop all the way around Clan territory and come in through ShadowClan. Or maybe head the other way around the lake, through RiverClan. I've only been on RiverClan territory once," she added reflectively, "and they caught me and sent me home with a scolding."

Alderpaw shook his head. "You're mouse-brained!" he responded.

Needlepaw turned to go on, and Alderpaw was about to follow, when he heard a soft cry coming from farther into the darkness, right against the wall of the tunnel. He froze, his ears pricked, and when the cry came again, he carefully padded toward it.

In the dim light Alderpaw could just make out a nest of moss and dry leaves, with something squirming inside it. At first he pulled back sharply; then he leaned forward again with a gasp of shock as his nose picked up the familiar milky scent of kits. A tiny black-and-white kit was lying in the nest, with a tiny gray one beside it, their colors hardly visible in the darkness.

The kits seemed to sense Alderpaw's presence, and they craned toward him, their eyes tight shut, their pink mouths open to let out high-pitched mews.

"What's the matter?" Needlepaw was bounding back down the tunnel toward Alderpaw. "Why are you—" She skidded to a halt as she spotted the nest.

"They're—" Alderpaw began.

"They're *kits!*" Needlepaw shook her head in disbelief. "Where's their mother?" she asked, glancing around. "Their eyes aren't even open yet. They can only be a few days old."

"And they're so thin," Alderpaw added. "I can tell they haven't eaten in a while."

"I'll go and look for their mother." Needlepaw bounded to the other end of the tunnel and wriggled out through the bars. Alderpaw could hear her calling outside.

Alderpaw stooped over the nest and examined the kits more closely. Both of them were she-kits, and under their fur they seemed to be just skin and bone.

"Hey, Needlepaw!" he yowled. "Forget their mother for now. These kits need to eat. Catch something, right away!"

"Okay!" Needlepaw yowled back. A few heartbeats later

she slid through the bars again and bounded along the tunnel again to join Alderpaw. She was gripping a fat vole in her jaws.

"That was quick!" Alderpaw mewed admiringly. "Now we chew up the meat and feed it to the kits."

When they had chewed some of the fresh-kill into a pulp, Alderpaw gently opened the gray kit's mouth and dropped the pulp in. The kit choked, spitting the meat out again.

"Oh, mouse dung!" Needlepaw sighed. "They're not used to eating this stuff yet. They need milk."

"Well, unless you have any, we have to keep trying with the vole," Alderpaw meowed determinedly.

He dropped more pulp into the kit's mouth, then massaged her throat so that she would swallow. The kit began choking again, but after a moment the chewed-up vole disappeared, and she began wailing for more.

"Thank StarClan!" Alderpaw exclaimed.

Needlepaw began to feed the black-and-white kit, and soon both tiny creatures were sucking eagerly at the pulp, desperate to fill their bellies.

"They would have starved without us," Needlepaw murmured, sounding unusually gentle as she blinked affectionately at her kit.

Unexpected warmth spread through Alderpaw. *I might have failed in my quest, but at least we saved these kits.*

"Now we need to get them warm," he mewed, when finally the kits stopped eating, their little bellies distended. They were already cuddling up to him and Needlepaw, drawn by the heat of their bodies. "Ow!" Alderpaw yelped as the gray kit batted him on the nose. "Your claws are sharp!"

He began to lick the gray kit, his tongue stroking backward from tail to head, to get her blood flowing. Needlepaw did the same for the black-and-white kit. Soon both kits were purring and sinking into sleep.

"It's a good thing we found them when we did," Alderpaw told Needlepaw. "I don't think they would have survived out here much longer."

Needlepaw murmured agreement. "I wonder what happened to their mother. Do you think a monster got her on the Thunderpath?"

Alderpaw shuddered at the idea. "I'm not sure. But I think we should bring these kits back to camp, where they can be cared for."

"Great idea," Needlepaw meowed. "And I think we should give them names. How about Violetkit for this little one?" she continued, stroking the black-and-white kit's head with the tip of her tail. "I'm picking up the scent of violets; I think their mother must have used some of the leaves for the nest."

"That's a good name," Alderpaw purred. "And I'm going to call this little one . . . Twigkit. She's as tiny as a twig!"

Needlepaw let out a *mrrow* of laughter. "Twigkit it is!"

As they rose, preparing to pick up the sleeping kits by their scruff, Needlepaw turned to Alderpaw with a smirk on her face. "When are you going to thank me for leading you into the tunnel?" she asked.

Alderpaw, still concentrating on the kits, gave her a confused stare. "What are you talking about?"

"Isn't it obvious?" Needlepaw looked even more smug. "These kits are *what you find in the shadows!*"

CHAPTER 23

❧

Alderpaw stood on the ridge, a stiff breeze ruffling his fur, and looked down the slope to where the lake lay glittering in the morning sunshine. He was gripping Twigkit's scruff in his mouth; the tiny kit was waving her paws around and letting out high-pitched squeaks. Alderpaw gently set her down in the rough grass.

"We're almost home!" he breathed out.

After they'd left the tunnel, he and Needlepaw had journeyed on until night fell, when they'd made a temporary den near the place where they had seen the Twolegs and eaten their food. Needlepaw had caught a couple of mice, and they had fed the kits again. Now the woods and moorland around the lake stretched in front of them, and before sunhigh they would be back in their own camps.

Needlepaw toiled up to the ridge and stood beside him, letting Violetkit down into the grass next to her sister. "Made it!" she panted.

"I guess we ought to say good-bye," Alderpaw began, feeling slightly awkward. "You'll want to go through RiverClan to get back to your territory—it's the quickest way."

"Yeah, I suppose so," Needlepaw agreed.

"Uh . . . Needlepaw . . ." Feeling even more awkward, Alderpaw turned to face her. "Maybe you could keep quiet about what happened in the gorge, at least until I've had the chance to talk to Bramblestar. I told you, the whole SkyClan thing is kind of a secret."

He cringed inwardly as he spoke, knowing how unlikely it was that Needlepaw would keep a secret to oblige a Thunder-Clan cat. He expected her to hiss at him in anger, but she simply stared at him, her mouth clamped shut.

"Okay, then." Alderpaw realized the best he could hope for was a quick getaway. "If you could just help me get Violetkit onto my back . . ."

Needlepaw's jaws gaped open at that. "What are you talking about?" she demanded. "I'm not leaving the shadow kits here. I helped find them! And which cat says that they're going to ThunderClan?"

Alderpaw could hardly believe what he was hearing. *She has got bees in her brain!* "If it weren't for my dream, and what Sandstorm told me, we never would have found the kits!"

Needlepaw's neck fur began to rise and she flattened her ears. "If it weren't for me," she pointed out, "and my idea to go through the tunnel, you would still be standing in front of that stupid Thunderpath trying to figure out what different *way of thinking* Sandstorm was meowing about. Are you kidding me?"

Alderpaw felt his own pelt bristling as anger swelled up inside him. "Are you kidding *me*?" he hissed. Part of him knew that he was wrong to let his fury out on Needlepaw, but he felt so frustrated that he couldn't help it. "This was my quest in the first place! Besides, do you really think I'd let you take the kits back to ShadowClan, where there aren't any rules, and apprentices run around thinking up new ways to break the warrior code? I might as well just take them back to the rogues in the gorge."

"Coward!" Needlepaw spat, her face full of disgust. "We never would have made it back here if we hadn't broken the warrior code a few times at least. Alderpaw, you're so blinded by rules that you can't see what's in front of your own nose!"

Alderpaw couldn't reply; the mewling of the kits was all that broke the silence. He and Needlepaw looked down at the squirming bundles of fur, and Alderpaw found his concern for them overpowering his anger at Needlepaw. He could see the same feeling in her green eyes.

"There's one fair way to resolve this," she mewed after a few moments. "We divide the kits up, and each take one back to our own Clan."

Alderpaw looked down at the kits, snuggled up together and mewling. An ache tugged at his heart. "We can't do that," he responded. "It would be wrong. Don't you see, Needlepaw? These kits only have each other now. It's like me and Sparkpaw: I don't always agree with her, but I can't imagine life without her."

Needlepaw was silent, gazing down at the kits. *I wonder if she has any cat she cares about as much as Sparkpaw and I care for each other,* Alderpaw thought.

Then, as Alderpaw kept watching Needlepaw and the kits, he was distracted by the yowling of a cat from farther down the slope. Instinctively he and Needlepaw moved in front of the kits to guard them. But when Alderpaw looked down and spotted the cat, he let out a yelp of delight.

"Molewhisker!"

His former mentor was bounding up the slope, with three other ThunderClan cats close behind him: Birchfall, Poppy-frost, and Berrynose. Alderpaw dashed down to meet them beside the horseplace fence.

Molewhisker's eyes were wide with shock and delight. "Oh, thank StarClan you're alive!" he exclaimed.

"So are you!" Alderpaw felt so light with relief that he could almost imagine floating away. "Are Cherryfall and Sparkpaw okay?"

"Yes, everyone's fine," Molewhisker assured him. "We got back to camp yesterday and told the others what happened. Every cat was devastated to think that you had drowned. We looked for you and Needlepaw back beside the river, but we couldn't find you."

"So this morning," Birchfall meowed, coming to stand beside Alderpaw, "Bramblestar sent us out as a search party, with Molewhisker to guide us back to the place where you went missing."

"However did you survive?" Poppyfrost asked, gazing at Alderpaw as if she couldn't quite believe he was there.

"Needlepaw helped me out of the river," Alderpaw replied. "She's here too, just a bit farther up the hill."

He began to retrace his paw steps, leading the other cats back to the ridge where he had left Needlepaw.

"Hi," the ShadowClan she-cat mewed as the ThunderClan patrol came up to her. "As you see, we've brought company." With one paw she swept the grasses aside to reveal the two kits, now dozing in a mound of fur.

Molewhisker and the others, murmuring in surprise, surrounded the kits and gazed down at them.

"They're adorable!" Poppyfrost exclaimed.

"Who are they?" Berrynose asked, giving them a suspicious sniff. "Where did you find them?"

"I can tell you all that later," Alderpaw replied, "but right now the kits need care. They're not well, so we were going to take them back to the ThunderClan camp to nurse them back to health."

Needlepaw glared at him. "Actually—"

"That's a good idea." Birchfall spoke with authority; clearly he was the leader of the search party. "Alderpaw, you're a medicine cat yourself, so you can help watch over them."

"But I found the kits too," Needlepaw objected, her shoulder fur beginning to rise again. "That is, we found them together. We think maybe the kits are . . . well, they're what StarClan wanted us to find."

The ThunderClan patrol exchanged surprised glances. "Do you believe that?" Birchfall asked Alderpaw.

"I think they *could* be," Alderpaw replied, "but I'm not sure yet."

"Then this is what we'll do," Birchfall decided. "We'll take the kits back to ThunderClan now, so that they can be cared for, and then—"

"They can be cared for just as well in ShadowClan," Needlepaw interrupted.

Can they? Alderpaw wondered. *ThunderClan has two medicine cats—three if you count me—while ShadowClan only has Littlecloud, and he's growing old.*

Birchfall gave Needlepaw a quelling look, as if he wasn't used to apprentices who argued all the time. "Let me finish," he meowed. "The next Gathering is in a few days, and we can bring the kits there to decide what will be done with them. Is that okay, Needlepaw? After all, we can all agree that what's most important is to get the kits well again."

Needlepaw ducked her head. "Okay," she muttered.

Alderpaw noticed that she looked almost chastened by Birchfall's decisive tones. *Well, I've never seen that before!*

"Are you okay getting back to the ShadowClan camp?" Birchfall continued to Needlepaw. "Should you even be out on your own?"

"I'll be fine, thanks," Needlepaw responded with a roll of her eyes. Clearly she was fed up with that question, and her respectful demeanor hadn't lasted long. Turning to Alderpaw, she added, "I guess I'll see you around, then."

Alderpaw stared at her, wondering if she had even taken in what he said about keeping SkyClan a secret. "I'll look out for you at the Gathering," he meowed.

As Needlepaw turned away, Alderpaw felt a claw-scratch of pain at his heart. *After all we've been through together, there should be . . . I dunno, more . . .*

He thought that Needlepaw looked sad, too, as she gave him a last look before bounding away down the slope in the direction of RiverClan.

Then, as he watched her, Poppyfrost brushed her pelt against his, her eyes glowing with admiration. "You've done so well, Alderpaw!"

"Yes, ThunderClan will be proud of you," Molewhisker told him. "And I can't wait to hear what Cherryfall says when she sees the kits!"

While Birchfall and Berrynose congratulated him, too, Alderpaw felt his chest swell with pride. *I feel like a hero! Oh, StarClan, it's so good to be home!*

CHAPTER 24

Alderpaw poked his head through the entrance to the nursery. "Is it okay to come in?" he called softly.

"Sure!" Lilyheart called back. "But watch where you're putting your paws."

As Alderpaw became used to the dim light of the nursery, he could see why Lilyheart had told him to be careful. Her own three kits, Leafkit, Larkkit, and Honeykit, were rolling around, play fighting on the thick moss and bracken that covered the nursery floor. Violetkit and Twigkit, their eyes open now, sat watching them.

"That's how you learn to fight when you're an apprentice," Leafkit told the younger kits, sitting up and shaking scraps of moss from her tortoiseshell pelt.

"What's an apprentice?" Twigkit asked.

"It's when you're six moons old and have a mentor, and learn how to become a warrior," Larkkit replied.

"And then you get to fight foxes and badgers and rival cats," Honeykit added. She leaped on top of her brother, growling fiercely. "Get out of our camp, stinky badger!"

"Stinky yourself!" Larkkit retorted, battering his sister with his hind paws.

Alderpaw skirted the battling kits and settled down in the moss beside Lilyheart. "You've got your paws full here," he mewed.

"I know, but I like it," Lilyheart purred. "I have Daisy to help. She's out hunting fresh-kill for us right now."

"That's great," Alderpaw mewed. "So how are you two doing?" he asked, stretching out his neck to touch noses with Violetkit and then Twigkit.

"We're fine, thank you," Violetkit replied.

Alderpaw could see that she was right. There was no need to worry about the kits' health anymore. In the few days they had been in camp, their little bodies had begun to plump up, and their fur was glossy. Their eyes were open now, wide and bright.

"It's so nice here with our mother," Twigkit added, leaning closer to Lilyheart.

"She's not your mother!" Leafkit piped up before Alderpaw or Lilyheart could respond. "She's *our* mother. You came from a long way away—beyond the lake, even."

The two younger kits glanced at each other, confused and a little hurt.

"Don't worry, little ones," Lilyheart mewed, bending her head to lick each kit around the ears. "I love you just as much as if I were your real mother."

"That's right," Alderpaw agreed, nuzzling the kits affectionately. "All you need to know is that you're very special."

Reassured, the two kits began to purr contentedly. For a moment Alderpaw gave himself up to the satisfaction of having saved them, whatever that might mean.

"They're lovely," Lilyheart meowed. "I'd be happy to keep them as part of my family. And my kits love them, too!"

Alderpaw nodded, but he knew that the real decision about the kits' future would be made at the Gathering that night. *I hope they'll be allowed to stay here,* he thought, realizing how attached to them he had become. *But that's not for me to decide.*

Emerging from the nursery, Alderpaw almost slammed into Jayfeather.

"There you are!" Jayfeather exclaimed crossly. "I've been looking everywhere for you."

"I've been to visit the kits," Alderpaw explained.

Jayfeather let out a snort. "I should have known. Anyway, you need to come with me. Bramblestar and Leafpool want to talk to you."

There had been a time when Alderpaw would have been worried by a summons from his Clan leader. Now, although he still felt slightly nervous, anticipation was stirring inside him.

As he followed Jayfeather, Alderpaw remembered his return to camp a few days before. All his Clan had been excited to welcome him back, and Sparkpaw had barely left his side since. This morning was her first hunting patrol without him, along with Cherryfall, Brackenfur, and Sorrelstripe.

Bramblestar had taken the first opportunity to draw

Alderpaw aside and ask for his view of what had happened in the gorge.

"It was so frustrating!" Alderpaw admitted. "We should have gotten there in time to save SkyClan from the rogues. I feel like I've failed."

Bramblestar rested his tail-tip briefly on Alderpaw's shoulder. "I'm puzzled," he confessed. "Why should StarClan send you a vision when it was already too late to do anything about it? But it wasn't your failure," he added hastily.

Alderpaw shrugged uneasily. "I feel like I've missed something important. . . . I feel like Sandstorm died for nothing, and it was my fault."

"You are not to blame for Sandstorm's death," Bramblestar assured him firmly. "I grieve for her, and so does the rest of our Clan. But going on the quest was what Sandstorm wanted. Remember how I tried to forbid her from going? She was determined, and you would never have convinced her otherwise."

"I guess so . . . ," Alderpaw mewed, though he still couldn't suppress his feelings of guilt.

"Meanwhile," Bramblestar meowed, changing the subject, "I've spoken to Molewhisker, Cherryfall, and Sparkpaw about keeping SkyClan a secret, at least for now."

"I hope it was okay to tell them . . . ," Alderpaw began apologetically, remembering once again that Needlepaw shared the secret, too.

"It's fine. You didn't have much choice."

"So what are we going to do about SkyClan, or what remains

of it?" Alderpaw asked, relieved by his father's approval. "And what about those horrible rogues in the gorge?"

"I've thought it over," Bramblestar replied, his amber gaze fixed on Alderpaw, "and I've come to the conclusion that there's nothing ThunderClan can do for SkyClan now."

"But—" Alderpaw began to protest.

Bramblestar overrode him. "SkyClan has scattered, and no cat knows where they have gone. Unless ThunderClan gets more information . . ."

Alderpaw felt the weight of his Clan leader's stare. *He means another vision.* Anxiety rose inside him like a gathering storm cloud. *Will I have one? What if I don't?*

"I told the rest of the Clan that you reached the place you saw in your vision," Bramblestar continued briskly, "but you found nothing there. That should be enough to keep Sky-Clan a secret until we get a stronger sign from StarClan. At least . . ." He hesitated. "What about Needlepaw?"

"I asked her to keep the secret," Alderpaw replied, "but I don't know whether she will."

Bramblestar nodded thoughtfully. "Well, it's the best we can do for now," he decided at last. "We'll discuss the kits later, with Leafpool and Jayfeather," he finished.

Thinking back to that earlier meeting, Alderpaw assumed that now he was being summoned to talk about Twigkit and Violetkit. *I hope they can stay with us,* he thought.

Jayfeather climbed up the tumbled rocks, neat-pawed and as confident as if he could see. Alderpaw scrambled up after him and found Leafpool and Squirrelflight already waiting with Bramblestar in his den on the Highledge.

"Good, you're here," Bramblestar meowed, sweeping his tail affectionately along Alderpaw's back, as if he was still amazed that his son was alive after all. "Have you recovered from your journey yet?"

"Yes, I'm fine," Alderpaw replied.

"Then we need to talk about the future," Bramblestar announced. "Most urgently, about Twigkit and Violetkit." With a wave of his tail, he invited the other cats to sit down. "Alderpaw, tell us what you know."

Alderpaw stayed on his paws as he described how Sandstorm had come to him in a dream, and given him the clue that allowed him and Needlepaw to find the kits in the tunnel.

"Needlepaw really helped?" Squirrelflight asked, sounding surprised.

"Oh, yes. It was her idea to go through the tunnel. And she helped me bring the kits back to the lake, and helped feed and care for them, too. She was really gentle with them."

"So the question remains about what to do with them now," Bramblestar continued. "Leafpool, Jayfeather, do you think that they could be 'what you find in the shadows,' according to the prophecy?"

Jayfeather wriggled his shoulders as if he felt uncomfortable in his pelt. "I'm not sure. It feels too simple. Maybe they're just a pair of abandoned kits. Their mother was probably killed on the Thunderpath, or maybe a fox got her."

"But Sandstorm told Alderpaw there was still time to succeed on his quest," Leafpool pointed out, her eyes briefly shadowed as she named her dead mother. "And then she told him how to find the kits. I think they could well be 'what you find in the shadows,' and if we embrace them, the 'sky will clear.'"

"Alderpaw, what do you think?" Squirrelflight asked.

Alderpaw blinked nervously at being put on the spot. "They *could* be," he replied, "but I think it's too soon to be sure. We'll know more when the kits grow older."

"Well said," Bramblestar mewed approvingly. "And that means we shouldn't give the kits up."

Jayfeather let out a snort. "I can't see ShadowClan agreeing to *that*! And much as I hate to admit it, they have a point. As Alderpaw tells it, Needlepaw was at least half responsible for finding the kits, and so ShadowClan has a claim on them."

"That may be true," Bramblestar agreed with a sigh, "but we'll wait and see what's said at the Gathering."

"We know what ShadowClan will say." Jayfeather twitched his whiskers. "Even though the last thing Rowanstar needs is two more young cats to keep track of."

Bramblestar let out a rumble of amusement from deep in his chest.

Alderpaw couldn't share it. The mention of ShadowClan had made him think of Needlepaw. . . .

A chilly wind ruffled the surface of the lake, breaking up the reflection of the full moon, which floated serenely in the sky above. Branches creaked and rustled in the blast, and dead leaves whirled through the air.

Alderpaw fluffed out his fur against the cold as he padded along the lakeshore with his Clanmates. Violetkit rode on his back, her tiny claws digging deep into his pelt. Beside him, Sparkpaw was carrying Twigkit.

"I don't think RiverClan and WindClan know anything about our quest to find SkyClan, or 'what you find in the shadows,'" she meowed to Alderpaw. "Won't they be surprised! I mean, that we found what lies in the shadows, anyway. They'll be furious enough to claw their own ears off when they discover that a ThunderClan cat found it."

"But Bramblestar isn't completely sure the prophecy refers to these kits," Alderpaw pointed out mildly.

"You mean he won't say," Sparkpaw responded. She gave an excited bounce, nearly dislodging Twigkit, who let out a squeak of alarm. "Oops, sorry, Twigkit. Anyway," Sparkpaw continued, "the kits totally are what you find in the shadows, and you'd have to be the stupidest furball in the forest not to know it!"

Alderpaw blinked contentedly and let her chatter on as they splashed through the stream and followed Bramblestar and the senior warriors alongside the lake through WindClan territory. It was good to be with Sparkpaw again and to bask in her cheerful confidence, after all the dangers they had suffered.

They were drawing near to the edge of WindClan territory when Alderpaw spotted Onestar and his cats streaming down the hillside and heading around the lake ahead of them, past the horseplace.

"Who are all those cats?" Violetkit asked, sounding nervous.

"Oh, that's WindClan," Alderpaw replied.

"Has no cat told you about the Clans?" Sparkpaw asked. "They should have! Honestly . . . Well," she went on, obviously delighted to show off her knowledge to the kits, "there are four Clans around the lake. We're ThunderClan—we're the best! Those skinny rabbit-chasers up ahead are WindClan, and then there's RiverClan and ShadowClan. You'll meet cats from all of them tonight."

"Yes, all the Clans meet at the full moon. It's called the Gathering," Alderpaw added. "On that island in the lake— can you see it?" He waved his tail toward the dark bulk of the island.

"I'm scared!" Twigkit mewed. "I don't want to meet so many cats."

"There's nothing to be scared of," Sparkpaw told her briskly. "Cats never fight at a Gathering. In fact, you're both very lucky. Kits aren't usually allowed to go to Gatherings. You're only here because you're special."

"Think what you'll have to tell Leafkit, Larkkit, and Honeykit when you get home," Alderpaw meowed. *If you get home,* he added silently.

Twigkit and Violetkit clung on tightly as Alderpaw and Sparkpaw carried them across the tree-bridge to the island. Pushing through the bushes to reach the clearing around the Great Oak, Alderpaw saw the open space filled with cats. The scents of the other three Clans hung heavily in the air, and he realized that ThunderClan was the last Clan to arrive.

He and Sparkpaw settled down with the kits in the shelter of a bush at the edge of the clearing, while the kits gazed around with huge eyes.

"I didn't think there were so many cats in the world!" Violetkit mewed.

Almost at once Alderpaw spotted Needlepaw at the far side of the clearing beyond the Great Oak. Her eyes widened at the sight of Alderpaw with the kits.

Alderpaw expected her to cross the clearing to meet him, but she didn't move until a white ShadowClan tom padded up to her. Needlepaw exchanged a few words with him, then turned her back on Alderpaw and walked away with the tom at her side. Alderpaw lost sight of her in the crowd.

An odd, empty feeling gathered in Alderpaw's belly. He was happy to be back with his own Clan, especially when his Clanmates were so pleased with him, but he still felt bad about the way Needlepaw had gone home alone without much of a farewell. He was nervous, too, about what she might have told her Clanmates about SkyClan. Part of him wanted to bound across the clearing and find her, but he knew that for now his place was with the kits. And when the final decision was made about their future, he and Needlepaw would be rivals.

Alderpaw realized that while these thoughts had been passing through his mind, the four leaders had leaped up into the branches of the Great Oak. The deputies had gathered on the roots, while the medicine cats sat nearby. Gradually silence fell over the cats in the clearing.

"I'll begin, shall I?" Mistystar began when she had greeted the Clans. "Prey has been plentiful in RiverClan, and—"

She broke off with an annoyed look as Rowanstar interrupted by rising to his paws and pacing to the end of his branch.

"Why are we acting like this is a typical Gathering?" the ShadowClan leader demanded. "I know that Bramblestar has news to share—don't you?" he added, turning to face the ThunderClan leader and giving him a hard stare.

Bramblestar froze for a moment. Alderpaw knew what he must be thinking, and he felt the same flare of panic. *Did Needlepaw tell Rowanstar about SkyClan?*

"News that might relate to the prophecy? Maybe about some young cats?" Rowanstar continued, his voice heavily sarcastic. "*Surely* you want to tell us all about that."

Alderpaw drew a long breath of relief. *She didn't give away the secret.*

Clearing his throat, Bramblestar rose to his paws. "Yes, there is news," he meowed, raising his voice so that every cat in the clearing could hear him. "But I'm not sure that it relates to the prophecy. Our medicine-cat apprentice, Alderpaw, went on a quest to find what lies in the shadows. Sadly, our wise elder Sandstorm died on that quest, and her whole Clan grieves for her. But on his way home, Alderpaw found those two kits"—Bramblestar pointed with his tail—"just outside our territories."

Alderpaw realized that every cat was staring at him and the two kits with him and Sparkpaw. He wanted to hide under the nearest bush, but he made himself sit still and meet the curiosity with a calm gaze.

"I don't think that's quite right, Bramblestar," Rowanstar went on. "Don't you mean that Alderpaw and Needlepaw found the kits, working together? Didn't Needlepaw save Alderpaw's life on the quest, helping him to shore when he was drowning?"

Bramblestar dipped his head. "Yes, that's true. But what was Needlepaw doing there in the first place? Is it normal for ShadowClan apprentices to wander off by themselves?"

"That's not your concern," Rowanstar snapped; Alderpaw could see he was embarrassed by the question. "ShadowClan can look after its own apprentices, thank you very much. What's important is that ThunderClan did not find these kits without help. And what I understand," he added, twitching his whiskers, "is that the kits were brought to ThunderClan for urgent care from your medicine cats, but that where they would stay permanently would be decided at this meeting."

Before Bramblestar could respond, Mistystar took a step forward. "I think Onestar and I would appreciate a bit more information," she mewed politely. "This is the first we've heard about this quest."

"You bet we would," Onestar growled from where he crouched on a lower branch, hardly more than his eyes visible among the leaves. "Or is this another case of ThunderClan thinking it can control the whole forest?"

"Not at all," Bramblestar replied; Alderpaw could tell that he was making an effort to hold on to his temper.

The ThunderClan leader launched into an account of the quest, although he left out any mention of SkyClan. "Sandstorm's spirit guided Alderpaw to discover the kits," he finished. "That makes me think that they must be important for us somehow, even if they're not 'what you find in the shadows' from the prophecy."

The cats in the clearing broke out into excited speculation and argument. Alderpaw was worried that the noise and curious glances would frighten the kits, but they seemed untroubled by it; they were curled up together, listening to what was going on but clearly not understanding that their future was being decided.

Up in the branches of the Great Oak, the leaders were wrangling too.

"You'll never convince me that those kits are what we were meant to embrace," Onestar grumbled. "I mean . . . they're kits! What do they know?"

"They don't have to *know* anything," Rowanstar pointed out with an irritated lash of his tail. "But StarClan guided us to them, and that's good enough for me."

Mistystar nodded in agreement.

"We can't be sure about this," Bramblestar meowed, his glance sweeping around to take in the other three leaders. "Not until the kits grow and reveal more about themselves. What is clear is that it's the Clans' responsibility to take care of them."

"That's all well and good," Rowanstar responded, baring

his teeth in the beginning of a snarl, "but it doesn't mean the kits need to stay in ThunderClan. Perhaps they belong in ShadowClan with Needlepaw, who helped find and care for them."

"But they're happy and safe now," Bramblestar argued. "It would be cruel to move them."

"You would say that, Bramblestar," Onestar hissed. "All that interests you is keeping the kits for ThunderClan."

"It looks like that, Bramblestar." Mistystar sounded almost apologetic. "But the prophecy came to every Clan, not just to ThunderClan. You don't have the right to keep the kits."

"That's so unfair!" Sparkpaw exclaimed, but Alderpaw waved his tail for her to be quiet. He didn't want to miss a single word of the argument.

"I accept that," Bramblestar meowed, to Alderpaw's dismay. "And I agree that ShadowClan has a claim to the kits—or at least to one of them."

"Then the only fair thing," Mistystar pointed out, "is for ThunderClan to keep one kit, and give the other to Shadow-Clan."

Alderpaw glanced down in horror at Twigkit and Violetkit. *Splitting them up would be so cruel!*

"What's happening?" Twigkit asked, blinking rapidly in agitation.

"Yes, why is every cat angry?" Violetkit added.

"It's okay, little ones." Alderpaw gave each kit an affectionate lick around the ears. "Clan leaders are always arguing."

The kits grew calmer, accepting what he said, while Alderpaw felt guilty that he might be lying to them.

"You don't think Bramblestar will really allow them to be separated!" Sparkpaw whispered into his ear.

"I don't know," Alderpaw murmured in reply, but inwardly he was afraid that their Clan leader would. *He doesn't really have any choice, with all the other leaders against him.*

When Alderpaw was able to listen to the leaders again, Bramblestar was speaking. "I'm not happy about this," he meowed, "but I feel I have to agree that one kit goes to ShadowClan."

"But that's not good enough!" Onestar protested, while Alderpaw felt cold all over with despair. "What about WindClan and RiverClan? Shouldn't all the Clans try to raise the kits together?"

His suggestion met with silence from the other leaders. "Is he mouse-brained?" Sparkpaw muttered to Alderpaw. "How would that work?"

Onestar just let out a hiss of annoyance and retreated even farther into the leaves, glaring out balefully.

The cats in the clearing were still whispering together. Some of them crowded around to get a good look at the kits. Twigkit and Violetkit shrank closer together, looking even smaller with so many full-grown cats looming over them.

"Back off, flea-pelts!" Sparkpaw hissed. "You're scaring them."

Up in the Great Oak, Mistystar was lashing her tail in frustration. "Is there any other business to discuss?" she called out, trying to make herself heard above the buzz of conversation.

"Don't be ridiculous," Onestar growled. "No cat is going to want to talk about day-to-day business after all this!"

"Then I declare the Gathering at an end," Mistystar announced. She jumped down from the tree and disappeared into a crowd of RiverClan warriors.

Alderpaw's heart pounded with apprehension as Bramblestar and Rowanstar leaped down together and thrust their way through the clusters of cats until they reached the bush where he and Sparkpaw waited with the kits.

"I can't believe you agreed to this!" Alderpaw burst out as his father approached.

Bramblestar's eyes were grave and he bowed his head as he replied. "There's no other way. Rowanstar, choose a kit."

Rowanstar hesitated, and Alderpaw sensed that he wasn't happy about the solution either. He would protect the rights of ShadowClan against any cat, but he wasn't cruel, and he clearly understood what he was doing.

"I'll take the black-and-white one," he meowed.

"That's Violetkit," Alderpaw told him, unable to stop his voice shaking. "Look after her, please."

Rowanstar dipped his head. "She will be well taken care of in ShadowClan," he promised. Then he gently lifted Violetkit by her scruff.

At last the kits understood what was happening. Violetkit began to wail in a shrill voice and lashed out helplessly with her tiny paws.

"No! No! Don't take her!" Twigkit screeched, flinging herself against Rowanstar's leg and raking her claws through his pelt.

"Alderpaw! Help me!" Violetkit begged. "I want to go home! I want Lilyheart!"

Alderpaw thought that his heart would shatter into icy splinters. Curling his tail around Twigkit, he drew her back from Rowanstar. "It's no use, little ones," he mewed. "This is the way it has to be."

"Take her quickly," Bramblestar snapped at Rowanstar.

Instantly the ShadowClan leader swung around and headed away to where his own Clan were gathering ready to leave. Dangling from his jaws, Violetkit twisted around so that she could still see her sister.

"Twigkit! Twigkit!" she kept on calling until she vanished from Alderpaw's sight.

Alderpaw imagined himself being separated from Sparkpaw, and how much it would hurt. But the pain that clawed through him now was even bigger than that. He felt that the Clans were being swept down a long, dark tunnel, and that this terrible separation was only the beginning of even more terrible troubles to come.

I should feel happy, he told himself. *I found the kits, and they might be the thing that will save the Clans if we embrace them.* But instead a sense of foreboding hung over him, like a storm cloud that was only waiting for the right moment to release its fury.

He was jerked back to the present by a sharp nudge from Sparkpaw. "Stop dreaming! Twigkit needs you."

The little gray kit had collapsed into a heap, letting out a desolate mewling. Alderpaw bent over her and licked her head and her ears. "Don't be sad, little one," he murmured. "We'll look after you. And you'll see Violetkit again, when you're old enough to come to Gatherings."

"But it's not the same," Twigkit whimpered. "I want Violetkit now! And what will she do without Lilyheart?"

"A ShadowClan cat will look after her," Sparkpaw promised. "A *nice* ShadowClan cat."

Alderpaw stroked Twigkit gently with his tail, and Sparkpaw nuzzled her from the other side, but the little kit wouldn't be comforted.

"The others are leaving," Sparkpaw mewed. "We should go too."

Looking up, Alderpaw saw that Bramblestar and his other Clanmates were gathering near the foot of the Great Oak, while the ShadowClan cats streamed past them on their way to the tree-bridge. Among them he spotted Needlepaw, with Violetkit riding on her back.

For a moment Needlepaw caught Alderpaw's eye, and Alderpaw stared back at her. His head was buzzing with questions, like they were bees in a hive.

Did you tell them about SkyClan? Will you? Will you take care of Violetkit? Do you miss me?

But Needlepaw's glance was not friendly, and almost at once she turned away and followed her Clanmates. Violetkit looked scared as Needlepaw flattened herself to thrust her way through the bushes. Then they were gone.

Alderpaw wondered what Violetkit's future would hold. He remembered the loneliness he had sensed in Needlepaw, and he wondered whether Violetkit would share it now that she had lost her sister. But he realized that there was nothing he could do to control what would happen to her. *I can take care of Twigkit,* he thought, looking down at the gray kit. *I always will, and I'll do everything I can to make sure that she's happy.* Touching his nose to hers, he felt a sense of warmth spreading through him. *If nothing else comes of my quest, at least I can make sure that this little one has a good life.*

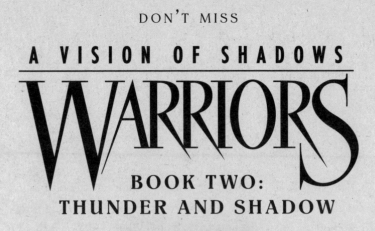

CHAPTER 1

Alderpaw's gaze drifted toward the trailing brambles at the entrance of the medicine den. Outside, leaves would be drifting into the hollow. Leaf-fall came so soon! Less than a moon ago he'd been trekking back from his quest beneath sunny blue skies.

"Alderpaw!"

Jayfeather's sharp mew snapped him from his thoughts. He turned his attention back to the leaves piled in front of him.

"You're meant to be separating the yarrow from the coltsfoot." Jayfeather glared at him with sightless blue eyes.

"Sorry," Alderpaw mumbled. Nothing he did seemed to please Jayfeather. Hurriedly, he began to peel the limp yarrow away from the dried coltsfoot.

Beside him, Leafpool reached deeper into the crack at the back of the cave. She hauled out another pawful of leaves. "I think that's the last of them. Once we've sorted them, we can decide what we need to gather before leafbare."

"We'll need catmint," Jayfeather mewed. "I want Spiderleg to be the last cat in ThunderClan who dies of greencough."

At the far side of the medicine den, Briarlight pushed herself up in her nest. "I can help with the sorting."

2

"Thanks," Jayfeather told her without turning. "But we've enough cats here already." His ears twitched irritably as he added, "And kits."

Alderpaw glanced guiltily at Twigkit. The young cat was playing with a leaf inside the entrance. She reached onto her hind legs, pawing the leaf high, then ducked as it drifted down to catch it on her back. As it landed between her shoulder blades, she gave a *mrrow* of delight. "I had to bring her with me," Alderpaw explained. "She didn't have anyone to play with."

"What about Lilyheart's kits?" Jayfeather snapped. "They're her nestmates aren't they?"

Leafpool pushed a pile of thyme to one side. "Lilyheart's kits are nearly five moons old," she reminded Jayfeather gently. "They're far too boisterous for Twigkit."

And they're not interested in having a young kit tag along. Alderpaw was grateful that Lilyheart had agreed to raise Twigkit along with her own kits, Leafkit, Larkkit, and Honeykit, but he wished the older kits had more patience with their foster littermate. They would be apprentices soon, and they were more interested in pretending to hunt and fight than in playing nursery games with Twigkit.

If only her sister, Violetkit, had been allowed to stay with her in ThunderClan. Alderpaw remembered with a spark of anger how callously ShadowClan had carried Twigkit's sister away from the Gathering, separating the littermates without worry for their feelings. They hadn't cared that they were separating orphaned kits. All they cared about was that

Needlepaw—one of their apprentices—had helped find them. Since the kits might be part of a prophecy sent from StarClan, Rowanstar was determined that one of them would belong to his Clan.

Anger surged through Alderpaw. *It was* my *prophecy! I led the quest that found them.* And yet that wasn't why he resented losing Violetkit so much. He felt sorry for Twigkit. And for Violetkit. Was ShadowClan taking care of her? Did she have a foster mother as kind as Lilyheart? Memories of his own kithood with his sister, Sparkpaw, and his mother, Squirrelflight, warmed his heart. *How would I have felt to be separated from them?*

Twigkit batted the leaf into the air once again, then leapt, her short fluffy tail whipping to balance her as she spun in the air. Nimbly, she caught the leaf between her forepaws.

"She's agile." Leafpool watched approvingly.

"She should be playing outside," Jayfeather huffed. "A medicine den is no place for kits."

"She could play with Briarlight," Alderpaw suggested.

Briarlight's crippled hind legs meant that it was important for her to keep her forelegs strong and active and her lungs clear. Chasing a leaf with Twigkit would be good exercise.

Jayfeather frowned, but Leafpool spoke before he could object. "That's a great idea, Alderpaw." She called to Twigkit. "Would you like to play catch with Briarlight?"

Twigkit blinked at Leafpool, her eyes sparkling with delight. "Am I allowed?"

"Of course," Briarlight purred. "You can play with me any time you like."

Jayfeather huffed again and began untangling the pile of thyme. "Does this mean she's going to be here even more?"

"Don't be so grouchy," Leafpool chided. "She's not doing any harm."

"I guess I only trip over her three or four times a day." Jayfeather snorted.

Alderpaw's pelt pricked with irritation. It was almost as though Jayfeather *enjoyed* being the grumpiest cat in the Clan.

"Get on with your work!" Jayfeather's ears twitched crossly. Not for the first time, Alderpaw wondered if the blind medicine cat could read his thoughts. Guiltily, he turned his attention back to the yarrow and coltsfoot.

As Twigkit carried her leaf toward Briarlight, the trailing brambles at the entrance rustled.

Graystripe popped his head through and blinked at Jayfeather. "Bramblestar wants to see you, Leafpool, and Alderpaw."

Alderpaw's heart quickened. *Why?*

He waited for Jayfeather to speak, but Graystripe went on. "Can I take some comfrey back to the elders' den?" The grey elder glanced at the herb piles hopefully.

Leafpool tipped her head. "Are your joints aching again?"

"Not mine," Graystripe huffed. "Millie's."

"Shall I come and check on her?" Leafpool was already rolling up a wad of leaves.

"There's no need. Unless you know a cure for aging." Graystripe pushed his way into the den. "Besides, I don't think you should keep Bramblestar waiting. Rowanstar's with him."

Jayfeather pricked his ears. "Why didn't you tell us?"

"I just did."

As Graystripe grasped the comfrey between his jaws, Jayfeather brushed past him and headed for the entrance.

Alderpaw glanced at Twigkit. Had something happened to Violetkit? Is that why the ShadowClan leader had come? "Stay here with Briarlight, okay?"

She nodded.

Alderpaw's heart was racing. He nosed his way through the brambles after Jayfeather.

Leafpool was following Graystripe from the den. Alderpaw hurried after her, the sharp sunshine stinging his eyes as he pushed his way from the shade of the medicine den.

Outside the nursery, Lilyheart stretched beside Daisy, soaking up the meagre warmth. There was a chill in the air but the cliff sheltered the camp from the blustery breeze that was stirring the branches at the top of the hollow. Leafkit, Larkkit, and Honeykit were nosing around the fallen beech, poking their noses through the gaps in the woven walls of the apprentices' den.

"There's so much room inside!" Leafkit gasped.

"I want a nest close to the middle," Larkkit mewed.

"Sparkpaw and Alderpaw's nests are there already," Honeykit sighed. "I can see them."

Leafpool's mew distracted Alderpaw from their chatter. "I hope the patrols come back soon," she mewed. "The freshkill pile's empty."

Alderpaw glanced at the empty patch of earth. Brightheart,

Whitewing, and Cloudtail paced beside it. Hadn't they brought prey back from their patrol? Perhaps they'd met Rowanstar before they'd had a chance to hunt. They gazed through narrowed eyes at the muscular ginger tom as he stood beside Bramblestar on Highledge.

Jayfeather was already beside him, fur pricking along his spine.

Alderpaw followed Leafpool up the tumble of rocks and stopped beside them.

Bramblestar gazed at them gravely. "Littlecloud is dying." He dipped his head to Leafpool. The two medicine cats had known each other a long time.

Leafpool's eyes darkened. "Is he suffering?"

"Dawnpelt's with him," Rowanstar told her. "She's giving him poppy seeds to ease his pain, but she doesn't know what else to do."

Leafpool flicked her tail. "If only you'd chosen a medicine cat apprentice moons ago," she fretted. "Littlecloud would have someone to care for him properly."

"And ShadowClan wouldn't be left without a medicine cat," Jayfeather growled.

Rowanstar's pelt ruffled. "I didn't come here to be lectured!"

Bramblestar stepped forward. "He came here for our help." He shot a warning glance at Jayfeather.

Alderpaw watched his father, impressed by his authority. Bramblestar clearly understood that it would do no good to rub mouse bile into ShadowClan's wound. More gentle treatment was needed. He stepped forward hesitantly. "Can *I* help?" he asked softly.

Jayfeather flicked him away with his tail. "You're not borrowing our apprentice," he told Rowanstar tetchily.

Alderpaw bristled. *Why not? You're always complaining I get under your paws.*

Rowanstar scowled. "I don't want an *apprentice.* Littlecloud needs proper care."

Alderpaw's pelt ruffled indignantly.

"I'll come," Leafpool offered.

"Thank you." Rowanstar leaned forward. "Grassheart's kits are due any day. Tawnypelt, Snowbird, and Dawnpelt will be able to help at her kitting, but it's Grassheart's first litter and I'd prefer to have a medicine cat close by if there are problems."

Alderpaw shifted his paws. It sounded strange to hear the ShadowClan leader talk with such concern about his Clanmates. Rowanstar had snatched Violetkit from the Gathering so callously that Alderpaw had decided the ginger tom must have no heart. Hope flickered through his fur. Had he been wrong? Perhaps Violetkit was as safe and loved in ShadowClan as Twigkit was in ThunderClan.

"I'll fetch herbs and come as soon as I can." Leafpool turned toward the rock tumble. She paused at the top and called over her shoulder. "Alderpaw. Travel with me. I'll need help carrying the herbs."

"To ShadowClan's camp?" Alderpaw blinked in surprise.

"Of course!" Leafpool whisked her tail.

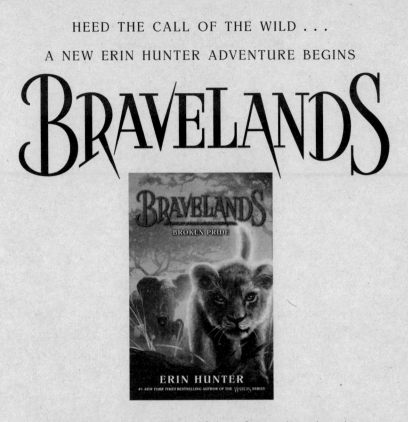

CHAPTER ONE

Swiftcub pounced after the vulture's shadow, but it flitted away too quickly to follow. Breathing hard, he pranced back to his pride. *I saw that bird off our territory,* he thought, delighted. *No rot-eater's going to come near Gallantpride while I'm around!*

The pride needed him to defend it, Swiftcub thought, picking up his paws and strutting around his family. Why, right now they were all half asleep, dozing and basking in the shade of the acacia trees. The most energetic thing the other lions were doing was lifting their heads to groom their nearest neighbors, or their own paws. They had no *idea* of the threat Swiftcub had just banished.

I might be only a few moons old, but my father is the strongest, bravest lion in Bravelands. And I'm going to be just like him!

"Swiftcub!"

The gentle but commanding voice snapped him out of his

dreams of glory. He came to a halt, turning and flicking his ears at the regal lioness who stood over him.

"Mother," he said, shifting on his paws.

"Why are you shouting at vultures?" Swift scolded him fondly, licking at his ears. "They're nothing but scavengers. Come on, you and your sister can play later. Right now you're supposed to be practicing hunting. And if you're going to catch anything, you'll need to keep your eyes on the prey, not on the sky!"

"Sorry, Mother." Guiltily he padded after her as she led him through the dry grass, her tail swishing. The ground rose gently, and Swiftcub had to trot to keep up. The grasses tickled his nose, and he was so focused on trying not to sneeze, he almost bumped into his mother's haunches as she crouched.

"Oops," he growled.

Valor shot him a glare. His older sister was hunched a little to the left of their mother, fully focused on their hunting practice. Valor's sleek body was low to the ground, her muscles tense; as she moved one paw forward with the utmost caution, Swiftcub tried to copy her, though it was hard to keep up on his much shorter legs. One creeping pace, then two. Then another.

I'm being very quiet, just like Valor. I'm going to be a great hunter. He slunk up alongside his mother, who remained quite still.

"There, Swiftcub," she murmured. "Do you see the burrows?"

He did, now. Ahead of the three lions, the ground rose up even higher, into a bare, sandy mound dotted with small shadowy holes. As Swiftcub watched, a small nose and whiskers poked out, testing the air. The meerkat emerged completely, stood up on its hind legs, and stared around. Satisfied, it stuck out a pink tongue and began to groom its chest, as more meerkats appeared beyond it. Growing in confidence, they scurried farther away from their burrows.

"Careful now," rumbled Swift. "They're very quick. Go!"

Swiftcub sprang forward, his little paws bounding over the ground. Still, he wasn't fast enough to outpace Valor, who was far ahead of him already. A stab of disappointment spoiled his excitement, and suddenly it was even harder to run fast, but he ran grimly after his sister.

The startled meerkats were already doubling back into their holes. Stubby tails flicked and vanished; the bigger leader, his round dark eyes glaring at the oncoming lions, was last to twist and dash underground. Valor's jaws snapped at his tail, just missing.

"Sky and stone!" the bigger cub swore, coming to a halt in a cloud of dust. She shook her head furiously and licked her jaws. "I nearly had it!"

A rumble of laughter made Swiftcub turn. His father, Gallant, stood watching them. Swiftcub couldn't help but feel the usual twinge of awe mixed in with his delight. Black-maned and huge, his sleek fur glowing golden in the sun, Gallant would have been intimidating if Swiftcub hadn't known and loved him so well. Swift rose to her paws and greeted the great lion affectionately, rubbing his maned neck with her head.

"It was a good attempt, Valor," Gallant reassured his

daughter. "What Swift said is true: meerkats are *very* hard to catch. You were so close—one day you'll be as fine a hunter as your mother." He nuzzled Swift and licked her neck.

"*I* wasn't anywhere near it," grumbled Swiftcub. "I'll never be as fast as Valor."

"Oh, you will," said Gallant. "Don't forget, Valor's a whole year older than you, my son. You're getting bigger and faster every day. Be patient!" He stepped closer, leaning in so his great tawny muzzle brushed Swiftcub's own. "That's the secret to stalking, too. Learn patience, and one day you too will be a *very* fine hunter."

"I hope so," said Swiftcub meekly.

Gallant nuzzled him. "Don't doubt yourself, my cub. You're going to be a great lion and the best kind of leader: one who keeps his own pride safe and content, but puts fear into the heart of his strongest enemy!"

That does sound good! Feeling much better, Swiftcub nodded. Gallant nipped affectionately at the tufty fur on top of his head and padded toward Valor.

Swiftcub watched him proudly. *He's right, of course. Father knows everything! And I will be a great hunter, I will. And a brave, strong leader—*

A tiny movement caught his eye, a scuttling shadow in his father's path.

A scorpion!

Barely pausing to think, Swiftcub sprang, bowling between his father's paws and almost tripping him. He skidded to a halt right in front of Gallant, snarling at the small sand-yellow scorpion. It paused, curling up its barbed tail and raising its pincers in threat.

"No, Swiftcub!" cried his father.

Swiftcub swiped his paw sideways at the creature, catching its plated shell and sending it flying into the long grass.

All four lions watched the grass, holding their breath, waiting for a furious scorpion to reemerge. But there was no stir of movement. It must have fled. Swiftcub sat back, his heart suddenly banging against his ribs.

"Skies above!" Gallant laughed. Valor gaped, and Swift dragged her cub into her paws and began to lick him roughly.

"Mother . . ." he protested.

"Honestly, Swiftcub!" she scolded him as her tongue swept across his face. "Your father might have gotten a nasty sting from that creature—but *you* could have been killed!"

"You're such an idiot, little brother," sighed Valor, but there was admiration in her eyes.

Gallant and Swift exchanged proud looks. "Swift," growled Gallant, "I do believe the time has come to give our cub his true name."

Swift nodded, her eyes shining. "Now that we know what kind of lion he is, I think you're right."

Gallant turned toward the acacia trees, his tail lashing, and gave a resounding roar.

It always amazed Swiftcub that the pride could be lying half asleep one moment and alert the very next. Almost before Gallant had finished roaring his summons, there was a rustle of grass, a crunch of paws on dry earth, and the rest of Gallantpride appeared, ears pricked and eyes bright with curiosity. Gallant huffed in greeting, and the twenty lionesses and young lions of his pride spread out in a circle around him, watching and listening intently.

Gallant looked down again at Swiftcub, who blinked and glanced away, suddenly rather shy. "Crouch down," murmured the great lion.

When he obeyed, Swiftcub felt his father's huge paw rest on his head.

"Henceforth," declared Gallant, "this cub of mine will no longer be known as Swiftcub. He faced a dangerous foe without hesitation and protected his pride. His name, now and forever, is Fearless Gallantpride."

It was done so quickly, Swiftcub felt dizzy with astonishment. *I have my name! I'm Fearless. Fearless Gallantpride!*

All around him, his whole family echoed his name, roaring their approval. Their deep cries resonated across the grasslands.

"Fearless Gallantpride!"

"Welcome, Fearless, son of Gallant!"

His heart swelled inside him. Suddenly, he knew what it was to be a full member of the pride. He had to half close his eyes and flatten his ears, he felt so buffeted by their roars of approval.

"I'll—I promise I'll live up to my name!" he managed to growl. It came out a little squeakier than he'd intended, but no lion laughed at him. They bellowed their delight even more.

"Of course you will," murmured Swift. Both she and his

father nuzzled and butted his head. "You already have, after all!"

"You certainly—" Gallant fell suddenly silent. Fearless glanced up at his father, expecting him to finish, but the great lion was standing still, his head turned toward the west. A light breeze rippled his dark mane. His nostrils flared.

The pride continued to roar, but with a strange new undertone. Fearless wrinkled his muzzle and tried to work out what was different. He began to hear it: there were new voices. In the distance, other lions were roaring.

One by one, the Gallantpride lions fell silent, looking toward the sound. Gallant paced through them, sniffing at the wind, and his pride turned to accompany him. Swift walked closest to his flank.

Overcome with curiosity, Fearless sprang toward the meerkat hill, running to its top and staring out across the plain. His view was blurred by the haze of afternoon heat, but he could see three lions approaching.

They're not from our pride, thought Fearless with a thrill of nerves. He could not take his eyes off the strangers, but he was aware that other lions had joined him at the top of the slope: Gallant, Swift, and Valor. The rest of the pride was behind them, all quite still and alert. Swift's hackles rose. Gallant's whole body looked taut, his muscles coiled.

"Who are they?" asked Fearless, gaping at the three strange lions.

"That is Titan," replied his mother. "The biggest one, there, in the center. Do you see him? He's the cub of a lion your father once drove away, and he's always hated Gallant for that. Titan's grown a fine mane, I see." Her voice became a low, savage growl. "But he was always a brute."

The three lions drew closer; they paced on, relaxed but steady, toward Gallantpride. Fearless could make out the leader clearly now: he was a huge, powerful lion, his black mane magnificent. As he came nearer, Fearless found himself shuddering. His mother was right—there was a cold light of cruelty in Titan's dark eyes. His companions looked mighty and aggressive, too; the first had shoulders as broad as a wildebeest's, while the other had a ragged ear, half of it torn away.

"Why are they in our territory?" asked Fearless in a trembling voice. He didn't yet know whether to be furious or very afraid.

Gallant spoke at last. "There's only one reason Titan would show his face here," he rumbled. "He wants to challenge me for leadership of this pride."

"*What?*" Fearless stared at his father.

"Come." Gallant turned and began to pad back down the meerkat hill.

Fearless followed with the rest, staying close to his sister's flank. "Valor, what does Father mean?" he growled. "Titan can't do that, can he? He can't just take over Gallantpride. It's not possible!"

For a moment Valor said nothing; he did not like the tension in her face. "I've heard of such things," she said at last, grimly. "It happened to Fiercepride, from beyond the forest. Fierce had been leader for ages, Mother told me, but he was challenged and defeated by a lion called Strong who'd recently grown his mane. And his family became Strongpride, and his pride had to live under Strong's rule. Fierce was forced to leave and live alone, and hunt by himself."

"That's horrible," breathed Fearless.

"Worse than that, Strong was a terrible leader. He was cruel and unfair and stupid; the pride fell apart in the end. He killed the cubs. Other lions died too."

Fearless gaped at his sister. "But that won't happen to Gallantpride," he insisted. "No lion can beat Father. He's the bravest fighter and the strongest lion in Bravelands!"

Valor didn't reply. Fearless looked around at the other lions of their pride, and a wave of cold rippled along his spine. None of them looked as confident as he'd hoped; they seemed nervous and edgy, as if an army of ants were marching across their paws.

Gallant was walking out onto the grassland now, toward Titan. When they were almost close enough to touch muzzles, both lions halted and stared into each other's eyes.

Titan was even more frightening up close, thought Fearless. His shoulders were broad and thickly muscled, and his paws were huge. There were deep, roughly healed scars drawn into his face and flanks, and when he opened his jaws to speak, his fangs were long, yellow, and deadly.

"Gallant of Gallantpride," he snarled in greeting.

"Titan, Prideless Lion," growled Gallant. "What is your business here?"

Titan drew himself up, his black mane rippling over his

powerful neck and shoulders. He slapped the ground with a massive paw.

"By the laws of our ancestors," he roared, "I, Titan, come to claim this pride of Gallant."

Gallant's muzzle curled back from his own long, deadly fangs.

"By the laws of our ancestors," he snarled, "I, Gallant, fight to keep this pride."

For a long moment they stared at each other, the air seeming to quiver with anticipation. Both huge males half crouched, their muscles coiled.

Then, as one, they launched their attacks, colliding with a terrible grunting roar and an impact that shook the ground. Rearing up, Gallant sank his claws into Titan's shoulders; twisting, Titan shook his huge mane, gripped Gallant's flank with his claws, and raked his flesh in return. They broke apart, only to slam together once more, jaws wide and claws tearing.

Fearless could hardly bear to watch, but neither could he look away. His heart was in his throat. Now that they were gripped in close combat, and he could see them together, the two lions looked equally matched.

The pride stood watching, their tails lashing with anxiety—all except Swift, who was pacing back and forth on the edge of the fight. She was the only one who was silent; the others roared their encouragement to Gallant, and snarled in contempt whenever Titan landed a good blow. But Swift said nothing, only paced and looked afraid.

"Mother," pleaded Fearless, unable to watch her fretting

anymore, "why don't we help Father? Together we can beat Titan, can't we? There's more of us!"

"We can't," said Swift, her voice choked with anxiety. "I'm sorry, my son. Those are the rules. The pride leader must win this fight alone."

There was a roar from the pride. Gallant had doubled abruptly and sprung for Titan, landing a mighty blow on the side of his skull. Titan reeled back, stumbled, then fell hard on his flank; Gallant pounced, slamming both his forepaws onto his fallen enemy.

"He's won!" shouted Fearless in excitement, as the pride roared its approval.

"Yes," cried Swift. "It looks like—" Then she gasped.

Titan's sidekicks, the two lions who had arrived with him, sprang suddenly forward, attacking Gallant from both flanks. They hung on him, claws digging in, dragging him down and away from Titan.

"Stop! No!" roared Swift, and the pride joined in her protest. "Cheats! Traitors—"

She leaped forward, but Titan was already back on his feet. He lunged, as fast as a snake, and sank his jaws into Gallant's exposed throat. Fearless saw his father stagger back, off balance, the two lions still fastened with their claws to his sides.

Swift and two other lionesses flew at Titan, but his companions released Gallant and turned on them, snarling and biting, holding them off. Swift gave panicked, snarling cries as she tried desperately to fight her way to Gallant, but the two big males were too strong.

As the rest of Gallant's pride joined the attack, the inter-lopers finally backed off, teeth bared and eyes defiant. With a crash and a grunting exhalation, Gallant collapsed to the earth, and every lion froze and stared. Titan stood over his fallen foe, his jaws still locked on Gallant's throat.

Fearless felt as if a cold night wind had swept through his body. Titan was not merely holding his father down. His fangs were buried in Gallant's flesh, and bright red blood was pooling under his great black mane. Gallant's paws, sprawled helplessly on the ground, twitched in a horrible spasm.

Swift gave a screaming roar. *"No!"*

"What— Mother, what—" Fearless's words dried in his throat, and he gulped hard. He had never seen a lion die, but he had encountered plenty of dead antelopes and zebras. That was how his father looked now: limp, blank-eyed, his lifeblood spilling into the dusty earth.

Father can't be dead! He is Gallant of Gallantpride!

The lions stood motionless, glaring at one another over Gallant's body. An awful silence hung over them. Fearless closed his eyes, desperately hoping it would all go away. But when he opened them again, his father was still lying on the ground.

ERIN HUNTER

is inspired by a fascination with the ferocity of the natural world. As well as having great respect for nature in all its forms, Erin enjoys creating rich, mythical explanations for animal behavior. She is also the author of the Survivors, Seekers, and Bravelands series.

Download the free Warriors app at www.warriorcats.com.

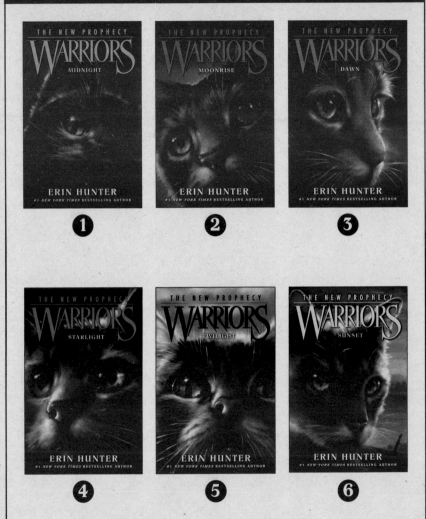

WARRIORS : THE NEW PROPHECY

In the second series, follow the next generation of heroic cats as they set off on a quest to save the Clans from destruction.

HARPER
An Imprint of HarperCollins Publishers

www.warriorcats.com

WARRIORS: POWER OF THREE

In the third series, Firestar's grandchildren begin their training as warrior cats. Prophecy foretells that they will hold more power than any cats before them.

HARPER
An Imprint of HarperCollinsPublishers

www.warriorcats.com

WARRIORS: OMEN OF THE STARS

In the fourth series, find out which ThunderClan apprentice will complete the prophecy.

WARRIORS: DAWN OF THE CLANS

In this prequel series,
discover how the warrior Clans came to be.

WARRIORS: BONUS STORIES

Discover the untold stories of the warrior cats and Clans
when you download the separate ebook novellas—or read
them in four paperback bind-ups!

WARRIORS: FIELD GUIDES

FOR THE ULTIMATE FAN!

Delve deeper into the Clans with these Warriors field guides.

HARPER
An Imprint of HarperCollinsPublishers

www.warriorcats.com